WELCOME, CALLER, THIS IS CHLOE

WELCOME, CALLER, THIS IS CHLOE

AMULET BOOKS · NEW YORK

Cataloging-in-Publication Data

Coriell, Shelley.
Welcome, caller, this is Chloe / by Shelley Coriell.
p. cm.
Summary: "When big-hearted Chloe Camden's best friend shreds her reputation and her school counselor axes her junior independent study project, Chloe is forced to take on a 'more meaningful' project by joining her school's struggling radio station" — Provided by publisher.
ISBN 978-1-4197-0191-7 (hardback)
[1. Interpersonal relations—Fiction. 2. Radio broadcasting—Fiction. 3. High schools—Fiction. 4. Schools—Fiction. 5. Grandmothers—Fiction. 6. Old age—Fiction.] I. Title.
PZ7.C8157Wel 2012
[Fic]—dc23
2011038227

Text copyright © 2012 Shelley Coriell
Book design by Maria T. Middleton
Photography © Jonathan Beckerman

Printed and bound in the U.S.A.
10 9 8 7 6 5 4 3 2 1

Amulet Books are available at special discounts when purchased in quantity for premiums and promotions as well as fundraising or educational use. Special editions can also be created to specification. For details, contact specialsales@abramsbooks.com or the address below.

THE ART OF BOOKS SINCE 1949
115 West 18th Street
New York, NY 10011
www.abramsbooks.com

To Lee

Sometimes change sneaks up on you, carried in on the breath of spring, sliding through the sun-soaked waves of summer, breezing along the whisper and crackle of fall. Other times change prefers a more direct route. It comes down fast and hard. *Wham!* Like a ginormous hammer.

—Chloe Camden, *Shut Up and Listen: A Junior Independent Study Project by a Queen Without a Castle*, p. 1

CHAPTER 1

I LOVED BEING A BURRITO.

Not the actual costume, a stinky ankle-length tube of compressed foam with scratchy shoulder straps. No, I loved the physical act of being a burrito—more precisely, of getting people to notice me—and I was good at it.

On the final Sunday of winter break I stood in full burrito glamour on the corner of Palo Brea and Seventh. The gorgeous winter sun, the kind created by the gods lucky enough to preside over Southern California, shone down on me. I waved at cars. Sometimes I blew kisses. Sometimes I handed out buy-one-get-one-free coupons for Dos Hermanas Mexican Cantina. And sometimes I performed my burrito shuffle dance in my way-hot peep-toe swing heels.

A woman on a Vespa puttered up beside me. "Nice shoes. Are they legit?"

I handed her a BOGOF coupon and flashed my ankle. "True-blue 1942."

"eBay?"

"Nope. Got them at a vintage shop off Calle Bonita near Minnie's Place Retirement Community. A real gold mine."

"Yum." The light changed and Vespa Girl drove off with a wave and serious shoe envy.

The sun glinted off my silver buckles. There was something deliciously romantic about slipping into shoes that had walked another time and place, something powerful about bits of leather that had survived more than a half century. What stories these shoes could tell if only they had a different sort of tongue.

When I aimed my swing heels toward the corner to hand out my last two BOGOF coupons, I spotted a car that sent me spinning in a happy burrito pirouette. A pearl-white convertible BMW stopped in the turn lane, my BF Brie Sonderby in the driver's seat. I hadn't seen Brie or my other BF, Mercedes, for almost three weeks, not since the night of the Mistletoe Ball, the most amazing night of my life. Unfortunately, it had been followed by the worst day of my life when World War III broke out in my living room.

It was a universal truth: When life turned hellacious, you needed BFs. To my extreme dismay, I'd spent all of winter break without mine because Brie had been on a ski trip in Chamonix with the parental unit, and Merce had been on the East Coast touring campuses with lots of ivy. Now Brie was reaching over the Beemer's passenger seat and gathering papers scattered on the floor.

"Looks like you could use a little help from a burrito with hot shoes," I said.

When she lifted her head, a gasp hitched in my throat. In addition to being one of my best friends on planet earth, Brie was one of the most beautiful human beings on planet earth, but not today. "What happened?" I asked.

Her fingers curled around the papers like dead, bleached coral. "Nothing."

Yeah, right. Her lips were the texture and color of ground beef, as if she'd been gnawing them for three weeks. She looked almost as bad as Mercedes did last year after her mother died.

I grabbed Brie's hand, which felt like a chunk of ice. "What is it? Did something happen in France? With you? Your mom?" I squeezed her fingers, sending warmth. "Hey, Cheese Girl, talk. It's me, Chloe."

Brie yanked her hand from mine. "You're the last person I want to talk to."

I steadied my hands on the car door. "Okay. Fine. You need some quiet. Pull into Dos Hermanas and let me drive. We'll pick up Merce, buy some Twizzlers, and—"

"Shut up, Chloe. Just! Shut! Up!" She pounded the steering wheel with each word.

I took a step back, my heel sinking into a divot in the asphalt.

Brie rested her forehead against her fisted hands, her usual gold and glorious hair falling around her face in a dull, tangled mess. "Go away. I can't deal with you right now."

I had no idea what was going on, but the heavens were

3

seriously misaligned. Confusion softened my voice. "Is it something I did?"

"You?" A strange sound—part sob, part laugh—fell from my BF's ground-beef lips. "Have you ever thought the world doesn't revolve around you, *Queen* Chloe?"

"I . . ." I had no idea what to say, other than who are you and what have you done with my best friend?

The light turned green, and Brie jerked upright, her eyes glinting with frost. "Sometimes you're so self-centered, I can't stand it." She punched the gas, and a blast of exhaust enveloped my peep-toe swing heels.

The BOGOF coupons fell from my hand as her BMW squealed around the corner and disappeared. What was that? *Who* was that? And why was she being so . . . so mean?

"Hey, Burrito Babe, move it!" A guy in a blue truck stuck his head out the window and waved a fist at me.

A wicked heat swelled beneath my burrito shell. On shaky feet I headed to Dos Hermanas. Something strange was going on in my world, and I needed an explanation, because of course there had to be an explanation as to why one of my BFs had gone mad-cow.

I drew in a deep breath as I entered the Mexican restaurant, which smelled of roasted chilies and a dash of lime. The smells soothed me, as did Larry, Moe, and Rizado, the three giant papier-mâché parrots hanging above the salsa bar. Everything about the tiny restaurant was in-your-face loud and bright, spicy, and bold. I loved it, and I loved the two sisters who ran it. Twenty years ago Ana and Josie left a dirt-poor village in Sonora, Mexico, and walked across the desert on bare feet in search of shoes and a better life. They found it here.

"Hey, Rojita, someone called for you." Josie handed me a piece of jagged brown paper, the kind that crackled out of paper towel dispensers. "She sounded—how you say—agitated."

The paper towel read: *Call A. Lungren pronto. School guidance center. ¡Emergencia!*

"You have problems with school?" Josie asked.

I shoved the note in my burrito pocket. "No." I had no idea who A. Lungren was, and frankly, I didn't care about her emergency. I had my own emergency.

Shut up, Chloe. Just! Shut! Up!

My BF had thrust a flaming arrow into the middle of my chest.

I was a lover, not a fighter.

When words collided and emotions exploded, my friends and fam could count on me for a pithy redirect or well-timed joke. But not today, not after my encounter with the angry zombie girl masquerading as one of my best friends. I quietly turned the handle of my front door and slipped into the entryway, ducking to avoid incoming missiles.

"You're not listening to me!" Grams yelled from the adjacent living room.

"I can't hear you when you're shouting at the top of your lungs!" Mom fired back.

The fiery ache in my chest expanded. This is how things had been between Grams and Mom since the day after the Mistletoe

Ball. There was no way I could attempt to broker peace between them. I slipped off my swing heels and tiptoed across the marble entryway, up the spiral staircase, and into the black hole. The massive second floor of my home was cold, dark, and as of five months ago, void of living matter. Except for me.

I beelined to my room to call Mercedes, the third member of our best-friend triumvirate. Mercedes and I met the first week of sixth grade at Del Rey Middle School when she rescued me from the dangerous white-water rapids of pre-algebra with daily tutoring. At the time I didn't know Merce was a social zero. All I knew was she was smart enough to help me get through math with a B, and she laughed at my jokes. While I had a million friends from elementary school, I hooked up with Merce in a fierce way. She was the kind of girl who spent lunch periods with her math book, alone and in need of a friend. A year later Brie moved to Tierra del Rey and rounded out our trio. I'm not sure why the überpopular Brie gravitated toward us. Maybe it was the whole balance thing. Brie was the beauty, Mercedes was the brains, and I was all personality. Together we were whole.

When I called Merce, I got her voice mail. "It's me," I said. "Give me a call as soon as possible. Emergency." *I'm bleeding to death.*

With the hope that Mercedes might be online, I logged on to OurWorld. When I tried to access Mercedes's page, *DENIED!* flashed on my screen. Was this some kind of site error? I clicked on the smiling avatar of Gabe, the founder of OurWorld, whose face always showed up in the top-right corner, and he reported no problems. I clicked on Brie's page. *DENIED!*

The single word stared at me, glowing red, pulsing, grotesquely alive.

A chat bubble above Gabe's avatar popped onto the screen. *Want to try another friend?* Gabe wrote.

"No, Gabe," I said. "I want my two *best* friends. I *need* my two best friends." I flicked off Gabe and ran downstairs to check the phone in the kitchen. Woot! Four messages.

"*Beeeeep.* Good morning, Chloe, this is Ms. A. Lungren from the Del Rey Guidance Center. There's a serious problem with your JISP. You need to call me ASAP."

I needed Ms. A. Lungren, whoever she was, to zip it.

I played the other three messages, all from A. Lungren. When her annoying voice finally tapered off, I noticed the quiet, so sudden and unexpected, it sent the hair along the back of my neck upright. What happened to Grams and Mom? Had they called a truce? I jammed the phone in the cradle. More likely they retreated to gather more things that went boom.

That's when I heard a soft creaking coming from the backyard. It was a low, steady squeak, familiar and comforting. I followed the sound beyond the fountain, pool, and terraced flower beds to the side of the house, where I found Grams. She sat on a swing of my old play gym, her orange Converse dragging along the pea gravel as she swayed.

The play gym groaned as I sunk onto the faded plastic seat next to her and started to pump. Brie had morphed into a zombie and was furious with me, Merce was MIA, and Gabe was directing me to other friends. I pumped harder, faster, the swing's chains creaking and spitting off bits of rust.

Grams's swing synched with mine, but she didn't say a word. Usually she knew when my world was falling apart and said and did appropriate Grams-y things. I watched her, noticing for the first time her slumped shoulders. She looked like she, too, had been bayoneted by her best friend. Pushing aside the image of Brie's frosty eyes, I asked, "What happened?"

Grams stayed tight-lipped for the longest time. Then she said, "I borrowed my neighbor's car."

I made a *hmmmmm* sound. Now I understood why Mom went ballistic.

"Why the hell won't everyone leave me alone?" Grams asked. "Damn it, I'm tired of everyone getting in my business. It's my business. Mine!"

Grams wasn't yelling at me. I knew that. Lately she'd been mad at the world. I stopped pumping. Was that Brie's problem? My BF's voice hissed inside my head. *Sometimes you are so self-centered, I can't stand it.* Was Brie mad at someone else and taking it out on me?

As we slowed, Grams kicked at the gravel, sending gray-blue pellets raining around us.

My parents and five older brothers always dealt with problems using their brilliant scientific minds. The family rebel, I traveled a different route. "What kind of car?" I asked with a tick of my eyebrow.

Grams booted another pile of pea gravel. "Miata."

"Red or white?"

"Red."

"With or without a spoiler?"

The corners of her lips twitched. "With."

I waited. This line begged for a dramatic pause. "At least it's better than the Dodge Duster you jacked last month."

Her face creased in a million lines, and she laughed, just like I knew she would, although the whole thing wasn't funny. The fine state of California had suspended her driver's license two months ago, after she plowed into an ATM.

"How about a ride to the Tuna Can?" I asked. Before she could argue, I added, "We can make twice-baked potatoes and pop in *Legends of the Fall*."

Grams stared at the pea gravel, but the faraway look on her face told me she saw something beyond little gray and blue stones. Where was she? I reached for her hand. Papery skin over old bones. "Grams?"

She blinked. "Huh?"

My eyebrows bounced. "You, me, potatoes, and Brad Pitt. How's it sound?"

Grams patted my hand, and she was the old Grams. Crooked grin. Eyes that had seen eighty-plus years but were ready for more. "You're the best, Chloe."

"Brie doesn't think I'm so hot," I said, more to myself than to Grams. And who knew what Mercedes thought?

DENIED!

"What's wrong, Poppy?" Grams tucked a curl behind my ear. At birth she nicknamed me Poppy because of my orange-red hair. *As bright and soft and wavy as a handful of poppy petals.* Still had the hair. Still had the name. Grams was my babysitter for the first six years of my life because my doctor parents worked a crap-ton of hours. There was little she didn't know about me. Even now.

I fiddled with the curl along my cheek. "Do you think I'm self-centered?"

"You? Of course not. You rescued me from *her* evil clutches, and you're serving me twice-baked potatoes with a side of Brad Pitt. Why would you ask?"

"Brie said I acted like the world revolved around me."

Grams patted my cheek. "You certainly spend your time in the spotlight, but in a good way. You're warm, kind, and funny. If Brie thinks otherwise, that's her problem."

My toes dug into the gravel. "No, it's, uh, kind of my problem."

"How's that?"

"We're friends. Best friends."

"And your point?"

"People need best friends." I waved my arms in the air. "Like oxygen. Without friends I'd die. I'd be all alone."

Grams snorted. "Since when is being alone a bad thing?"

SUBJ: URGENT: Your JISP—Villainous Vixens
FROM: a.lungren@delreyhs.edu
TO: QueenChloe@yahoo.com

Ms. Chloe Camden:

I have tried repeatedly to reach you via phone over winter break. However, I've been unsuccessful. Your former guidance counselor (Mr. Hersbacher) has opted to take an early retirement, and I have been assigned to take over his roster of students.

In reviewing the Junior Independent Study Project (JISP) proposal you submitted on September 15 (*Villainous Vixens: The Not-So-Squeaky-Clean Women of Daytime Soap Operas*), I've determined this project does NOT meet the criteria outlined in sections 2, 5, and 6 of the JISP guidelines. As you are aware, unless you complete a successful JISP, you will receive a "FAIL" mark on your permanent record. DEADLINE for JISP approval is tomorrow at 7 p.m. PST.

Please come to my office (room 107) first thing in the morning to select your new JISP. I look forward to assisting you with this challenging yet ultimately rewarding project meant to change your life and those of others.

Anne Lungren
Guidance Counselor
The Del Rey School

You must be the change you want to see in the world—Gandhi

CHAPTER 2

"SIT."

A. Lungren, my brand-spanking-new guidance counselor, pointed a sharp-tipped finger at the chair across her desk.

I was so not in the mood. Call me cranky, but getting called self-centered by one of my BFs left me a wee bit irritable. I still didn't understand what happened in the street with Brie during my burrito shift. I left eight messages for her last night. She hadn't returned my calls. When I drove to Brie's house this morning, no one answered the door. Ditto for Merce.

DENIED!

Only A. Lungren showed any interest in me. "This is bad but not hopeless," A. Lungren said as she leaned over her desk toward me. With her twitching nose and upturned glasses, my new counselor reminded me of a cat, the annoying kind that tangled itself around your legs and left cat hair on your 1984 turquoise suede slouch boots. "But I'm here for you, Chloe. You realize that, don't you? You're not alone as we dig you out of the colossal hole you're in with your JISP."

"Sure." I searched the bookcase behind her, looking for root beer barrel candy. When I visited my former counselor, Mr. Hersbacher, he always gave me a root beer barrel candy from the old Red Velvet Pipe and Tobacco tin he kept on the bookcase, and we talked about his feet. When I first met Mr. H. my freshman year, he had a midfoot joint spur, and I hooked him up with my podiatrist father. Mr. H.'s and my relationship had been delightfully pain-free ever since. My new counselor did not have a tin of root beer candy, only a cheap metal picture frame with her college diploma. I squinted. Great. Wet ink. Brand-new and still thinking she could change the world one misguided high school student at a time.

I crossed my ankles, enjoying the way the light bounced off my 1948 black patent-leather wing tips. After that conversation with Brie yesterday, I needed a pick-me-up. What I did not need was A. Lungren changing my world or interfering with my perfectly wonderful JISP.

Juniors at the Del Rey School were required to do in-depth independent study projects on subjects they felt passionate about. We had to write a twenty-page report and give a fifteen-minute oral presentation to peers and faculty. The whole JISP-y thing was pass/fail, and I had no doubt I'd pass. Failure on all things academic was not an option in the Camden universe.

". . . do you not agree, Chloe?" A. Lungren stared at me with wide cat eyes.

"Uh, about what?"

"About the problems with your current project. Weren't you listening?"

"There's nothing wrong with Villainous Vixens."

A. Lungren cleared her throat as if she were hacking up a fur ball. "Let me go over this again. First, your topic, soap opera villainesses, is unacceptable."

"It's a subject area I'm passionate about," I argued. Since before I could walk, I'd been watching the soaps with Grams, who'd been the editor of the popular soap opera blog, *Soap Rants and Reviews*. "Passion is the number one criteria on the guideline worksheet. And . . ." I held my breath. Watching the soaps, I learned a good deal about dramatic delivery. There was power in a pause, in the words not yet spoken, words that hovered, like a hammer waiting to drop. I turned to the final page of my JISP notebook. ". . . and my old counselor already approved it. Here's his signature."

Wham! Take that, Evil Kitty Counselor.

A. Lungren looked at me with lifted furry brows, then tore the paper from my bright blue JISP notebook. It sounded like the earth ripped in half. "Mr. Hersbacher is no longer here. I am, and I say watching soap operas does not provide a meaningful contribution to your community. Nor does it provide leadership opportunities or the potential to create positive change or action."

"But—"

"No buts. From what I heard, Mr. Hersbacher was way too

14

indulgent with you these past three years. My colleagues say you were one of his favorites. You may have sweet-talked him into approving this topic, but I went to the JISP review board, and they, too, deemed it unacceptable. You must have a new topic by seven tonight."

A. Lungren slapped shut my JISP notebook, the rush of air a smack across my face.

Whispers moved through the Del Rey School like the long, wispy tentacles of jellyfish. They wore glowing skirts of sparkly blue, swanky black, and brilliant yellow. I bolted from the ridiculous meeting with my guidance counselor, at first hardly aware of the jellyfish whispers, because I was singularly focused.

Find Brie and Mercedes. Find Brie and Mercedes.

FINDBRIEANDMERCEDES.

Friends needed friends when counselors with sharp kitty claws shredded their JISPs. My throat thickened as I raced across campus to Our Tree.

The Del Rey School was huge. Grassy areas with leafy shade trees surrounded more than a dozen adobe buildings where clans of students had long ago staked their territories. Jocks hung out in front of unit two, band geeks gathered at the tables in front of the library, and stoners did what they did near the auto shop building. As for Brie, Merce, and me, we owned the ficus tree in the quad, one of the school's most coveted outdoor hangouts. We hung out under Our Tree every day before school. Every. Day.

But when I reached Our Tree after meeting with A. Lungren, they weren't there.

A tight fist clamped around my chest.

That's when I first noticed the whispers.

"Is that her?"

"Yep. That's Chloe . . ."

I spun. The two girls who'd been talking about me passed, their heads bent, their voices soft, but loud enough for me to hear one gasp and the other giggle.

That's when I noticed another oddity. No one had plucked one of my pin curls and said, "Hey, Chloe, happy Monday." No one had pointed at my shoes and said, "Sa-weeeeet!"

The bell for first period rang. I stood frozen. Alone. Except for the jellyfish whispers.

I hurried into the cafeteria at lunchtime and spotted Brie and Merce at table fourteen, Our Table. If the cafeteria was a castle, table fourteen would be the royal throne. Queen Brie had made sure our trio had seats there since our freshman year.

That afternoon Brie and Merce looked totally normal as they laughed and talked with the rest of the A-listers. The vise around my chest loosened. The whispers and slights I imagined yesterday and this morning were no doubt a byproduct of watching one too many daytime dramas.

I beelined toward my besties. "Are you ready for a laugh?" I waved the folder A. Lungren had given to me at our meeting. "My new guidance counselor axed Villainous Vixens and suggested I do my Junior Independent Study Project at the Eastside Community Blood Bank."

Mercedes barked out her seal-like laugh, the one I'd heard almost every day for the past six years. The sound was low and choky. Wonderful. "No way," Merce said.

"Way." Blood was fine. Necessary. The problem? I couldn't stand to look at it, another sign of my genetic mutation. My podiatrist father and heart surgeon mother had no issue with body fluids of the red variety, nor did my five doctor and doctor-in-training brothers. Even Grams could sit through a season of *General Hospital* without fainting. Not me. "Scootch over." I pointed to the crowded bench. "I need hugs."

The chatter of voices and crackle of lunch bags at table fourteen stopped.

"There's no room." Brie slipped a spring roll in her mouth.

"None," someone at the far end of table fourteen echoed.

"Excuse me?" I popped my palm against my ear, vaudeville style.

No one smiled. Mercedes examined her veggie burrito. I knew it was a veggie burrito because Mercedes ate veggie burritos every Monday. Best friends knew stuff like this.

"What's going on?" I asked. All eyes turned to Brie, who took another bite of her spring roll. It was so quiet I heard her molars grinding rice and seaweed.

Mercedes put down her burrito. "Sorry. With you being late, we couldn't save you a seat."

"Hell-o-o. I was late because I waited thirty minutes at Brie's locker for you two. Why did you leave without me?" The panic nipping at my wing tips all morning skyrocketed up my body and shot off my tongue. "Where were you this morning? What's wrong with everyone? Why are people whispering about me?"

Brie waved her napkin toward the freshmen at table twenty-one. "Why don't you move over there?"

One by one heads at table fourteen dipped in a puppetlike nod. Brie had that effect on people. When she said, "Jump," they said, "Would you like a double stag or a spread eagle?"

I almost laughed. I should have laughed. But Brie was serious. The lunch bell rang, and for the rest of the day, I kept hearing my name in whispers. After school I caught snatches of a conversation from the row of lockers behind mine.

"Brie said . . . Mistletoe Ball . . ."

". . . disgusting! Then Brie . . ."

I popped my head around the lockers. "Then Brie did what?" I asked with a smile. "I'd like to be in on the joke." Because surely this was a joke. My two BFs dissing me. The entire school whispering about me.

The girls shut their lockers and rushed by, eyeing me as if I needed psych meds.

I slammed my locker, ready to hunt down Brie when A. Lungren slinked toward me on little cat feet.

Bad kitty. Go away. Go far, far away.

"Chloe, I'm glad I found you," A. Lungren said. "I just learned about a JISP opportunity right here on campus."

At the word *JISP*, I wanted to bang my head against my locker. I needed a project by seven to keep the word *fail* off my permanent school record and to keep my dad and mom from going postal. Like my two best friends. Like the entire school. Like my annoying new counselor, who was excitedly waving a flyer in my face and going on and on about the purrrrrfect JISP.

I knew the Del Rey School had portable classrooms and storage units on the east side of campus, but I didn't know one housed a radio station—a real one, with an antenna, call letters, and a sign on the door that read, Toxic Waste. Keep Out!

According to the flyer from my counselor, KDRS 88.8 The Edge was a low-wattage, student-run radio station broadcasting from campus, and they needed promotions help. On the assumption radio promos did not involve blood, I agreed to look into it.

Dark, musty air swallowed me as I walked into Portable Five. At first glance, it looked empty, but as my eyes adjusted to the gloom, I noticed other students. Noticed but didn't recognize. *Outsiders*, Brie would have called them, people who didn't have seats with the clans in the lunchroom or spots on the quad before school.

I squinted through the semidarkness and made out a tall, thin guy with a set of earbuds around his neck, two young dweeby guys who were arguing with each other, a girl with crinkly black hair and a shiny nose ring, and a blond girl licking a candy cane who sat in front of a DVD player in the corner of the room. A faded pair of jeans with a tool belt around the waist jutted from under a large piece of buzzing equipment by the back wall. Everyone but the tool-belt guy looked at me. No one said a word.

"Hi, I'm Chloe." I waved the flyer. "I'm here about the promo position."

Nose Ring Girl's nostrils widened in a dragon flare. "What promo position?" She grabbed the flyer from me. "What's this? What the hell is this?"

No one seemed concerned that she was screaming at the top of her lungs.

"Taysom, did you post this?"

The guy with the earbuds scanned the flyer. "Nope."

"Frick, Frack?" she asked the two freshman types, and they stopped squabbling long enough to shake their heads.

The electronic equipment regurgitated the guy in the tool belt and faded jeans. Him, I recognized. Fellow junior. We had first-period economics together. He sat two rows behind me, and he never talked. Maybe it was because he was an outsider, or maybe it was because he slept through econ. On most mornings soft snores wafted from his direction.

For being regurgitated, Mr. Tool Belt didn't look bad. A ruddy red brushed his pale cheeks, and his thick black hair was messy, like he'd been out in the wind. A nubby scarf looped his neck. I could picture him perched alone on a rugged, windswept Scottish moor.

"I posted the flyer." His voice was barely audible over the buzzing box, or maybe it seemed that way because he stood at a distance from everyone. He turned to Nose Ring Girl. "We need a new power supply."

Her nose ring quivered. "That means we'll have to crack the emergency fund."

Mr. Earbuds shook his head. "Empty."

"Music? You bought more music!" Nose Ring Girl's eyes bulged.

"Music's the heart of our programming," Mr. Earbuds shot back.

Other voices erupted, and I wanted to cover my ears, like with Grams and Mom. I waved a hand in the air. "Excuse me, I'm still here. Chloe. Chloe Camden. Ms. Lungren from the Guidance Center said you need promo help."

"Oh my gawwwwwd. We have a freakin' JISP. We so do not need this." Nose Ring Girl stomped toward the back of the cave. Mr. Earbuds popped in his buds, the two freshmen types started arguing again, and Candy Cane Girl turned to her DVD. It was one of the most bizarre scenes I'd ever seen.

But I needed a JISP. ASAP. "I've done some promo work for a local business, Dos Hermanas Mexican Cantina, and I'm in the drama club, so I'm used to getting attention. I may be able to help. Why don't you tell me about the station?"

A growl erupted from Nose Ring Girl's corner of gloom. "Someone shut her up or I will."

My feet twitched.

Mr. Tool Belt flicked a switch, and half the lights sputtered on. In the half-light I could now see the main room was filled with a maze of wounded furniture and dusty storage boxes lined up like tombstones. Years ago someone had painted KDRS 88.8 The Edge in giant, jagged black letters on a wall, but most of the letters had faded to a phantom gray. The place looked like a school supply graveyard.

"Sorry about the dark," Mr. Tool Belt said. "I can't run my multimeter with the lights on. Crappy wiring." As if on cue, the lights flickered, and a screech tore from one of two glass rooms at the rear of the building. "Welcome to KDRS Radio, which is about to breathe its last breath."

Candy Cane Girl glanced up from her DVD, clutched her throat, and made a soft, choky sound.

Mr. Tool Belt slipped a hammer into one of the leather rungs on his belt. "I'm Duncan Moore, and that's Haley. She handles arts and entertainment." In the half-light, I could see Candy Cane Girl's hand now rested on her rounded belly. Pregnant?

Duncan pointed to the others. "Taysom with the earbuds takes care of music. The newbies are Frick and Frack. They handle sports and public service announcements. Miss Congeniality"— he pointed to Nose Ring Girl—"is Clementine, our general manager."

"Seriously, are you a JISP?" Clementine looked at me as if I were something scraped off the underside of one of the freshman lunch tables.

I squared my shoulders. "I'm undecided. Right now I'm looking into a few options."

"Options? And if we're lucky, you'll pick us?" She snarled the words.

"Someone yank too hard on your nose ring?" I asked.

Candy Cane Mom made a *ca-ching* sound. However, I wasn't trying to score points. It was a joke meant to lighten the gloom. I smiled at Clementine. She growled and stomped into one of the glass rooms.

Duncan wound an extension cord in a complicated series of figure eights, keeping space and the cord between us. A chill prickled my palms. Why were people keeping their distance from me?

"Sorry about Clem." Duncan took a deep breath as if readying himself for an unpleasant task. "Today's a tough day for us." He looped the cord over his shoulder, where it tangled with his scarf. I noticed a tiny, lopsided red heart stitched into one of the ends of the scarf. It looked oddly cheery in this dark place. "We just found out school admin won't renew KDRS funding for next year. With no money for equipment replacement and maintenance, music, supplies, and licensing, we're officially off the air in May. If we want to continue broadcasting, we need to find people and businesses willing to underwrite programming. This semester we're literally fighting for air."

I could do this promo job standing on one way-hot vintage shoe, like Burrito Girl for Dos Hermanas. But I wasn't too keen on hanging out in this gloomy place with these less-than-friendly people.

The Edge. I stared at the gray, jagged letters. There was

something edgy about this place, about these people. Even Duncan, who had invited promo help, was keeping his distance.

Something beeped, and Duncan pushed a small button on his watch. "I need to go. Clem can answer any questions."

Candy Cane Mom made a *pffft* sound.

Duncan went into one of the glass rooms and flicked some switches. When he came out, he announced, "Ghost is set for the night." He headed for the door, but before he walked out, he finally met my gaze. His eyes were a soft, misty gray. "Thanks for coming. I hope you can help us out. We need . . ." He shook his head. "We need something."

The door closed behind him. Without him and his nubby scarf, a chill settled over the radio station, but no one else seemed to notice. Haley watched her DVD, Taysom fiddled with his iPod, and Frick and Frack were arguing again. A loud click sounded, and Clementine's voice boomed over a speaker. "Hi-ho, hi-ho, it's time for you to go." She waggled her fingers at me.

This was not a Chloe-friendly zone. This radio gig was not for me. I returned the waggle and hurried away from Portable Five. I didn't need KDRS Radio. I needed a JISP by seven, something I was passionate about. I had no passion for 88.8 The Edge. Until today I'd never even heard of 88.8 The Edge.

So where did my passions lie? Easy. My friends. Family. Dos Hermanas. Soap operas. Shoes. Definitely shoes. Preferably of the vintage variety. I squinted at my wing tips. Vintage shoes weren't foot apparel for the masses, but everyone needed a good, sturdy pair of shoes. I slowed. There were many who couldn't afford even that, like Dos Hermanas, who walked barefoot across the desert all those years ago. I stopped. What about a shoe drive? I rotated my foot, letting the sunlight flash off the patent leather. And why not for barefoot children in Sonora, Mexico? I flashed the ankle of my other shoe. Brilliant. And, unlike the radio gig, perfect for me.

With a jaunty click of my heels, I walked toward A. Lungren's cat den. Then my cell vibrated, indicating an incoming text flagged *Urgent*.

URGENT
Stop by tuna cn. Prob. No nd 4 guns.
Brad Pitt w%d b nce. Dnt sa NEfin 2
HER.
Grams

A dame that knows the ropes isn't
likely to get tied up—Mae West

CHAPTER 3

I SAW THE BLOOD BEFORE I SAW GRAMS. ON GRAMS'S PORCH,
a silver dollar–size circle of shiny red puddled near a ceramic
squirrel sporting an ear-to-ear grin. A tidal wave of nausea rolled
over me.

Grams stumbled out of her trailer, her arm held high. "Thank
God you're here, Poppy, we need to . . . oh holy hell!" She took a
wobbly step toward me and pushed my head between my knees.
"Deep breath in. Deep breath out. That's a girl."

When the haze cleared, I raised my head. "What happened?"

"I was trimming the dwarf palm and got my thumb." She
raised her hand, which she'd wrapped in a dish towel. A stream
of blood trickled down her wrist.

I swooned and ducked my head between my knees, where I
found myself face-to-face with the grinning ceramic squirrel.
"You should have called Mom."

"You are not allowed to talk about *her* in my presence." Grams huffed out a growl. "And you will not tell *her* about this." She jabbed her bloodied hand in the air.

Another wave of wooziness shook my head. "Let's, uh, call an ambulance."

"Let's not. Nosy Noreen next door will see and call *her*." When Grams spoke next, some of her bluster had faded. "You don't have to stay. Just drop me off at the ER."

I straightened. Grams needed me, and I would be there for her. That was my MO. Need a friend? Call Chloe. How about a laugh? Enter Chloe with joke book in hand. But right now, I needed help. Holding on to the porch railing, I picked up the phone handset near the porch swing. "Why don't you get your purse while I make a few calls?"

I dialed Brie and got her message machine. Déjà-bloody-vu. But it was time for best friends to step up to the BF table. "Brie, emergency with Grams. I need to get her to the hospital. Call me ASAP." How's that for subtlety?

Thankfully, Mercedes was home and answered the phone. I wondered if it was because I was calling from Grams's phone, which wouldn't come up on her caller ID. "Emergency at the Tuna Can," I said. "I need someone to drive Grams and me to the ER."

Mercedes paused. "I can't. I'm working on college scholarship essays tonight."

Who cared about college? "My grandmother's bleeding to death."

"Stop exaggerating. If that were the case, you would have called 911. Brie's right, you're such a drama queen."

While Grams was not dying, she was growing paler as the dish towel around her hand grew redder. My fingers tightened around the phone. "Mercedes, I need you."

"You don't need me, you need a driver. Call a cab."

"No, I don't need a cab. I need *you*." The porch groaned as I sunk onto the wooden swing hanging from the awning, the full force of the last few days slamming me. Brie and the jellyfish whispers. A. Lungren and my stupid JISP. The battle at home. "The day after the Mistletoe Ball Grams and Mom started World War III, and I'm in the middle of it. Picture Switzerland without the Alps for protection."

A low grumble sounded on the other end. "I don't have time for this today."

She didn't have time for my bleeding grandmother? For me? My mouth felt dry, scratchy, as if filled with sun-soaked beach sand. "What's going on? Have I broken some kind of best-friend rule? Screwed up the secret BFF handshake?"

"Life isn't a big joke."

"No, it's not, but there's nothing wrong with a little laughter, especially when things are completely out of whack." That's what I needed, a little whack to knock some sense into my world, into my best friends. "Why are you and Brie being so . . . so mean?"

Mean. What an ugly four-letter word.

Silence, heavy and cold, pressed down on me. I took a breath, forcing air and a calmness I didn't feel into my chest. "Talk to me, Merce. You owe me an explanation." I stared at the grinning ceramic squirrel. "Especially after last year."

Last year, the year her mother died, had been brutal for Mercedes. I stood at her side through it all: the chemo, the funeral, and the hell of learning how to live without a mother. I offered her Twizzlers when she needed comfort, jokes when she needed laughter, and hugs for everything else. Best friends stood beside you. Always.

Mercedes didn't say anything, and for a horrible moment I thought she had hung up. At last she sighed. "Brie's really upset over the whole Mistletoe Queen thing."

I almost fell off the porch swing. "A fungus crown? Is that what this is all about?"

"You know she was nominated for Mistletoe Queen, too."

"Of course Brie was nominated for queen. She's on every court and has been since the time we were freshmen. She's royalty. Everyone knows that. Everyone also knows Mistletoe Queen is hardly a popularity contest. The president of the National Honor Society won the crown last year, and before that, I think it was the first-chair violin."

"But Brie was counting on it. She bought that new dress."

I remembered Brie's dress. Who wouldn't? White and wispy with frosty gems, the dress made her look like an enchanted ice queen. I'd worn a slinky red sweater dress with an antler headband.

"This one was important to her," Merce went on. "She needed something good in her life that night."

"It's not like I had any control over who won. School clubs nominate nicey-nice people from their ranks, and a committee of teachers looking for do-gooders makes the final selection."

Another long pause boomed on the other end. "But you made such a big show of it."

The Mistletoe King and I spent the evening knighting royal subjects and creating wacky royal decrees, like anyone caught kissing on the dance floor had to do the Chicken Dance. "We were all having fun. You laughed so hard, you fell off the sleigh."

"Not everyone had fun. For crying out loud, Chloe, Brie spent most of the night bawling her eyes out in the bathroom. Don't you remember, or were you too blinded by your shiny new crown?"

"Of course I remember. I also remember Brie saying she was upset over her idiotic parents, not me."

"And?"

"And what?" This was not the time for twenty questions. Grams was bleeding, and I needed some support.

"Don't you remember what Brie said after that?" Merce didn't let me answer. "She said she needed us. Me *and* you. She needed to talk. She needed hugs. And you know what you told her? You said, 'Give me fifteen minutes, Cheese Girl, and I'll be here for you.' But you never came back. You spent the next hour laughing and dancing and shooting fake snowballs through the gym's basketball hoops. You even went out for the late-night mini-chimi platter at Dos Hermanas with your stupid Mistletoe Court after the dance. You totally abandoned Brie when she needed you. When I needed you. God, Chloe, you know I'm horrible at that kind of stuff."

My stomach twisted into a tight, hot knot. Not one of my more brilliant moves. Okay, it was a major friendship fail, but it wasn't the end of the world. "So slap me with a major BFF violation, but in my defense, I tried to get in touch with her the next day. I contacted you both through OurWorld."

"Sure you did. You went on and on about some problems between your mom and grandma. Not once did you ask about Brie's problems with her family. The weekend of the Mistletoe Ball was horrible. All of winter break was horrible. Brie's family didn't go skiing in France because it was so bad."

The past few years Brie had her own version of war on the home front, and when her parents' arguing got too overwhelming, she would escape to my house. "Make me laugh, Chloe," Brie would say. "Make me forget about how much they hate each other."

My parents weren't perfect—always working, especially my dad, who this year was named dean of the university's school of podiatric medicine—but my home had always been a happy place filled with laughter and my loud-but-loving brothers.

When I was four, I remembered crawling onto Mom's lap after dinner one night and declaring with great seriousness that this would be my last dinner *ever* with the family.

"Why's that?" Mom asked as she stroked my hair.

"I'm going to Russia to become the star of the Bolshoi." I'm not sure of my motive back then, but it had something to do with Grams and me starting a mother-granddaughter ballet/tap/jazz class on Saturday mornings.

"Russia's a long ways away," Mom said with a straight face. "We'd miss you very much."

Dad nodded. "With you gone, who would make us laugh? Who would slide under the sofa to look for Grams's remote controls? And who would Zach sneak his lima beans to?"

"I'm afraid we have a much bigger problem than lima beans," Jeremy said with a severity that quieted the table. "Poppy can't go to Russia and join the Bolshoi because they don't make tutus in her size. Too little."

I scrambled up from Mom's lap and onto the dining room table, balling my hands on my hips. "I'm *not* too little. Luke, tell Jeremy I'm not too little."

Luke, the oldest and in my mind wisest of my brothers, took his fork and used it as a ruler to measure my left foot and right earlobe. "According to my calculations, you're definitely classified as Too Little to Join the Bolshoi."

I placed my hands on my cheeks. "Oh no!"

"She could wear a tall hat," Max said, putting a bread bowl on his head.

"Or Grams's red high heels," his twin, Sam, added.

"Wait! I have a plan!" Zach jumped from his chair. "We'll stretch her. Luke will take her right arm, Jeremy can take her left. Sam and Max, you grab her feet."

Within seconds I was stretched and hovering over the dinner table, then flying around the dining room amid peals of laughter. I remember at one point hanging from the chandelier and Zach laughing so hard he snorted a lima bean he'd hidden up his nose.

Yes, unlike Brie's home, mine had rung with laughter for years.

I sighed into the phone then said to Merce, "I'm sorry. I had no idea things with Brie's parents were that bad during winter break."

"That's part of the problem. You had no idea. You were too busy basking in your queenliness. Face it, Chloe, you screwed up. Royally."

I swallowed the knot that had crept up my throat. Merce was right. I abandoned Brie at the Mistletoe Ball, and Grams's health issues slammed me over winter break. "I'll talk to Brie, apologize, and let her know I haven't jumped the BF boat."

"I think you need to give Brie a little space."

"Space?" I was tired of *space* between me and my BFs.

"Seriously, Chloe, she needs time away from you."

"No, she needs—"

"Me, too." Merce hung up.

The phone felt like a brick of ice. Brie and Merce were abandoning me over one lousy night and one stupid mistake. For a very un-Chloe-like moment, I wanted to throw the phone at the grinning squirrel, but then Grams walked out of the Tuna Can, her bloody dish towel held high, a dribble of slick red trickling down her arm and plopping off the tip of her elbow.

Deep breath in. Deep breath out.

I helped Grams down the porch steps, my shoes clanking on the metal.

Shoes. My JISP. I needed to call A. Lungren and tell her about my new JISP project, explaining about the medical emergency with Grams and that as soon as I got access to a computer, I'd shoot her all of the wonderful shoe-y details.

Economics was a required course, and most juniors hated it. Some juniors even slept through it, like Duncan Moore, the tool-belt, faded-jeans guy from KDRS. Only this morning, he was wide awake and scribbling like a maniac on a sheet of lined paper.

"Finishing the essay on excise taxes that's due in seven minutes?" I stopped next to his desk as the first-period bell rang. Duncan smelled nice this morning, like soap and an ocean breeze.

He didn't look up, but a wave of red crept along the part of his neck not covered by his scarf. "I'm *starting* the essay on excise taxes that's due in seven minutes."

A page of bright white sat on his desktop. Seriously, he was on the first paragraph of a three-page essay. "Wow, Dunc, you could use some serious time management lessons."

He looked at me through the wings of his eyelashes. "That or a few extra hours in the day. If you have some, send them my way."

There was something serious in his storm-colored eyes, too serious, and I almost reached out to smooth the sharp line creasing his forehead, but I stopped.

Eyes were everywhere.

My feet shifted. Nothing had changed since yesterday. People were still looking at me strangely and whispering behind my back. Touching outsider Duncan Moore's troubled forehead would send another wave of jellyfish whispers rushing through the turbulent seas of my life. I clasped my hands behind my back. "I'll see what I can do about rustling up a few extra hours." I winked at Duncan and headed to my desk, my gold sparkle Socialites with rhinestones, circa 1960, making happy, tapping sounds.

That morning I could do anything. After all, I'd handily taken care of Grams, A. Lungren, and my new JISP.

Last night after the ER adventures with Grams, I filled out a whole new JISP book, titled *Barefoot No More*, which included details about childhood poverty in Sonora, Mexico, shoe collection sites, a budget, strategies, and timeline. Then I scanned the masterpiece and e-mailed a copy to A. Lungren. For good measure, I left a second message on her phone at 7:22 p.m. reminding her again of Grams's medical emergency. That morning I slipped the new and improved JISP notebook into A. Lungren's slot in the guidance office.

With my JISP tied in a shiny bow, it was time to tackle Brie, Merce, and the jellyfish whispers. Merce said Brie was upset because I wasn't there for her the night of the Mistletoe Ball when she was in crisis. But I was now.

When the bell rang announcing the end of first-period econ, Duncan fell in step beside me. He wore another lumpy scarf, this one black and red with another lopsided red heart stitched into one of the ends. I wondered if he had a novice-knitter girlfriend, someone to smooth the harsh lines on his face. The Del Rey School was huge, more than four thousand students, and we had a few classes together over the past three years, but I'd never seen him at any football games or dances or in the lunchroom.

Outsider.

Brie's word for people who didn't have a place in our world popped into my head again. Outsiders weren't bad, but I couldn't imagine life spent on the outside looking in.

"Did you get your econ essay finished?" I asked, trying to shake off the image.

"Turned in with ten seconds to spare." Duncan didn't smile, but the line carved in his forehead disappeared.

"Is it just econ, or are you one of those thrill seekers who likes living on the edge with all your classes?"

"Thrill seeker? In my dreams." Up close I could see dark half-moons under his eyes, as if he was not getting enough sleep or having bad dreams. He reached into his back pocket and took out a piece of paper. "Speaking of edges, here's an emergency memo from Clementine. She e-mailed it last night. All Edge staffers must attend today's emergency meeting after school."

With both hands I waved off the paper. "I'm not a staffer. I'm doing a different JISP." I flashed him my ankle. "Something to do with shoes."

That deep, vertical line divided Duncan's forehead again. "You should check in with Clem. For some reason she thinks you're an official staffer."

"You had no right!" I slammed the KDRS memo on A. Lungren's desk. "No right to commit me to a JISP with that radio station."

"Your JISP was due last night at seven, and you failed to meet the deadline, which means you would fail your JISP and put a dark mark on your permanent record. As your guidance counselor, it is my duty to keep that from happening."

"I was in the ER with my injured grandmother. You need a doctor's note?"

"No, Chloe, I need you to calm down." A. Lungren's voice was a low purr. "I'm sorry about your grandmother, and I got your phone messages and e-mail, but your project came in twenty-two minutes after the deadline. This is a perfect example of how the real world doesn't always go according to our plans. Real-world issues need to be dealt with in real-world ways. Your JISP is a tool to help get you ready for this kind of world."

I pictured the dark, gloomy radio station and the crazy staff. "I don't want to work at the radio station. I want to collect shoes for barefoot children in Mexico. I want to set up collection boxes in the quad and at lunch table fourteen and get donations from shoe manufacturers."

"Chloe—"

"I want to go door-to-door and get pledges to sponsor entire schools of shoeless Mexican children."

"Chloe—"

"I want—"

"Chloe! Be quiet!" A. Lungren steadied her cat glasses on the bridge of her nose. "The JISP review board has made its decision. For the next few months, you will do promotions work at the school's radio station."

"Do you know anything about the station?" A tremor edged my words. "KDRS is not a good place for me. It's insane over there. Everyone fighting. Equipment breaking. They have no money and are going off air at the end of the semester." I had enough disasters with my BFs, and I didn't need any more with my JISP. "The radio station's a lost cause."

"Not necessarily." A. Lungren's feline features grew animated. "I did some research and discovered that, until four years ago, KDRS was a thriving part of the Del Rey School community. During radio classes, students learned about news and feature writing and ran the radio station for credit. Unfortunately, the English teacher who oversaw the program for decades retired. Admin discontinued the radio classes because they couldn't get a qualified teacher on board. A few die-hard students have held things together as an after-school club, but things are looking bleak."

As was I. Because I was shackled with a counselor who couldn't resist a lost cause.

"It's clear, Chloe, that KDRS needs a hand, and you can start by putting together a promotions plan for today's emergency meeting."

A hand? I wanted to give A. Lungren the Hand.

"By the way, you'll need this." A. Lungren handed me a composition notebook.

I was four again and standing on the edge of the Pacific Ocean getting battered by waves, but it wasn't fun, and Grams wasn't there holding my hand. "For what?" I asked.

"Your progress reports. You must turn in a report to my office once a week."

"Why do I need to turn in weekly reports? That's not a normal part of the JISP."

"The reports are for your parents."

"My parents?" Heart surgeons and deans of podiatry schools didn't have time for parent-teacher conferences or JISP reports. That was a job for grandmothers who ran award-winning soap opera blogs from tuna cans.

"I spoke with your parents this morning, and they are extremely concerned about your lack of progress. They've been through this with your brothers and know your JISP is a permanent mark on your school transcripts, one that highly desirable, highly competitive universities will look at in determining admissions."

I stared at my shoes. What if I didn't want to go to a highly desirable, highly competitive university? I wasn't like my brothers. I didn't have college plans and my career mapped out. I didn't even know what I wanted to be when I grew up.

With a final kitty grin, A. Lungren escorted me out of her office.

JISP intervention complete.

I stood in the breezeway, where voices chimed, and laughter, too, but it was all muted, as if something stood between me and the rest of my world. Space. Lots of space. As I made my way down the hall, one voice and one laugh were strangely clear—painfully familiar. The voice was low and breathy, and the laugh belonged to a friendly seal.

I gravitated toward those sounds and fell in step behind Brie and Merce. Habit? Stupidity? I shook my head. These were my people, my clan with whom I shared a woven plaid, and not just any plaid. We wore one of the fanciest, most coveted plaids in the school.

Brie stopped at her locker. My feet slowed, and I fidgeted with a pin curl. Brie and I needed to talk. We were best friends, and that's what best friends did. When life was good we talked. When it was disastrous we talked. When it was confusing we talked. Yes, I should have talked to Brie the night of the Mistletoe Ball. I should have put my best friends above a stupid fungus crown. I screwed up, landed myself in a queenly quagmire of my own making, but it was time to right the universe.

I opened my mouth as Brie looked over her shoulder. A smile that didn't reach her eyes slid across her frosty pink lips. Words froze in my throat as she linked arms with Merce, who didn't once look my way. One by one other girls from table fourteen linked up with my two best friends, and they sashayed down the hall arm in arm. I thought of all the times I'd linked arms with them and bent my head for private talk meant for our ears only. It wasn't a vicious gesture, not meant to exclude. Girlfriends did it all the time, a friendly way of saying, *We support each other. We are one.*

Today the intertwined arms looked like barbed wire.

SUBJ: KDRS Emergency Meeting
FROM: Clementine.Radmore@gmx.com
TO: KDRS Staff

Emergency meeting today after school. Miss it, you die.

Clementine
Aut vincere aut mori.

CHAPTER 4

WHEN LIFE GIVES YOU THE STOMACH LINING OF A COW, MAKE menudo.

It was Josie's twist on the whole lemon-lemonade thing. As I walked into Portable Five after school, I told myself I wouldn't think about friends with barbed-wire arms or get into a catfight with the world's most annoying guidance counselor. Instead, I'd embrace KDRS promotions and help with whatever emergency plagued the station.

I'd make menudo.

Inside Portable Five no one seemed to be doing anything urgent. Frick/Frack sat in one of the two glass rooms in front of a microphone. Haley, who today was Tootsie Pop Mom, sat in her corner with her DVD player, her feet resting on a giant stack of movies. Taysom of the Earbuds flipped through a box of ancient vinyl record albums, and Clementine of the Nose Ring was hunched over a laptop in the main room.

Only Duncan, who stood on a ladder in a corner hammering the cover of a light fixture into place, acknowledged my presence. He stopped tapping long enough to give me a look that asked, *What are you doing here?*

No, I don't belong at KDRS, I thought. These days I didn't belong anywhere. Not at lunch table fourteen. Not in OurWorld. My heart rate quickened, and I hugged my bulging JISP folder to my chest and focused on menudo.

"Everyone ready to talk promo?" I pumped enthusiasm into my voice. When no one said anything, I asked Clementine, "Aren't we having an emergency meeting?"

Clementine didn't look up from her laptop. "Twenty minutes."

Good, in twenty minutes I'd reveal the ideas Dos Hermanas and I brainstormed to grow the radio station audience and attract advertisers. Instead of sitting alone in the cafeteria for lunch and advertising my absolute friendlessness, I had hid out in my car talking on the phone with the sisters about promotions and menudo.

"Do you want to see my notes first?" I asked Clementine.

"No."

"I have this great idea about—"

"Later."

I tapped my shoe. "What can I do until then to help?"

Without missing a keystroke Clementine said, "Shut up."

I turned toward the guidance center. *Do you see me, A. Lungren? I'm trying. I'm really trying.*

Duncan climbed down the ladder and packed his tools.

44

"You need some help?" I asked.

He shook his head and carried his things through a door at the far right side of the building I hadn't noticed before. The air cooled and thinned. Yesterday Duncan had been the only friendly, albeit distant, being at KDRS Radio, the only one who wanted me around, and this morning he went out of his way to make sure I knew about the emergency meeting, like he cared if I showed up. Had he changed his mind and joined the Anti-Chloe Club?

"Stop making noise," Clementine said with a dragon snort.

"I didn't say anything."

"Your shoe sounds like a jackhammer."

I plunked my eyes closed. Thanks to growing up in a house with five older brothers, I was used to noise. When I could, I slept with my window open to hear the rush of the ocean, and when I was a kid, I used to fall asleep on Grams's chest listening to her heart beat.

"And stop that, too," Clementine said.

"Stop what?" I searched for a peaceful place, a soothing place. The ocean at sunset.

"Breathing."

My eyes flew open. "You want me to stop breathing?"

Clementine smirked. "Would you?"

Taysom chuckled, and Tootsie Pop Mom, Haley, made a gurgling sound at the back of her throat, rolled her eyes, and thwunked her head on her desk as if dead.

I ground my back teeth. They were all wack jobs, and thanks to A. Lungren, I was forced into their wacked world.

I hurried across the station and through the door Duncan used to a narrow room full of maintenance equipment and janitorial supplies. Duncan stood at a sagging workbench, where he was prying the cover off an ancient clock and studying its intestines.

"Get the possessed lights fixed?" I asked. It sounded so much less pathetic than *Would you be my friend?*

Without looking at me, he nodded and popped the cover off another clock. He took apart springs and gears and hands and placed them in a neat line on a workbench.

Voices had always surrounded me—my five older brothers, Grams, the soap opera divas on TV, Merce, and Brie. In my world, someone was always talking, and if not them, me. "I have some great promo ideas, some creative, low-cost stuff we can do right here on campus that will build our audience." I watched as Duncan tugged and twisted various clock parts. "And after we get more students listening, we can promote the station to the general public. You know, other schools, the neighborhood, local businesses. Then we'll start calling on advertisers."

When I stopped to take a breath, he slid the cover onto one of the clocks, secured it with duct tape, and looked at me, that line creasing his forehead. "I thought you picked a different JISP."

"It's Clementine. She's my crack." I waggled my eyebrows. "I crave daily insults."

Duncan's gaze softened. "Great voice. Perfect delivery." Turning the knob on the bottom of the clock, he set the time. The second hand started to *thudda-click* as it chased itself around the clock face. "You'd be good on air."

"Over my dead body," Clementine said as she jerked to a halt in the supply room doorway.

I made evil finger–twitching motions and cackled. "I'm sure we can arrange that."

Her glare said, *Bite me*, but the expression fell away as she turned to Duncan. "Meeting starts in two minutes. You sticking around?"

He held up the clock. "Need to go."

"Anything to add to the agenda?" Clementine asked.

"No, I'm good," Duncan said. Yes, Duncan was good. He fixed broken lights and old clocks. He cared about the station enough to bring in someone to help keep a sinking ship afloat.

Clem gave me another fiery dragon glare and stormed off, her wild hair whipping me in the face.

"She's not usually this bad," Duncan said. "The idea of the station closing in May kills her. Radio's a hobby for most of us, but it's Clem's life. She wants to own her own station one day."

I ran the toe of my shoe along a crack in the linoleum. How nice to have your future planned, like my brothers. As for me, I liked old shoes and spicy Mexican cantinas with stuffed parrots perched on top of salsa bars. And honestly, I could get into KDRS radio if the staff wasn't so anti-Chloe. The promotional work, not to mention the idea of going on air, made my toes tingle.

"What about you?" I asked. "Why are you at the station?"

Duncan unbuckled his tool belt and hung it on a hook. His

back was to me, and I watched the muscles along his broad shoulders and arms bunch under his faded T-shirt. I wondered at the loads he carried on that muscled back. He didn't say anything.

"Do you want a career in radio?" I asked. "Did you fail to make the badminton team?"

He faced me, his stormy eyes steady. "Do you always talk this much?"

My breath caught in my throat. "Does it bother you?"

He reached for the cord hanging from the bare lightbulb overhead with both hands but didn't pull. After an eternity, he shook his head, and I let out the breath I'd been holding.

"So why are you here?" I asked again.

Duncan wrapped the cord around his fingers three times. "It's fun."

"Fun? KDRS is fun?"

"Yeah. Fun." His shoulders lifted in an awkward shrug. "Sometimes that's hard to find."

I searched his face. He had to be joking. But Duncan, with his stormy eyes, was no jokester. "Fun is everywhere," I said. "You just have to find it. Or make it."

He leaned toward me, his fingers pulling the cord tight. "Tell me, Chloe, exactly how do you make fun?" His face looked earnest, but there was something else there, something that settled around him like a swollen storm cloud.

Duncan Moore didn't have much fun in his life. The realization slammed me, knocking me breathless. I couldn't imagine a life without laughter and friends and fun.

I reached for both ends of his scarf, wanting to draw him away from the heaviness of his world and into mine, at least the one I'd known until a few weeks ago. "The recipe for fun's a top-secret formula." I pulled him toward me to whisper in his ear, mock severity lining my brow. "If I told you, I'd have to . . . you know . . . kill Clementine."

Duncan stared at me, a strange look on his face, as if he'd come across a beached whale carcass, fascinating but in a grotesque way. I dropped the ends of his scarf. "Okay, so my sense of humor is warped, don't mind—"

A soft laugh rumbled around his broad chest, wound through the crowded storeroom, and wrapped around me in a hug. What a wonderful sound. I'd heard so little laughter the past few weeks.

His watch beeped, and his laughing tapered off. "I need to go."

I fought the urge to beg, *Don't go. Stay and laugh with me.*

He pulled the cord, extinguishing the light. When he reached the storeroom door, he placed both hands on the door frame, as if forcing himself to stay, and looked at me over his shoulder. "I'm glad you're here, Chloe." Did he like laughing with me? Or was he simply being a *nice* guy? Could he tell I needed nice? "Someone like you can make a difference."

He turned to leave, and I reached for his scarf again, looping my thumbs through the ends. "Someone like me?" *Say something nice. Say something to make me forget that my best friends hate me and the whole school is whispering something about me that's not nice.*

He stared at my thumbs. Like my science-minded brothers,

Duncan was an observer. In his quietness, did he see things others didn't?

"Yeah, someone like you," he said. "Someone with a big personality and a big heart. People like you can do big things." Not mean. Definitely not mean.

As if embarrassed by the sweet words, Duncan unhooked my thumbs, which sparked and heated, like two stubby candles. How crazy was that? Thumbs were . . . thumbs. As I contemplated the tingly heat, he hurried into the main room, where he climbed onto a wobbly desk and centered the clock above one of the glass windows. Then he slid out the door.

Thudda-click, thudda-click, went Duncan's clock.

Duncan said I had a big heart. I always felt things in a big way, joy on the night of the Mistletoe Ball, worry about Grams's health, guilt for ignoring my best friends at a time when they needed me, confusion over all the whispers. I definitely felt big emotions; maybe I could do big things.

"Get your butt over here, JISP Girl."

Time to pour my big heart into my big pain-in-the-butt JISP.

The radio staff and Mr. Martinez, an English teacher who had joined the group while Duncan was wreaking havoc with my thumbs, sat in a horseshoe with Clementine at the center. I took out my promo notes to hand to Haley when Clementine snatched them from my hand.

"The world doesn't revolve around you, JISP Girl. You're last on the agenda. Now sit down and shut up." She turned to the rest of the staff, her voice less snappish as she said, "Bad news.

Since the wrestling team got knocked out of the Winter Trophy tournament, we have a two-hour program hole to fill this Friday. I don't want clutter. What do you all have?"

"I can get interviews with the wrestling coach and captain," Frick said.

"I'll take another hour on my format clock, expanding my grunge band segment," Taysom added. "And isn't there an indie film festival coming to town next week? Maybe Haley can do a preview. I can help with bites." Haley reached for another Tootsie Pop and gave a thumbs-up sign. Mr. Martinez, head bent as he graded a stack of papers, saluted with his red pen.

Problem fixed. It was strange seeing this little dysfunctional family at work. Clementine took the staff on an hour-by-hour walkthrough of the week's programming. When she was done, she closed her eyes, as if trying to find a Zen moment. "Okay, JISP Girl, talk."

I'd been uncharacteristically silent through the meeting because they weren't talking a language I understood. Program holes. Format clocks. Clutter. Bites. Sweepers.

However, promo was something I knew and loved.

I looked at every staff member. The soap villainesses had taught me that delivery was just as important as content. I leaned forward, my eyes wide. "Free burritos."

A loud, hot rumble tumbled from Clementine's dragon snout.

"You want to give our listeners burritos?" Frick said. "That's . . . uh . . . kind of weird."

"Not at all," I said. "We need more listeners to attract advertisers."

Clementine smacked her hands on either side of her head. "Would someone shoot her and put me out of my misery?"

"What's wrong with what I said? If we have a broader audience, we'll have more impressions, so we'll be more attractive to advertisers. It's basic marketing."

Clementine's nostrils flared. "We're a noncommercial station. FCC says we can't have *advertisers*." She turned to the rest of the staff. "See, she knows nothing about radio. She doesn't belong here."

Wrong. I belonged here thanks to my JISP. "Bad choice of words. Duncan called them . . . what? Sponsors?"

"*Un-der-wri-ters.*" Clementine enunciated each syllable as if I were dense.

"Okay, un-der-wri-ters like lots of listeners, and one way to attract listeners is to give them free things." I explained about Dos Hermanas' buy-one-get-one-free burrito special. "After starting BOGOF, Sunday sales skyrocketed. People like freebies. I'm suggesting we have a contest for listeners, and the winners get something free."

"What type of things?" Taysom asked.

"We don't have any things," Frick said.

"N-n-none." Frack. Was that snide laughter?

"Stoo-pid." Clementine.

Tootsie Pop Mom hummed a funeral dirge.

"Stop." I jammed both hands in the air. This wasn't fun. This should be fun. Why did Duncan have to leave? "We get donations. I can ask Dos Hermanas if they'd give us a gift certificate. We need eight items." I pointed to the faded KDRS logo on the wall. "My idea is, 88.8 The Edge, your home to the Great Eight Giveaway. But that's only the first step. As we're getting out the word to all of our shiny new listeners, we'll need to find out about"—another well-timed dramatic pause—"refritos."

Clementine slammed her forehead on the table.

I ignored her and explained that last year Dos Hermanas won Best Refritos awards from a dozen web dining guides. Prior to getting the award, Ana and Josie spent months talking to customers about what type of refried beans they wanted. Black beans or pintos? With or without onions? Light spice or high kick? "People will keep returning to a restaurant if they like the refritos, and they'll keep tuning in to our station if they like our programming."

"And how do we find out what kind of . . . refritos they like?" Taysom asked.

"Burrito costumes."

Clementine's head popped up, fire flying from her ears. "You want us to dress up as freakin' burritos!"

No, what I wanted was to sic my evil kitty counselor on dragon Clementine and see which one came out on top. "Not necessarily, but we need to draw attention to ourselves. Costumes, posters, flyers. When we get their attention, we have them fill out a survey about what kind of radio programs they want, and after they fill out the survey, they get entered in a drawing to win free stuff."

Cricket. Cricket.

"Come on, people," I said. This was all about my JISP, and thanks to A. Lungren and AWOL BFs, my JISP was my life. "We can hold the survey and prize drawing in the lunchroom. Frick and Frack, you can take first lunch. Taysom, you and Haley take second." I gave Clementine my most winsome grin. "You know you want to."

Laugh. Please, please, somebody laugh.

Without a word, Clementine stalked to one of the glass rooms and slammed the door. The glass rattled, and I ducked, half expecting little shards of window to fly across the newsroom and straight at my chest.

With a final deep breath, I faced the rest of the staff and Mr. Martinez. "Okay, that's a no." Sure, I was a lover with a big heart, but I could fight when I had to, when things I cared about were on the line. Like a passing JISP. Like trying to forget images of best friends with barbed-wire arms. "What about the rest of you? Are you with me?"

WIN A $25
GIFT CERTIFICATE
TO
DOS HERMANAS
MEXICAN CANTINA!

Stop by Cafeteria Table Fourteen

and fill out the first-ever

KDRS 88.8 The Edge Radio Listener Survey!

CHAPTER 5

THE NEXT DAY I SAT AT TABLE FOURTEEN WITH ONLY A PLATE OF tamales de dulce to keep me company.

Sitting alone in a school cafeteria was akin to screaming, *Look at me, world! I have no friends!* All around me different clans talked and laughed and shared oatcakes and haggis. When Kim and Leila from the drama club walked by, I shot out my hand. "Hey, guys. Come check out our radio survey. We have some cool swag."

They looked at each other, shuddered, and hurried away.

I waved at Liam across the aisle. He'd been the king to my Mistletoe Queen and had sworn his love and fealty at the ball. Today he refused to look me in the eye.

I wanted to stand and scream, *What's going on? Why's everyone treating me like a pariah?* But I stayed seated because the almighty JISP demanded I stay seated.

Thanks to my persuasive presentation yesterday, everyone at

the KDRS staff meeting but Clementine agreed to help with the survey and Great Eight Giveaway.

During the first two lunch periods, Frick, Frack, Taysom, and Haley manned table fourteen, the undisputed hub of the cafeteria, and managed to gather more than four hundred completed surveys. I'd hoped to have Duncan at my side for the final lunch bunch, but he hadn't shown to first-period econ. Had he slept in? Was he finishing a last-minute paper for some other class? Or like everyone else, did he not want to be seen with me?

"This is stoo-pid."

My shock gave way to twisted delight as Clementine sat on the bench next to me. "You want to help with the survey?"

"I want to make sure you don't do anything to lead to the ruin of my radio station." She hauled out a copy of *Time* magazine and stuck her nose in it. The pope's face was on the cover. He looked peaceful, holy, and hilarious with Clementine's crinkly bush of hair.

I swallowed a nervous giggle and glanced at the cafeteria doors. Still no Brie. I fidgeted with the plate of tamales at my elbow. Brie was the other reason I suggested we set up the survey at table fourteen. I needed to get her attention. She and her whispering legions may have declared war on me, but I had enough battles at home. I needed peace. I'd given her a few days to cool off. Now it was time to talk, stop the whispers, and share tamales.

It's funny. Grams is the only person with whom I share DNA who doesn't have a bunch of letters after her name, but when it comes to people and relationships, she can give plenty of lessons to the PhDs and MDs in my family. Last night when she noticed my less-than-sunny disposition and I told her about my BF woes, she proclaimed, "This calls for tamales."

The first time Brie came to my house in the seventh grade to hang out with Merce and me, she didn't laugh at my jokes, nor did she quite know what to say when Merce, trying to impress her, straightened one of those retro Rubik's Cubes in less than thirty seconds. In the awkward silence, Grams suggested we make tamales de dulce. For two hours we worked side by side as we simmered corn husks, mixed the raisin-walnut filling, and steamed the tamales. By the time we ate the sweets, we had sugar in our hair, masa on the ceiling, and laughter riding the waves of steam throughout the kitchen.

Since then, Brie, Merce, and I have made tamales de dulce at least once a year. Sometimes we used raisins and walnuts, other times blackberries or figs or chopped apples. For Brie's sixteenth birthday Merce and I made her a complicated but delicious batch with toasted coconut and candied pineapple.

"You and Brie have had some sweet times together," Grams had said. "She needs to be reminded of that."

So last night Grams helped me make a dozen tamales de dulce.

The lunch bell rang, and students started pouring into the caf, including Brie. When she reached table fourteen, her beautiful face twisted in an ugly scowl. She looked at Clementine and wrinkled her nose. I could see the thought bubble over her head. Outsider.

"This is *my* table." Brie's lips barely moved.

My hands grew sweaty, which was crazy. This was Brie, one of my BFs. She knew my fears and dreams. I knew hers. We steamed tamales together. "We need to talk," I said.

"This is my table." Her lipstick, Iced Cotton Candy, was frosty pink, cold. Behind her a crowd gathered, probably the other A-listers who claimed a spot at table fourteen, but I saw only my best friend's face.

I wasn't a mean person; the idea that I hurt my BF made me sick. "Listen, Brie, I'm sorry about the Mistletoe Ball. I'm sorry I was AWOL during winter break. I had issues with Grams and Mom—huge, universe-altering issues—but that doesn't excuse me not being there for you."

Brie's face remained as hard as the diamond studs glistening like glaciers in her ears.

"I made a mistake," I went on. "I know you felt like I abandoned you when you needed me, but I'm here now." I slid the tamales toward her, relief washing over me. It was like handing her my heart, and as Duncan had said, it was a big one.

Brie picked up a tamale and studied it with unblinking eyes.

I licked my lips. "I have no idea what you said to everyone to make them whisper about me, but honestly, I don't care. I want what we had, and I'll do anything to get that. Anything. What do you want me to do, Brie? What do you need from me?"

Brie blinked, and with a flick of her hand, she flung the tamale across the room, where it smacked into the side of a garbage can. "You're such a loser, Chloe. The only thing I need is for you to get away from my lunch table and out of my life."

The cafeteria silenced. Trays clanked, mouths moved, but I heard nothing except Brie's words. They sliced through me with razor sharpness. At some point someone with crinkly black hair ushered me to table twenty-one, where I sat and tried to stanch the flow of blood from the middle of my chest.

When the lunch bell rang, I gathered surveys with Clementine. Or was it the pope? After school I went to Portable Five and helped the radio staffers log survey results into computers, but the numbers were a mishmash of squiggly lines. When I got home, I saw Grams and Mom in the throes of battle, but I didn't hear any explosions. I was in a daze, numb but for the ache in my chest.

That night tears rushed down my cheeks and soaked my pillow, which according to Grams should have been a good thing. During my hormonal junior high years when I came home from school sobbing at least once a week, Grams explained tears were good. She claimed they washed away the bad and nourished the soul. Mom explained that tears helped our bodies release toxins that build up during stressful situations. They contain beta-endorphins, natural pain relievers.

Both were dead wrong.

Sleep and the morning sun burned off some of the haze, and an odd, hollow feeling settled in my bones. Brie, one of my two best friends, had slammed me publicly and decisively. She booted me from the clan, stripped me of my plaid.

I was cold and naked.

As I arrived at school the next morning, my bruised and bloody heart convinced me it was time to give Brie and Merce the space they needed. For now. Despite the tamale incident, I wasn't ready to give up on my two best friends, but I needed a little space, too.

All that week I worked on my Junior Independent Study Project, with the emphasis on *independent*. No one waved at me in the school parking lot when I arrived every morning. No one invited me to eat lunch in the cafeteria. I spent my lunch hours in the safety of the library studying the school's large but dated collection of broadcasting books, because it was clear I knew something about promo, but nothing about radio. After school I went to Portable Five, where I silently hammered away on my promotions plan as the rest of the radio staff broadcast live programs and ignored me.

My weekend was equally painful and silent. I received no messages on my OurWorld account, no phone calls inviting me to the basketball game. No one texted me to get the latest econ assignment or asked to borrow a kickin' pair of boots.

By Sunday afternoon I wanted to pull every orange curl from my head. I was officially the most unpopular student in the history of every high school on every planet in every universe.

When I got to school on Monday, I almost broke out in song and dance when I found Duncan waiting for me at the door to our first-period econ class.

"We need to get to the station," he said. "Emergency."

"Did Clementine snort too hard and melt Haley's DVDs?"

A half smile curved Dunc's mouth. It was the most wonderful

sight I'd seen in days. "Clem got called into a meeting with school admin this morning, and she said she needed to talk to all of us, including you."

When we arrived at Portable Five, the entire staff gathered in a tight knot around Clementine. She wiped dampness from the red shiny tip of her nose. "Three weeks. We have three freakin' weeks until admin yanks us off the air."

"W-w-what?" Frack

"No way!" Frick.

"They can't do that," Taysom said. "We're funded through the end of the semester."

"We may be funded, but we aren't *wanted*." Clementine shoved a stapled bunch of papers at me. They were results from last week's lunchroom survey.

I scanned the numbers and cringed.

"Admin was not impressed that of the seven hundred seventy-two students who answered the survey, only four had tuned in to 88.8 The Edge during the past month," Clementine said. "Given our dismal audience, admin decided the radio station should be dismantled and Portable Five used for storage. This way they can get rid of two of the mobile storage units they're currently renting."

"Wait a minute." Duncan took the papers from me. "How did admin get the results? You haven't even given this to Mr. Martinez, and raw data only went to staffers."

Clementine turned her dragon glare at me.

"No way." I placed my fingertips on my chest. "You can't

blame this one on me." Clem sent out an e-mail with the report last week, but I'd been too busy nursing my bleeding heart to do much with it. "Until today, I hadn't seen the data."

"Apparently Ms. Lungren has."

"My JISP adviser? How did she get hold of the sur—" The words ground to a halt in my throat as I pictured my weekly progress report, the one that included half a ream of paper with my action plan, notes from my promo discussions with Dos Hermanas, and printouts of staff e-mails. "Okay. She got it from me, but she's hardly the type to rat us out to admin. She's all about rescuing me from JISP failure and saving the station. Heck, she wants to save the entire teenage population from unsightly facial blemishes."

"*Your* counselor may have good intentions, but she also has a big mouth and no idea how cash-strapped the school is this year. She asked the vice principal of activities for additional funding to help promote poor, dismal KDRS and showed him the survey to prove how much freakin' help we needed." Clementine positioned her index finger and thumb in the shape of a gun, aimed at me, and pulled the trigger.

I lowered my hands. "I'm sorry. I didn't think she'd—"

"Exactly, Chloe. You didn't think." Clementine swiped another hand at her red nose. "You come in here with your big mouth and lame ideas and screw up everything."

Frick and Frack were oddly still. Taysom wouldn't look at me. Haley, the human sound-effects machine, had switched to off. Only Duncan made noise as he turned report pages.

"This is your fault. Your fault!" Clementine said.

No. Clementine was wrong. This JISP was wrong. Space between me and my BFs was wrong. Everything in my life was wrong. I lunged for the door, needing to escape the cave.

"Wait!" Duncan tapped his index finger on the report. "Have you all looked at question ten? The one where we ask what kind of programming listeners want? More than music or news or sports, listeners want interactive programming. They want their voices heard. They want a talk show."

"What does a talk show have to do with keeping us on the air?" Taysom asked.

Duncan waved the papers at me. "Don't you remember Chloe talking about refritos? We find out what kind of refried beans our target market wants, and we give it to them. If we give them what they want, they'll tune in, and if enough of them stay tuned in, we're sure to pull in underwriters, and if we have an abundance of underwriters, the station will have so much extra cash we can pay the school for the extra storage space."

Clementine shook her crinkly mane of hair. "Talk shows are beasts. Controversial topics alienate listeners. Stuff could happen that would get us yanked off the air in a heartbeat. We don't do talk shows. Never have. Never will."

"Maybe we should," Duncan said. "Ninety-eight percent of respondents want one."

Taysom scanned the report. "Dunc's right."

"Anyone willing to handle callers in a talk-show format?" Duncan went on.

Taysom shuddered. Haley made a *splat* sound. Clementine said, "Hell no!" Everyone looked at Frick and Frack as they shook their heads.

"Seriously, Chloe's funny and articulate, and she never shuts up," Dunc said. I'd never seen his gray eyes so bright. "She'd be a great talk-show host."

"She knows squat about radio," Clementine said, her voice screechy.

"She can learn the technical stuff," Duncan argued. "The important thing is she has an engaging personality. We need her."

"My gawwwwwd, people. No one's going to want to talk to Chloe. She fracked Mr. Hersbacher, the head of the Mistletoe Ball committee, to win a stupid crown. Brie Sonderby saw everything."

The hit was straight on, Clementine's right fist to my already-bleeding heart. This was the big secret behind the whispers. This was the heart of the rumors Brie spread to turn the entire school against me. Surprisingly, Clementine's words didn't storm through my head. Nor did Brie's lies, because they were so ludicrous, so ridiculous, I would have laughed if I wasn't thinking about Duncan's wonderful words.

We need her.

When you've been out in an ocean, stung by jellyfish, battered by waves, and circled by sharks in frosty pink lipstick, you grab at the first life preserver tossed your way. I wrapped my arms and mind around those words.

We need her.

I faced every member of the KDRS radio staff. I wasn't naked. I wasn't alone. And according to Duncan, I was needed.

"You're wrong, Clementine. Brie Sonderby lied. I did nothing inappropriate with my old guidance counselor to win the Mistletoe Crown, and I could spend time and energy fighting Brie, but I have something more important to do. Duncan's right. You need me here at the station, and I can prove it . . ." I inserted a dramatic pause worthy of a Daytime Emmy–winning soap queen. ". . . with rotten salsa."

"Oh my gawwwwd!"

Hear Ye! Hear Ye!

CHLOE, QUEEN OF THE UNIVERSE,
WILL ASCEND TO THE RADIO THRONE
THIS FRIDAY FROM 8 TO 10 P.M.

BY ROYAL PROCLAMATION,
ALL SUBJECTS ARE REQUIRED
TO TUNE IN TO 88.8 THE EDGE.

Royally Yours,
Queen Chloe

CHAPTER 6

"TAKE OFF THAT STUPID TIARA."

"And happy Tuesday to you, too, darling Clementine."
I slipped off my tiara and positioned it in the middle of my
desk, which was a dented whiteboard supported on either
end by storage boxes and shoved against the north wall of
Portable Five. Welcome to the glamorous home of *Chloe, Queen of
the Universe*, KDRS's exciting new radio talk show, debuting this
Friday.

Clementine had kicked and screamed, fighting the idea of
me hosting a talk show. While I wasn't a fighter by nature, I was
needed, and I needed someone to need me. So I fought back with
Dos Hermanas' salsa. I explained to the KDRS staff that last year
nine customers got sick after eating salsa at Dos Hermanas. FDA
investigators eventually discovered salmonella-tainted tomatoes
distributed by a local commercial grower and ordered a massive
tomato recall. Dos Hermanas was not at fault, but they got tons of

bad publicity. The weird thing? Two months after the salsa fiasco, sales at Dos Hermanas skyrocketed.

"In the end, people forgot about rotten salsa but remembered Dos Hermanas," I'd told the staff. "Publicity, even bad publicity, can be a good thing. The fact that Brie Sonderby is spreading juicy lies about me can help boost our number of listeners. People know about me. They're curious about me. They'll tune in to hear me. Duncan's right. You *need* me."

Rotten tomatoes won out. Clementine was the lone "no" vote. The other KDRS staffers hadn't been totally enthusiastic, but I think with the radio station scheduled to shut down, they were willing to try anything. Kind of a let's-throw-her-against-the-wall-and-see-if-she-sticks attitude.

Mr. Martinez, the radio club adviser, who teaches English and pops in and out of the station throughout the week to make sure the KDRS clan isn't doing anything illegal or offensive, also approved my proposal. But he wasn't optimistic. "The school is financially strapped, and nonacademic programs are the first to go, especially programs that appeal to so few students," Mr. Martinez said. "I'm afraid, Chloe, you've hitched your wagon to a dead horse."

Only Duncan seemed to think the idea of a talk show featuring me could save the station. Once again, he was the lone body standing in my corner. Maybe he liked girls with good taste in shoes, or maybe he was simply a nice guy.

I looked around the newsroom and didn't see him or his tool belt. He'd been absent again in econ this morning. I was surprised at how often I checked that empty seat behind me and how cold class was without him and one of his nubby scarves.

"Anyone seen Duncan?" I asked.

Next to me Clementine stiffened. Taysom, who'd been scribbling on a notepad, looked up, as did Frick and Frack. Haley, who was watching *The Wizard of Oz*, hit the Pause button, stopping Dorothy and Toto in mid-skip on the yellow brick road. Their collective gaze settled on Clementine, who pressed her lips together. "Duncan won't be in today."

"Everything okay?" Frick asked.

Clementine nodded.

Taysom pulled out his earbuds. "Does he need a ride?"

The GM shook her head. "He said he has it covered."

"What about homework?" Frick asked.

"I got it for him." Clementine.

"What's going on?" I asked. "Is Duncan in some kind of trouble?"

Around me long gazes locked over my head. Bodies shifted. It all meant something to everyone but me. At last Clementine turned to me and aimed a pointed finger at my tiara. "Are you going to sit there all day and admire your idiotic crown, or are you going to get to work on saving the universe?"

I picked up my crown and watched the flickering light glint off the stones. "This, Clementine, is not an idiotic crown but a masterful marketing tool. Do you know how many people asked me about it?" No one in the newsroom looked at me. "Twenty-eight, and I told them all about my show this Friday. Not bad, huh?"

Okay, some of it had been bad, like the message *someone* left in frosty pink lipstick on my locker after lunch.

Chloe, Queen of the Losers!

I squeezed my hand tight and rubbed away those words until the slick writing was an oily smear of pink. Forget all that crap about sticks and stones. Words, especially those written in your best friend's curly handwriting with her favorite shade of lipstick, hurt.

But Brie's lies and taunts would soon be old news, like rotten tomatoes. And eventually the demons possessing my best friends and the rest of the school would be exorcised, and my universe would be in perfect alignment.

I plopped the tiara on my head and opened my JISP notebook, where I'd been jotting pages and pages of notes for my queenly radio debut.

Thwack. A dusty, five-inch-thick binder slammed onto my desk. "For you," Clementine said. The spine read *KDRS Operations Guide*. Everything for the care and feeding of a high school radio station.

I fanned away the dust. "What am I supposed to do with it?"

"Become one with it."

"You want me to read the whole thing by Friday?"

"No, just the pages ending in two and seven." Dragon rumble. "KDRS is not some after-school playground for people who like to hear themselves talk. We're licensed by the FCC, and we follow FCC regs and school policy for all broadcast activities. Our goal is to provide our listeners with quality, professional programming.

Anyone who doesn't work to that end will get dragged through and roasted over the fires of hell." A sunny glint sparked in Clementine's eyes as she leaned closer. "After you get your music selected, get your teasers done. I also want to see your format clock with all stop sets noted, and I'll need to approve any drops, stagers, and other production elements you plan on using. Since you're not certified, you won't be running the boards or keeping the log, but you will study the op notes on how the board works and how to screen live calls. Got that?"

I got that she wasn't quite speaking English.

"I want you in here during your lunch period for the next five days with your mouth shut and eyes open," Clementine continued. "The best way to learn this stuff is to watch. Radio isn't rocket science, but it's not as simple as sitting your butt in a chair and yakking away. And one more thing—I expect you to know step-by-step how to deal with VSPs. One mishandle of a VSP, and you're gone."

"VSP?"

Clementine's gaze stayed on me so long my feet started to squirm. "Very Stupid Person," she said. "They can kill a show, literally get us kicked off the air. Now get your music prepped. You need to record dry track today so Taysom can mix your teasers and sweepers."

"Huh?"

Clementine leaned against the wall, her arms crossed. "Your format music, the standard theme music we'll play as openers and closers and with your promos."

Taysom must have seen the huge question mark over my head. "You haven't selected theme music?" he asked.

"Uh, no. Do I need theme music?"

Taysom looked as if I'd asked him if I needed a left ventricle. "Music belongs everywhere. It's essential to all radio programming, even news and talk shows. Music is an expression of your radio personality, something that announces your unique presence."

Unique. I liked that. Unique things stood out, they made a statement, like vintage shoes. I considered my show title, *Chloe, Queen of the Universe*. I'd kicked around a dozen names, including *Chloe Nation* and *Life According to Chloe*. At one point I reached for the phone to call Mercedes to get her analytical input, but fortunately, my synapses fired before I opened that can of stupid. Turning to BFs for issues big and small was simply a habit. In the end, Grams weighed in.

"*Chloe, Queen of the Universe* is a little over the top and totally fun," Grams had said. "It's catchy, but more importantly, it's *you*."

Thanks to Grams, I had a name, but no music. "I guess we could go with queenly music, kind of royal sounding."

"Oh my gawwwwwd," Clementine said. "She'll sound like the Plumber King." The Plumber King was a local contractor with cheesy commercials featuring a plumber wearing a gold crown and sitting on a royal toilet throne.

From the corner, Haley made a flushing noise.

I looked at my show title scrawled across the whiteboard desk.

"We could also play on the universe theme and use something celestial. Harps and lutes, kind of angelic."

Clementine made a gagging noise, and I envisioned a volume knob on her forehead and me turning it down. No, I wasn't exactly an angel, but I was trying to help *her* station stay on the air.

"A successful *Chloe, Queen of the Universe* show means more listeners," I said. "More listeners mean we have a better chance of luring underwriting funds, and those funds mean we could keep KDRS from crashing and burning. You realize we're on the same team, don't you?"

Clementine smacked her forehead. "Oops, I forgot my Go-Chloe-Go T-shirt and freakin' pompoms." She stormed into one of the little glass rooms at the back of the portable.

I rubbed my temples. Why did Clementine dislike me so much? Surely it couldn't be Brie's attempt to turn me into a pariah. Clementine, like the rest of the radio staff, was an outsider. She didn't seem like the type to give a rat's heinie about the Brie Sonderbys of this world.

"How do you envision interacting with your audience?" Taysom asked.

My show. My JISP. It was a ball and chain around my ankle. I flattened my hands on the two-ton binder. No, it was an anchor, keeping me steady. After getting kicked out of my clan, I floated alone with nothing to hang on to. I needed KDRS.

"I don't want to come across as arrogant," I told Taysom. "I want to be more like the queen next door, everyone's friend."

Because on the night of the Mistletoe Ball, I hadn't been a friend to

Brie when she needed me. Ever since my talk with Merce on the day Grams cut her hand, the thought had been sneaking up on me and echoing through my head.

"That's a start," Taysom continued. "Now, what type of stuff are you going to talk about? Newsy current events? Softer human-interest topics? This type of stuff drives your format music."

With zero social obligations I had plenty of time to brainstorm content, and when I was thinking about talk show topics, I turned to the Question Bag.

Grams made the Question Bag for my seventh-grade birthday party. She'd taken a small brown-paper lunch sack and drew question marks all over it. Fat ones. Skinny ones. Curly ones. Blockish ones. Inside she put more than one hundred slips of paper with questions. We used the Question Bag at my party, a huge blowout with every seventh-grade girl at school in attendance. Throughout the party, we'd draw questions and people would shout out answers. It was a good way to get to know one another. To connect.

Grams, being Grams, hadn't included expected questions like, *What's your favorite TV show?* or *Who's your favorite singer?* Grams's bag of questions forced us into deeper waters.

You won a million dollars, but you can't spend it on yourself. What would you do with it?

You have a chance to have dinner with one famous person, living or dead. Who?

I proclaimed to my birthday guests I'd have dinner with Charlie Chaplin. Merce announced she'd dine with Copernicus. Brie had surprised me. She was new to the school and model gorgeous, so I expected her to say something completely superficial, like some Hollywood hunk or supermodel.

"I'd have dinner with God," Brie said. When I gave her a curious look, she shrugged. "I have big questions."

The next week we made tamales de dulce and officially became a trio. Since then Brie, Merce, and I would haul out the Question Bag during sleepovers, on lazy summer afternoons at the beach, even during finals when our brains were about to burst. Over the years we added our own questions, from the silly to the serious.

Would you go without bathing for one year if you got paid $50,000?

If your best friend planned on getting an abortion and needed money to pay for it, would you loan it to her?

I turned to the KDRS staff. Grams always said I poured my heart into everything I did, and my radio show would be no different. "I want to talk about stuff people care about, stuff that makes them think . . . and feel. We'll talk about what pushes our buttons, what soothes our souls. We'll talk about our dreams and fears. We'll go deep, to heart-level stuff."

A hush fell over the newsroom. Everyone focused on me. A nice fluttery feeling expanded my chest, but my smile faded when I saw Clementine staring at me from one of the glass rooms, her glare like Brie's: so icy, it burned.

As I pulled into my driveway that night, my house stared at me with dark, lifeless eyes. I fiddled with my keys but didn't turn off the ignition. I'd forgotten Dad was at the university teaching a late class, Mom had a full day of surgery, and Grams had some kind of appointment. On nights like this I usually called Brie and Mercedes, and we went to Dos Hermanas for dinner.

I tried to picture Clementine and me sharing chips and salsa. Oh my gawwwwwd. No, the GM and I weren't destined to swap friendship bracelets, especially after the latest frosty look. However, I wouldn't mind getting to know Duncan better. Again, I wondered where he'd been all day. KDRS was a much warmer place with him around.

Just the way my home was a warmer place with people in it. My youngest brother, Zach, had left for med school in August, leaving me the sole inhabitant of the second floor. The black hole loomed before me, ready to suck me in.

I jammed my car in reverse and backed out of the driveway.

By now, Mom should be out of surgery and finishing her notes. Like me, she probably felt tired but accomplished. Today my surgeon mother mended a few hearts while I worked on creating the best talk-radio show on planet earth.

I drove to the hospital and found Mom in the CICU. She stood in front of a large window that framed a gray-haired, gray-faced man hooked to beeping and buzzing machines. Mom's forehead rested on the window.

"Looks like you could use a red chili chimi," I said.

Mom opened her eyes and offered me a tired smile. "Sounds good, but not tonight." She jutted her chin toward the man. "I can't leave Mr. Dominguez for another hour or so."

I frowned. If I didn't hate hospitals so much, I'd wait with her.

"Why don't you stop by the Tuna Can?" Mom suggested. "Grams could use a pick-me-up. She spent the afternoon visiting senior assisted-living facilities."

I lunged for Mom and frantically patted her arms and back.

Mom's weary face wrinkled. "What are you doing?"

"Looking for bullet holes."

My mother rumpled my hair. "A woman who specializes in helping people like your grandmother transition into assisted-living facilities took her out today."

"And they both survived?"

"Last I heard." Mom rested her forehead on the window. "But your grandmother isn't happy. She was in such a state this afternoon that she lost her keys and couldn't get in the Tuna Can, so she broke a window and tried to crawl in. Noreen next door found her stuck in the bathroom window."

I sunk onto the chair outside Mr. Dominguez's CICU room. I refused to look at the man whose heart my mother touched today, but not because of my fear of blood and general dislike of hospitals. In his pasty skin and bandaged chest I saw Grams, whose heart was breaking at the idea of giving up the Tuna Can, her teeny tiny corner of the universe.

This had been the root cause of World War III. Six months ago Grams's doctors told her that because of her progressing Parkinson's disease, she needed to think about new living arraignments, something where she wasn't alone all the time. Grams, being Grams, had refused to consider it. But the night of the Mistletoe Ball everything changed. That evening Grams took a walk on the beach, became disoriented, and couldn't find her way back. When her neighbor Noreen noticed that Grams had not returned home, she called my mom, who called the police. The beach patrol found Grams after three in the morning, shivering under a lifeguard tower with a near case of hypothermia.

"She's a danger to herself," Grams's doctor told my parents. "And it's not going to get better."

The day after the Mistletoe Ball, Mom and Dad invited Grams over for a giant spread of twice-baked potatoes. To her credit, Mom tried to put a positive spin on moving out of the Tuna Can, calling it a new and exciting episode, and she put many options on the table: a live-in aide, a roommate of Grams's choice, an assisted-living facility.

Grams lobbed her potato in the garbage.

War ensued.

At one point during winter break, it got so bad that Grams and Mom refused to be in the same room. They sent messages to each other through me. My mom has a medical degree and Grams has eighty years of life lessons, but I swear I was back in junior high. *This* was the type of stuff that kept me snowed under during winter break.

Since that time, I'd been stewing over an idea, but I figured Mom would shoot it down. But if I could tackle a radio show, I could take on anything, right?

"Grams could live with us," I said to my shoes. I held my breath, half expecting my mom to explode.

Instead, Mom's shoulders bounced in a silent chuckle. "I

suggested that long before the incident at the beach. I told her with your brothers gone, we'd move you downstairs to the den, and she could have the entire second floor."

This would restore life to the black hole. I jumped up. "Perfect."

"She told me to shove all eight rooms up my heinie." Mom sighed and reached for a clipboard on the door to the CICU room. "Now, why don't you stop by and see how she's doing? You're the only one who can make her smile these days."

Grams smile? After a day of looking at assisted-living facilities? I'd have better luck getting Clementine to braid my hair. Again I thought of that nasty, very Brie-like look on Clementine's face and shivered. But Mom was right; Grams needed a dose of Chloe cheer.

As I pulled out of the hospital parking lot, plotting witty and highly entertaining ways to pull Grams out of her funk, I spotted a metallic green bike on the side of the road. A lone figure hunched over the duct tape–dotted frame, a wrench in one hand, an oily bike chain in the other.

I punched the gas and pulled up next to him. "You look like you could use a little help from a girl with a big heart."

Duncan sat on his heels and stared at the night sky. In the moonlight I could see the circles under his eyes had darkened. Grease streaked his jeans and blood seeped from a knuckle on one of his hands. He threw the chain to the ground. "I could use a new bike."

"Can't help you there, but how about a ride?"

Duncan's forehead lined, as if he didn't understand my offer. Or didn't want it. I recalled the KDRS staffers saying he didn't need any help. Duncan was a person used to going it alone. Even at the radio station he held himself distant. Apart. An outsider among outsiders.

He stared at the bike, then at the hospital, rubbing his hand across the bridge of his nose and leaving a grease spot. "Yeah. I'm late."

Duncan,

Something died in one of the recycling bins in Schnepf and
Stromberg. The stench is unbearable. Please check into it
and let us know if this is a rodent issue.

Dina Jimenez
Asst. Property Manager
Executive Office Properties

CHAPTER 7

"PLEASE TELL ME THAT'S NOT A DECOMPOSING RAT." I HELD
Duncan's scarf over my nose and mouth and tried not to breathe
the air in the executive break room of Schnepf and Stromberg
Accounting. It stunk so bad Duncan's ruddy, wind-kissed cheeks
were tinged green.

"It's not a rat." Duncan spoke without taking a breath. "I'm
pretty sure it's a sub sandwich. At least it *was* a sub sandwich."
With a dust pan, he scooped a six-inch oozing brown mass from a
bin marked Cans Only and dropped it into a small plastic bag he
plucked from his trash cart. He wrapped the decomposing blob
in two more bags and shoved it deep into a bin on his cart. With
a spray bottle marked Pine Fresh, he cleaned the bin and doused
the air. "Got it."

"And the crowd goes wild." I threw my hands in the air and
made mass cheering noises. "Another garbage crisis deftly dealt
with by . . . Trash Man!"

Duncan winced as he pushed his cart into the hallway, the wheels squeaking softly. "Trash Man?"

I fell in step beside him, our way lit only by the after-hour security lights glowing a soft orange. "Do you prefer Garbage Guy? Rubbish Rescuer?"

He groaned.

I fingered the edges of his scarf, which still hung around my neck, noting that this one, too, had a lopsided red heart stitched onto one end. "How about Junk Hunk? Debris Dude?"

"You're a warped soul, Chloe." He didn't laugh, but that half smile curved his mouth. Mission accomplished.

Duncan ducked into the next office in search of more garbage, which he sorted into the two circular bins on his cart. He worked quickly, efficiently. Duncan Moore was a guy who knew his garbage. He also seemed more at ease here than at school. On the ride from the hospital parking lot, he'd been stone still, but here in the office building, his face no longer looked carved in granite.

"You've been doing this a while?" I asked. When I rescued Duncan and his broken-down bike on the side of the road, I'd expected to take him home. Instead, he directed me to a commercial office complex north of the hospital.

"A few years. I have six office buildings where I handle trash."

"Must take a while."

He poured the contents of another trash can into his bins. "I'm home a little after eleven."

"Which explains why you sleep through econ."

"Doesn't everyone sleep through econ?" He tilted his head, his gray eyes sparking with silvery bits.

"I kind of like econ." I took a small waste basket of paper and emptied it in the bin marked Recyclables. "All those business models, market analyses, supply-and-demand charts. It's fun."

Duncan grabbed another trash can. "Like I said, Chloe, you're a warped soul." Yes, he was definitely different with his garbage. Almost relaxed.

In a communal office area, he emptied a trash can and something clanked. He dug around and hauled out a dinged box with a frayed cord and said, "Yesssss!"

"What's that?" I asked.

"A treasure."

"Uh, Dunc, it's a pencil sharpener."

"Same thing."

"Exactly what are you going to do with it?"

"Fix it."

"Why?"

He stared at the scuffed, dented box, then me, clearly not understanding the latter. "Because it needs fixing."

I pictured Duncan working on the transmitter, the lights, and the clock. "You like to fix things, don't you?"

The trash cart's wheels jangled and squeaked as he pushed them out of the office area. "Yeah, I guess so. After school I work in a thrift store fixing broken appliances."

"You have two jobs? No wonder you have no time for fun."

"It's not bad." He didn't seem upset, more resigned, as if working two jobs was a fact of life.

"So what kinds of things do you fix at the thrift store?" I asked.

"Everything. Radios, dishwashers, old movie projectors, snow skis. And toasters. Bet you never met a guy who's fixed a hundred toasters."

"I'm impressed. I bet you can fix anything."

The squeak of wheels softened as he slowed. "Some things can't be fixed."

Like friendships broken by lies and frosty pink slurs. The thought slammed me. Could I fix the growing gulf between Brie and me? Did I want to? I slid my pin curls behind my ears. Of course I did. Despite the horrible words and flying tamale, Brie wasn't a villainess. I believed that with all my heart because I knew I could never be friends with someone who had an evil heart. We were still connected.

Long ago I figured out the BF connection, the invisible thread that linked friends. This thread was responsible for the times you finished each other's sentences or showed up to school wearing the same color shirts or your hair in matching messy ponytails. Sometimes this invisible connection woke you in the middle of the night and demanded you text your BF. That was when your BF texted back: *Mom gon. I'm @ d hsptl. I nd u. Merce.* I'd been connected to Merce and Brie for years, and some part of me still hadn't let go.

While I thought about the BF thread, Duncan, too, had traveled in his head to a deep, thoughtful place. His garbage cart was still, his gaze pinned on something across the darkened corridor. Was he thinking about the things he couldn't fix? Without the scarf around his neck, I could see his pulse slamming below his jaw.

I grabbed the trash cart and sent it rolling down the hall. "Okay, time for a little fun."

Wide-eyed, Duncan stared from me to his runaway trash cart and back to me. "Fun? Here?"

"As someone very wise and with wonderful taste in old shoes once said, fun is everywhere. We just have to make it."

Duncan headed for his trash cart. "Hate to burst your bubble, but garbage is not fun."

With his trash cart once again in hand, he squeaked down the hall, leaving me looking at his broad shoulders and the curve of his faded jeans. The pocket was torn, but someone had attempted to patch it with lopsided stitches, and I pictured Duncan's own hands fixing that tear. Always fixing things. Always working.

I whipped off the scarf, tossed it through the air, and looped it around his neck, drawing him back to me. That wonderful sea-swept smell mingled with pine cleaner.

When he turned to me, he looked more curious than angry.

"Time to play," I said.

"Play what?"

I reached for the trash bin marked Recyclables. "Garbage Games."

Duncan whistled. "I'm impressed."

"You should be." I made the final two folds on my paper wings.

"It's my special variation of the Sparrow, and last summer it obliterated my brother Zach's Canada Goose."

Duncan studied his airplane, which was also impressive, nose heavy with a good deal of surface area. He spent the past ten minutes constructing it, and it was fun to watch his concentration. He liked to work with his hands, and he was good with them. I remembered his fingers sliding along my thumbs and the bubbly heat. That had definitely been a nice feeling.

"Your family's into paper airplanes?" Duncan asked. Thankfully, he was not looking at my flushed face but at the Sparrow.

"No, only my youngest brother. He taught me how to make them when I was five or six." Zach had been infinitely patient and indulgent. He was also the brother who packed me in his backpack when I was two and tried to take me to his second-grade class for show-and-tell. "We have this ongoing paper airplane competition. When I was little, he let me win some to keep things close, but now it's pretty serious. He started med school in August, and before he left, I debuted the Sparrow and nudged into the sweepstakes point lead. I haven't lost once with it. Ready to fly?"

Duncan stared at his plane as if he didn't know what to do next.

"You didn't race airplanes as a kid?" I asked.

Head shake.

"Never?" My eyes grew wide.

His shoulders bunched in a nonchalant shrug. "I had a deprived childhood." I could tell he'd meant it to come across as flippant, but truth weighed his words. His hand curved about his plane, and I thought he'd crush it.

"The deprivation stops here." I hopped off the desk I'd been sitting on. "Let the games begin."

I explained we'd fly the planes down the office corridor, earning points for distance and hang time. Not surprisingly, Duncan's carefully crafted plane gave my Sparrow a run for its money. I won the first round in both distance and hang, but he swept the second. By the third and final round, he was checking the air for wind drift from the vents. A nice red flushed across his cheeks, and his eyes seemed more silvery than gray, like starlight on the ocean at midnight. "Final heat," Duncan said. "Winner takes all and gets major bragging rights."

Someone in the office had turned down the heat, so the air had grown cool, but next to me, Duncan was toasty warm. I'd had too many cold shoulders lately. Brie. Merce. Clementine. I moved a bit closer. Duncan lifted his plane. "Ready?"

I nodded. On the count of three, we released our planes, but I didn't watch them. Instead, my gaze stayed on Duncan. Upturned lips. Wide shoulders edging his plane farther. Face relaxed. He was such a different person here with his trash cart.

"Niiiiice," he said, and I figured the race must have ended. I didn't look to see who won. His face had that little half smile, and it sent something tingly swirling the length of my body.

Yes, I thought. Duncan Moore was very, very niiiiice.

When I pulled my car into the driveway at the Tuna Can later that night, I still felt the wonderful rush of heat from my evening with

Duncan. After our airplane race, he went back to emptying trash, but not before admitting he had fun.

One dose of Chloe cheer: Check.

Now time for another.

I walked into the Tuna Can just as a pair of scissors whizzed through the kitchen and pierced the wall.

Grams tossed a cellophane-wrapped DVD on the kitchen table and glared at her hand, which was curved in a rigid half curl. "Piece of crap scissors," she said under her breath. "Don't work worth a damn."

I didn't bother to dislodge the scissors from the wall, nor did I offer to help open the DVD case, which had obviously been giving Grams fits. Instead, I sat at the table and said, "If you want to get the scissors fixed, I know a guy who's good at fixing things."

Grams blinked, as if she hadn't realized I'd walked in the door. She patted my hand. "I'm sorry, Poppy. I'm not the best company tonight."

"I am." Thanks to Garbage Games and queenly radio shows about to debut. "And because I'm in such a stellar mood, I'm going to take you to the movies."

Grams picked at a smear of dried jelly on the table. To my knowledge the Parkinson's hadn't affected her hearing, although last week I noticed her speech slurred and she swallowed as if she had too much saliva in her mouth. "Or maybe we can do it this weekend," I added. "I know you had a busy day."

The memory of looking at assisted-living facilities must have flicked a switch. Grams jumped from the chair and grabbed her purse from the counter. "You fly, I'll buy."

Relief washed over me. This was my old Grams.

By the time we got to the theater, Grams was in high spirits. "Man, that's one smokin' hot heinie." She pointed to the life-size cardboard cutout of Brad Pitt promoting his upcoming release. "You know he got his start on *Another World*, but some dipwad in casting canned him after two episodes. The moment I saw Brad on *AW*, I knew he'd be a megastar. I mean, with a heinie like this." She patted Brad's cardboard butt, her cheeks flushed.

At times like this Grams seemed so normal, like the Grams who'd walked me to school, attended my parent-teacher confer-ences, organized my birthday parties, made question bags, and taught me to make tamales de dulce. She was nothing like the woman who drove her Jeep into an ATM and was found half fro-zen on the beach at three in the morning.

Before the movie, Grams needed to use the bathroom. "You go inside and get us a seat, Poppy. I'll be out in a flash."

I pretended to check my watch. "We have a few more minutes. I think I'll stay out here and enjoy the view a little longer." I tilted my chin toward Brad Pitt's butt.

"That's my girl!" Grams went into the bathroom, and I waited.

While I would never admit it to Grams, I wasn't hanging around to ogle Brad's butt. I wanted to keep an eye on her, like she used to wait for me when I was six. My toe tapped against the nubby carpet. Ten years ago when she stood outside a public bathroom and waited for me, did she worry about me not being able to work the lock on the toilet stall? Was she concerned I might slip on the water on the floor near the sink?

I stopped tapping and hurried toward the bathroom. As I reached for the handle, the door swung open, and I stumbled to a stop.

My former BF seemed equally surprised. Her eyes bright, she curved her lips in a soft, frosty pink O before her whole face twisted into a villainous vixen glare. That initial glint in her eyes gave me hope. The BF thread still connected us. There in the bathroom doorway, it tugged at my chest.

"Hi," I said as Brie slipped her tube of lipstick into her purse. "You here to see the late show?"

"I'm on my way out. Merce and the gang are waiting for me in the car. We're heading to Extreme Bean."

To talk. Brie, Merce, and I had spent hundreds of hours talking at the coffee shop. I tucked my hair behind my ears. Talk. Brie and I needed to talk now, to heal this thing that had festered between us. "Was the movie any good?"

"Yes." Brie snapped shut her purse. "Here *alone*?" The last word sounded like some kind of disease.

"No, I'm here with a friend." She didn't need to know aforementioned friend was my eighty-two-year-old grandmother.

"Nose Ring Girl?"

My toes curled. Brie had always been one to label others. Outsiders had been her brainchild, although I, too, had labeled Clementine Nose Ring Girl. Suddenly, it sounded mean.

"Her name is Clementine, and no, I'm here with someone else."

"How nice. You have two friends." Brie's breathy laugh was cold, and I took a step back.

Just then the bathroom door opened, and Grams walked out, passing us without a word. Her shirt was untucked, and a giant water spot soaked the front of her sweater. "Chloe? Chloe?" Grams called, her high-pitched voice wobbly.

"Grams." I waved, trying to get her attention. She wandered a few steps to the right then left, her gaze clouded. "I'm right here," I said louder.

Grams stared at me with a slack expression and shook her head before spinning toward the theater. A long piece of toilet paper trailed from her waistband and tangled around her orange Converse. She stumbled, bumping into the wall. Righting herself, she shook the toilet paper from her shoe. "Piece of crap carpet."

Next to me Brie let out a loud laugh as she waggled a hand at the toilet paper still bobbing behind Grams. Others in the lobby turned and twittered. Then Brie gave me an evil soap-opera-villainess grin.

As a rule, I didn't hate. *Hate* was another ugly four-letter word. So I had a hard time putting into words how I felt toward Brie as a confused Grams stared at all the people laughing at her, but it wasn't nice, and it wasn't very Chloe-like.

My computer dinged.

Chloe, Are you still there? Gabe wrote. *Do you still want to cancel your account?*

I stared at Gabe's avatar in the corner of my screen. My stomach churned like a whirling pool of seawater, frothy and angry.

Merce, Brie, and I joined OurWorld three years ago. We'd created the social networking accounts so we'd be only a click away from one another at all times. Gabe and OurWorld had connected us during times of boredom (*What is lip gloss made of?*), times of excitement (*Ohmygosh! Alex asked me to homecoming!*), and times of heart-shredding sorrow (*Is it okay to be pissed off at my mom for dying?*).

Gabe's avatar waved at me. *Select* Yes *to cancel your account. Select* No *to maintain your account.*

My mouse hovered over the *Yes* button. Was I ready to disconnect from Merce and Brie? To snap the thread?

Pictures of Brie making fun of Grams in the movie theater flashed in my head.

I clicked *Yes.*

Once you leave, you lose all files and friends, Gabe wrote. *Are you sure you want to cancel?*

Two months ago I couldn't have imagined life without my two best friends, the two human beings who knew my thoughts before I said them, who hurt when I hurt, who knew my deepest dreams and fears.

My hands started shaking. Best friends *knew* you. They knew where you were vulnerable, and that was the heart of the issue with Brie. She knew I hated being alone. She knew I needed people like I needed air. She had taken that from me, or at least she'd tried to. Despite her lies and gossip, despite her power as high school royalty—Brie had not turned everyone against me. I had Duncan and the rest of the radio staff. I was not alone.

My mouse attacked the *Yes* button.

Gabe's virtual hand reached out and grabbed the hand of my avatar, walking me past an image of a globe. As I walked off screen, Gabe waved. The globe and Gabe faded away.

My heart constricted, and I couldn't breathe. It was as if Gabe had taken all of the oxygen with him.

Deep breath in. Deep breath out.

How silly. My virtual world with my former BFs was ending, but I had a very real, very good world, an entire universe, without them.

Dead Air: Silence on the radio when there is no audible transmission.

*— **KDRS Operations Guide**, p. 482*

CHAPTER 8

"AND THIS"—DUNCAN OPENED THE DOOR AND MOTIONED ME inside the small room fronted with glass—"is the queen's castle."

"Don't expect me to freakin' bow," Clementine said with a snarl. She sat in one of two chairs before a long table piled with electronic equipment. The control room was small, about ten feet square with one wall of glass that looked over the newsroom. Gray egg cartons covered the other three walls.

For the past few days Duncan and Clementine had been giving me a crash course in all things radio during my lunch hour. Along with Mr. Martinez, they schooled me in broadcast writing, interview techniques, FCC regs, and program production.

I ran my fingers along the chair that in a few days would be my queenly throne. "This is where I'll do my entire show?" The station ran live programming Monday through Thursday after school until six and on Friday until ten. My show would be the bright, shiny star of the Friday night eight-to-ten slot.

Duncan pointed to Clementine's chair. "And I'll sit there." To my immense joy and relief, Duncan had agreed to run the control board for *Chloe, Queen of the Universe*. He knew all the tech stuff and was certified, which meant all I had to do was talk and reel in a sea of KDRS listeners. And there'd be no stinging jellyfish allowed in this corner of the ocean. After Brie publicly ridiculed Grams, I decided what she said and did and who she got on her side didn't matter.

My JISP mattered. My show mattered. Duncan and his soft, scraggly scarves mattered.

Clementine hooked her thumb toward the glass room next door. "And I'll be in the production studio making sure you don't screw up. By the way, that voice-over you did yesterday is total garbage. You sound like you have socks in your mouth. You'll need to do it again. And the sales kits you put together to give to potential underwriters are useless. You didn't include my e-mail address or the radio station's direct telephone number."

Even Clementine mattered.

Duncan motioned to the other glass-fronted room. "Clementine will sit next door in the production studio and screen the calls, and I'll patch them through. Have a seat, and I'll show you how to use the mic."

A tingle ran through the tips of my fingers as I sat. I would use this mic to reach out and charm the masses. This morning I'd sweet-talked the vice principal into plugging my show during the morning announcements. The publicity team for student council agreed to post a blurb about my show on the school's event blog.

And on Friday after school I planned to stand in the parking lot in my tiara and hand out more flyers. With all the promo work, we'd have hundreds—no, thousands—of new listeners.

Clementine let loose a low growl.

"What did I do now?" I asked with an eye roll. Clem may matter, but that didn't mean I had to like her.

"Frack's here." Clem aimed her chin at the newsroom, where Frack was unloading his backpack on his desk. She turned to Duncan and shook her head. "Martinez axed Frack's proposal for live coverage of next month's Tardeada because it runs on a Saturday, and he doesn't want to come in and supervise stuff here at the station. Not that I need any supervision." Clementine gnawed the end of her pencil. "Frack put a lot of time and research into that proposal, lining up live interviews of musicians and speakers. He even had some cool ideas on how to cover chili and corn roasting demonstrations." Clementine nudged Duncan. "How about you talk to him, Dunc? You're good at fixing things."

Duncan held up his hand, palm side facing Clem. "I'll leave the people stuff to you."

Clementine bit her pencil, and the wood split. She spit out the splinters, one of which landed on my right 1957 marabou glide.

I flicked it off with a jaunty kick. "Try the sandwich method."

"The what?" Clem asked.

"The sandwich method. It's a way of telling someone craptastic news. You say something nice, slip in the bad, and slap on another slice of nice." Clementine looked at me as if I were speaking Swahili. "So tell Frack the feature he did on the local Red

Cross rocked. Then tell him it's a no-go on the Tardeada. Finally, tell him you need another one of his marvelous public service announcements, this one on Save the Blue-Footed Booby Week."

Clementine threw her pencil on the desk. "Sandwiches are about as dumb as burritos."

"Just watch." Before Clem could argue, I popped into the newsroom and took a seat on Frack's desk. Within three minutes, he was smiling and surfing the web for blue-footed-booby news, and I was in the radio control room, bending in a deep bow. "And that, Clementine, is how to make a *sandwich*."

Clem turned a dial so hard, the knob snapped off. "No, that's you sticking your nose into business that doesn't concern you."

"Frack's happy."

"Damn it, Chloe, I manage the staff here, not you." She threw the knob on the desk and jerked out of her chair. "Watch the board for a few minutes, Dunc, while I go make sure Frack isn't choking to death on his sandwich." Clem stormed out of the control room.

"Talk about someone with serious control issues," I said. "I was trying to help. What's wrong with that?"

Duncan said nothing as he picked up the knob, bent something on the underside, and snapped it back in place. He pulled a clipboard from the top of one of the machines but didn't look at it. "How do you know so much about dealing with people?" He pointed the clipboard at Frack, who was showing Clem a website with pictures of blue-footed boobies. "You're not some kind of psychologist in training, are you?"

Cue the laughter. "To my parents' dismay, I am definitely

not headed for a doctorate of any kind." I took a seat in the chair behind the mic. "I guess when you're around people all the time, you watch them, study them, kind of learn how they tick. Some people know about clocks and toasters. Some people know about . . . people."

Duncan seemed to consider my words long and hard, but in the end, he shook his head. "I'll stick to toasters." He ran a hand along the four-foot piece of electronic equipment with a hundred dials and levers. "Meet the control board. She's the heart of the radio station." Pointing to one of the knobs, Dunc started my lesson on Radio Tech 101.

After he explained how he switches from the live mic to recorded programming, he pointed to a series of brightly lit bars. "When the bars disappear, you have dead air. It happens when equipment malfunctions, common here because everything is so ancient. We also have dead air when the DJ screws up or when lightning or wind messes with our antenna."

I thought about the past few weeks: my silent phone, my friendless OurWorld page, my lonely walks through the hallways and breezeways of the Del Rey School. "Silence is the evil of all evils," I said softly.

"Exactly." Duncan looked like he wanted to give me a gold star. "Dead air will kill your show. It'll make listeners push a button and move someplace else on the dial."

Like best friends moved out of your life when threads snapped.

Duncan finished with the control board and reached for a headset. His hands were pale but strong, a callus on the side of his right index finger. They were hands that didn't play enough, although he seemed relaxed now as he dangled the headset before me. "You'll wear this for your entire show. I can dial it in so you can hear Clem in the production studio, the staff in the newsroom, or your callers on the landline."

He slipped the headset over my head, and his finger brushed my earlobe. A bolt of electricity, which had nothing to do with wires and knobs, fluttered and warmed my ear. My *ear*. I didn't know there were happy nerves in an ear.

"You want it tight," Duncan went on as he adjusted the band that went over my head, "but not too tight."

I wanted Duncan to touch my other ear. I lowered my gaze and pretended to study the mic's on-off switch. Last year I went out with one of the busboys at Dos Hermanas, who had a killer collection of Doc Martens. On our second date he kissed me. The kiss had been nice, warm, but nothing like the high-voltage jolt Duncan left on my ear.

For his part, Duncan seemed oblivious. His eyes were bright, but that was most likely because we were surrounded by machines. Midway through Duncan's tutorial on the Ghost, the computer that ran the automated programming, his watch beeped. His lips folded in a frown as he turned it off. "I need to go."

"You *need* to go?" I asked. Yes, I was stalling, keeping Duncan around as long as I could.

He yanked on the ends of his scarf and wound it around his neck. "Yeah, I *need* to go. I have to take the quiz I missed in econ the other day."

I'd been raised with five brothers and a drama-queen grand-mother. I had no problems speaking up. "But do you *want* to go?"

Duncan's cheeks warmed, and he concentrated on flicking a series of switches on the Ghost. When he looked at me, his gaze was steady. "No, Chloe, I don't *want* to go."

The warm tingle at my ear shimmied over my entire body. Duncan Moore liked being with me. The shimmy stopped. Or maybe he liked being with his radio equipment. I shook my head. It was probably a wonderful combination of the two. I hopped from my chair. "We'll finish tomorrow?"

"Yes, tomorrow. Definitely tomorrow." A half smile parted his lips as he walked out of Portable Five.

Even when dragon Clem came back into the control room and huffed out fiery snorts during the rest of my lunchtime radio lesson, I couldn't stop smiling. Duncan promised me tomorrow, and for a guy who worked two jobs and lived by the beeping of a watch, that was the equivalent of a ten-pound box of chocolates and two dozen red roses. My marabou glides barely touched the ground the rest of the day.

After school, my very happy feet fluttered across campus as I posted more flyers for *Chloe, Queen of the Universe*, which would debut this Friday. When I reached the bulletin board near the student parking lot, I spotted Kim and Leila from drama. Together we'd starred in four productions since our freshman year. Kim was the president of the drama club and had nominated me for Mistletoe Queen.

"Any news on the spring musical?" I asked. "Once the cast is selected, I'd love to have you on my radio show." I reached into my bag and took out a flyer. Both girls just stared at it.

"I heard rumors we'll be doing *Fiddler on the Roof*," I went on. "Fernando would make a great Tevye, don't you think?"

Kim's bottom lip trembled before she blurted out, "Why don't you throw yourself off the roof of a seventeen-story building?"

My head snapped back as if she'd landed me an uppercut to the jaw. "Excuse me?"

A tear trembled on Kim's eyelashes. Leila put her arm around her friend's shoulder. "She's not worth it," Leila said. "Let's go."

Kim threw off the touch. "Not before I say it to her face." A single tear fell, followed by another. "How could you, Chloe? How could you post all those pictures? They've gone viral, and now I'm the *butt* of hundreds of jokes. You're horrible and ugly and . . . mean!"

With a sob Kim ran to a small red hatchback, and I turned to Leila. "What's she talking about?"

"Don't act like you don't know about the pictures, because you're a lousy actor. And a lousy friend."

I shifted from one foot to the other, feeling uncharacteristically unsteady on my glides. "What pictures?"

"The ones you posted this morning on your OurWorld page."

"What? I canceled my OurWorld account last week. I haven't posted on OurWorld since winter break," I said, but Leila didn't hear me because she hurried after Kim. I ran after her, but she slammed the car door in my face.

Sweat slicked my palms, and I almost dropped my cell phone as I called up OurWorld there in the middle of the parking lot. I canceled my account, so there was no way I could have shared hurtful pictures of Kim. No. Way. I tried to log in using my old access information. To my shock, Gabe accepted my user name. With trembling fingers, I punched in my password. *DENIED!*

Have you forgotten your password, Chloe? Gabe asked.

Cars whirred around me, but I didn't move as I logged in to Merce's OurWorld account. Of course I knew her log-in info, because that's the kind of stuff best friends shared. On her Neighbors page, I clicked on the Chloe avatar and landed on "Chloe's" home page. My stomach lurched as I stared at the photos I'd taken at the Del Rey School's fall production of *A Midsummer Night's Dream*. Someone had Photoshopped each image, and not to whiten teeth and airbrush zits. In a photo of Kim leaping across stage in a pair of tights as she played Puck, someone had enlarged her butt so it resembled two giant cantaloupes and added the caption, "Kim Ramon in Her Big A$$ Role".

Definitely mean.

Someone had reactivated my OurWorld account and smeared Kim and the entire drama club. In my world, only two *someones* knew my original password and log-in ID.

My fingers curled tighter around the phone. Like Dos Hermanas' rotten tomatoes, the Mistletoe Ball had become old news, but Brie, for some twisted reason I still didn't understand, continued full steam ahead on the bash Chloe train.

Beeeeep.

Good morning, Chloe, it's Ms. A. Lungren. I wanted to wish you the best of luck on your radio program this evening. I'm thoroughly impressed with the amount of work you've put in this week preparing your show's content and learning the technical aspects of radio. I'm confident that you are fully prepared and capable of excelling in this exciting new endeavor. Believe in yourself, Chloe. Believe!

Beeeeep.

End of messages.

CHAPTER 9

I SAT AT MY WHITEBOARD DESK FRIDAY NIGHT STARING AT MY
I. Miller blue satin platform lifts with rhinestone buckles, circa
1950. Tonight I needed the extra bling. Unfortunately, the bling
wasn't shiny enough to distract me from my serious case of
nerves.

I was about to reach for the supersize bag of Twizzlers I tucked
in my purse when a piece of paper soared across my desk. It was
intricately folded and had spectacular hang time. The Sparrow,
but not my version. This one had a longer tail and flaps on the
back stabilizer. It floated onto my lap, where I noticed writing on
the wing.

Stop worrying. It'll be FUN.

When I glanced into the control room, I met Duncan's calm,
steady gray eyes. Yes, fun was everywhere, in empty office
buildings with garbage and in graveyard portables—with struggling radio stations with a bunch of misfits. Duncan was right. I

needed to stop worrying about those horrible OurWorld photos and Brie's continued vendetta against me. I had to focus on the debut of *Chloe, Queen of the Universe*, which was going to rock the radio world.

"Get your butt in the control room, JISP Girl!" Clementine's fiery voice roared through Portable Five, and I jumped, dropping the paper airplane. Singed hair and flaring nostrils hovered over me as Clementine dragged me to the control room and pointed to the chair next to Duncan. "Sit."

"You know, people would be much more apt to follow your direction if you were a little less . . . oh, I don't know . . . fascist." I sat and winked at Duncan. He hid a smile in his scarf. Tonight's nubby neckwear was soft blue and green, like the ocean on a misty morning. The missed stitches and ragged tails of yarn looked like bits of seaweed. And of course it had the crooked red heart stitched on one end.

Having Duncan at my side for my first show felt good. Sparring with Clementine felt good. Knowing the entire staff was in the newsroom felt good.

"Breathe between units of thought, not randomly." Clementine picked up my headset.

"Been working on it for sixteen years."

She slipped the headset over my head and adjusted the band. "If you read, hold your copy in front of you so you don't look down. Keeps the airway open."

"Of course, closed airwaves would kill my show."

To her credit, Clementine ignored my stupid chatter. "Elbows on the table make for a more conversational style," she continued in a steady, calming voice.

"Elbows positioned."

She rested her hand on my knee, stopping the *clackity-clack* of my shoe. "And if you feel like you're going to hurl, do not blow chunks on my equipment, got it?" She looked at the ceiling. "Seriously, if you get nervous, close your eyes and pretend you're talking to a friend. Okay?"

"I'll picture you."

Dragon sigh.

Clementine knew her stuff. All of this was designed to create a more natural radio presence that would appeal to listeners.

I adjusted the cord on the mic. If we had any listeners tonight. Had my week-long promotional efforts drummed up any? Had Brie with her continued smear campaign, which now included a gallery full of less-than-complimentary drama-club photos, turned them away? My throat tightened. Or worse, would Brie try anything on air?

"Tell me again about the Great Silencer," I asked Clementine. "The one I can use on VSPs."

"We went over it five minutes ago." Clementine yanked at my headset, repositioning it. "Weren't you listening?"

Of course I was listening. And worrying. I looked at the clock. Two minutes. "Tell me again."

Clementine wagged her crinkly hair and hissed. "Okay, we run live shows on a seven-second delay. It's an intentional delay that allows us to deal with any technical problems, which occasionally happen, given our ancient equipment, but we can also use it to cut off objectionable material, like profanity, before it goes out onto the airwaves."

I wasn't worried about profanity. I was worried about Brie Sonderby.

Clementine leaned toward me, the heat of her stare like red-hot coals. "You're not going to wig out on us, are you?"

"No, of course not." I was ready for this. Duncan was at my side. It would be *fun*. "Sound the trumpets. The queen has arrived."

Clementine grumbled and hurried next door into the production studio. She slipped on her own headset, and her voice echoed through mine. "On the beam."

I positioned myself in front of the microphone.

"Four, three, two, cue music . . ."

Duncan punched a button, and my rumbling theme music filled the air. Taysom had unearthed a 1940s retro piece, upbeat and classy, not too brassy. It was perfect. It was me.

I stared at the microphone and pictured invisible airwaves connecting me to hundreds, thousands of listeners. Maybe even Brie. Mean, mean Brie.

As the music tapered off, Duncan pointed to me, but when I opened my mouth, my throat constricted.

Words.

Where were the words?

Why couldn't I talk?

I always talked.

Something warm and firm settled on my knee. Duncan's

hand. I focused on that hand, the one that made a tricked-out Sparrow with the words *Stop worrying. It'll be FUN.* The one that now created little fiery sparks on my knee. My knee? Why did Duncan have such an effect on my odd body parts? And why was I thinking about Duncan when there was dead air everywhere?

Across the glass, Clementine rolled her hand in a circle, as if she was motioning me across a school crosswalk. She looked so calm.

Why was dragon Clementine being so calm?

Because I was freaking out.

Panic bubbled in my chest. If I opened my mouth, I'd make frothy, dying sounds. Or puke. Or start babbling about tingly knees and earlobes and thumbs.

If you get overwhelmed, Clem had said, *pretend you're talking to a friend*.

What friends? I was no longer connected to Brie and Merce. The drama club despised me. The entire school was whispering about me again.

No, not everyone.

I stared at Duncan. Garbage Games. Paper airplanes. Even Clementine didn't look so dragonish. I cleared my throat. "Uh, this is uh, 88.8 The Edge." I licked my trembling lips. "Uh . . . welcome to the realm. Uh . . . this is Queen Chloe, and I'm glad you tuned in."

Duncan nodded. Clementine nodded. Haley, Taysom, Frick and Frack, and even Mr. Martinez, who sat in the corner grading papers, nodded, nudging me on.

With the first words out, the rest came easier. "Uh . . . we're starting something new here at The Edge, a call-in show starring me, Queen Chloe, and of course *you* in our first-ever live talk show. Tonight we're going to kick off things and talk about pet peeves. You can learn a good deal about people if you know what pushes their buttons. As for your queen, something that makes me want to stomp my royal feet is TMI.

"That's right, minions, too much information. These days people talk, talk, talk, which is a good thing for our show, and your queen, she loves to talk. But I want you to think about those times where you're minding your own business and . . ."

I pointed to Duncan. He cued stinger number one.

Wham! The banging-hammer sound effect poured out seamlessly.

"You get hammered with TMI," I continued. "Over winter break I was at the grocery store minding my own business when a woman in the produce department started comparing the oranges to certain body parts she'd had implanted. At first I thought she was talking to me. Exactly how do you respond to this type of comment? But then I realized she was using a Bluetooth. I mean, really, did I want to hear this? Should I be hearing this?"

Duncan's shoulders jiggled, a wonderful, silly movement that stole my breath. But I managed to keep chatting another ten minutes until Clementine gave me a break signal. "Okay, minions, after the break, I'm opening the phone lines and it's your turn. Let me know about your TMI troubles or tell me a pet peeve of your own." I gave our call letters and the station's phone number.

Duncan dialed up a PSA and school announcements. The On Air light went dark. Over the speaker came a dragonlike growl. Across the glass in the production room Clementine gripped the sides of her head as if her hair were on fire.

"What?" I asked. I'd been shaky at first, but I'd pulled it together. Kind of.

"You called our listeners *minions*," Clementine said with a hiss.

"I'm playing up the whole queen thing."

Clementine's head hit her desk.

"What's wrong with 'minions'?" I asked her crinkly hair.

"You're insulting our audience."

"No, I'm establishing a rapport with them. I'm using fresh, original, memorable language that our growing, faithful audience will associate with my show." In the talk shows I'd studied I noticed most of the successful hosts had certain phrases and gimmicks unique to them.

Clementine dragged her body upright. "Calling someone a minion is not going to endear them to us. They aren't going to listen to radio programming that insults them."

"Wanna bet?" Duncan pointed to the phone bank. Three lines blinked red.

Clementine went off mic and picked up the phone. Her job was to screen callers and make sure they weren't on crack. She'd patch them through to the phone in the control room, and Duncan would activate the call. The rest would be up to me.

After the break, Duncan cued the music, and the On Air light came on again. "Welcome back, minions, glad you stuck around. Tonight we're talking about pet peeves, and the queen hates too much information. Now it's your turn to dish. Up first"—I looked at the slip of paper Clementine held and smiled—"Josie from Tierra del Rey. Welcome, caller, this is Chloe."

"Hey, Your Majesty, love the show. I agree. People don't know when to shut up. It's like—how you say—irritating. I run restaurant, Dos Hermanas on Palo Brea and Seventh. Last week this woman buy takeout and talk about her sick kid and she say how green stuff come out his nose looks like the tomatillo salsa in the salsa bar. *Aye-yae-yae.* We no need to know that."

Ana called in next, followed by Noreen, Grams's neighbor, my dad, two of his students, and my brother Zach's old girlfriend. Yes, I knew them personally, and, yes, I begged all of them to call in, but that didn't mean they weren't bona fide listeners.

In the next segment I introduced a new topic. Comfort foods. Thanks to Brie and Mercedes, not to mention Grams and Mom, I'd been inhaling plenty of Twizzlers lately.

"Hey, minions, your queen now wants to talk about the food you love and need when life gets rough. When you get a Rudolph-size zit on the end of your nose right before the big dance. When you get into a fender bender with Daddy's new car. Visualize with me, minions, you're down, you're beaten, and you need munchies to make it better.

"In the queen's castle, the royal comfort food is"—I reached into my bag and took out a Twizzler and crinkled the plastic in front of the mic—"Twizzlers. Soft, sweet, and oh so comforting.

The last time I had more than the recommended daily allowance was the day a certain guidance counselor, who shall remain nameless, disemboweled my Junior Independent Study Project, a story that could be a whole show of its own. But back to comfort foods. What food soothes your battered heart and calms your tattered soul?"

I stared at the phone bank. It stared back. Dark. Unblinking. I should have told the sisters they could call in twice, but no problem. I was ready for this. I was not going to sound like an idiot on the air. I was going to have *fun*.

"While you're all running to your phones, we'll chat about some traditional comfort foods. January is National Soup Month, and soup is undoubtedly one of the world's greatest comfort foods. Who doesn't like a steamy bowl of chicken soup when you're sick? Or how about a hearty bowl of chili when it's cold and rainy?" The phone bank remained frighteningly dark. "Hey, is chili even a soup? I'm not sure about that. We need some data, minions. Yep, we have serious data deprivation here."

Across from me Clementine rolled her eyes.

"Hey, Clementine, can you do a quickie Wiki check and let me know if chili is considered a soup?" Clementine shook her head and glared. "You minions remember Clementine, right? She's our news guru, and she's in the castle with me tonight, not on a throne, mind you, but on a stool next door in our production studio. A *jester's* stool. Hey, Jester Clem, pop on and greet the minions."

Another crinkly head shake.

Dead. Air.

"Hi," Clementine said.

"No, the queen wants you to say, 'Greetings, minions.'"

In the newsroom all gazes snapped to Clementine. "Greetings, minions," Clem said between clenched teeth.

"Jester Clem's a bowl of laughs, isn't she? But she's a whiz with information. Dominates the data. And she's fast, too. As we speak, she's crunching data." I pointed at Clementine's computer and mouthed, *Wikipedia*. I bantered about soup and a minute later asked, "Okay, Jester Clem, what do you have for the minions? Is chili a soup?"

"Inconclusive," Clementine said, her words clipped. "Some call chili a one-pot meal, others group it with soups and stews."

"Inconclusive, huh? Okay, I'm making a royal decree. Chili is a soup. With that out of the way, we're ready to take calls, so dial up."

Still no flashing red lights. I pictured my friendless OurWorld page and empty voice mailbox. My fingers circled the mic, my knuckles whitening. "Ooo-kay. How about you, Jester Clem, when life gets you down, what do you like to chow on?" She shook her head and ran her jutting hand across her throat in a slicing motion.

I shook my head and mouthed, *Talk!*

"Beets." Clementine looked like she wanted to beat me over the head with a hammer.

"I told you, minions, she's a royal jokester. Seriously, what's your fave comfort food?"

"I'm serious," Clementine insisted. "I like beets."

"As in purple, bulbous root vegetables?"

"What's wrong with purple, bulbous root vegetables?"

"They're weird."

"They're not weird."

"They taste like dirt."

"They taste sweet and crunchy."

"And have you always had a love affair with beets?"

Dragon sigh. "I guess so. I first ate them years ago at my grandparents' farm in Temecula, where I spent my summer vacations. Grandpa and I picked the beets, and Grandma and I canned them."

"Hmmmmm. Summers at a nice family farm. Fun time with Pops and Grams. Have you ever thought beets are comforting because you associate them with people you love?"

Clementine tilted her wave of crinkly hair. "Could be."

One of the phone lines blinked. Clementine held a sign with the caller's name. "And good, calls are rolling in. Ernie's on the line. Welcome, caller, this is Chloe. What's your favorite comfort food?"

"Pizza. The mega-meat kind. Pepperoni, sausage, hamburger, and bacon. I also wanted to say I agree with you, Queen Chloe, beets are weird."

"A brilliant minion. I think I'll make you a knight of the realm." I pointed to Duncan, who played a blare of trumpets.

Two other lines blinked red. Another caller found comfort in mashed potatoes with butter. "Beets are not weird," she said.

"Nor is Jester Clem. She has different tastes. We need to respect her choices."

Clementine turned on her mic and piped in, "Can you knight her?"

I cleared my throat. "Only one knight a night, but I'm making a royal decree. We must respect Jester Clem, and . . . we must respect beets."

For the next forty-five minutes we talked about comfort food. At one point, Clementine popped on air and talked about foods scientifically proven to alter moods. "Chocolate increases endorphin levels, making you happier, and turkey is loaded with amino acids that make you calm."

Note to self: Give Clementine a chocolate-covered turkey for Valentine's Day next month. She was working as hard as me to pull this off.

When we reached the top of the final hour, the phone bank was full. I had to turn away callers. People wanted to spend time with me. *Me.*

"Unfortunately minions, it's time for the queen to abdicate the throne, but only for a week. Be sure to tune in next Friday for the only show with one queen, one universe, one Chloe. KDRS 88.8 The Edge."

Duncan cued my theme music and set the Ghost to run the automated programming for the rest of the night. I left the control room, my ankles wobbly. But in a good way. I gave the KDRS staffers a queenly wave (elbow, elbow, wrist, wrist, wrist), and slumped into the chair in front of my whiteboard. "Well?" I asked.

Mr. Martinez, who was gathering the papers on his desk, saluted me with his red pen.

"You didn't do anything to get us kicked off the air." Clementine's concession trilled through my head. I hadn't tanked. I filled two hours with witty and engaging conversation. I made Duncan smile. And I hadn't had to deal with Brie. "How many total callers did we get?"

Frack looked at a notepad.

"Come on, Frack, let's hear," I said. I wanted specific numbers, proof that people liked my show, that they liked me.

"S-s-seventeen."

I thumped Frack's back. "That's more than four times the four listeners who admitted on our survey to tuning in." Note to self: Include data in weekly JISP progress report to A. Lungren.

"Don't forget we had to turn away four at the end," Frick added. "We could have easily gone on another ten minutes."

"Chloe's survey suggested it, and tonight's show proved it. Our listeners loved being on the air," Taysom added.

It was odd, sitting around the graveyard radio station on a Friday night with a family of sorts. Didn't these people have places to go? Friends to see? Movies to watch?

Speaking of movies, I turned to Haley, who had finished watching her DVD and was writing on a notepad. "How was the movie?" I asked.

"Four out of four comets."

"What was it?"

Haley tossed me the DVD. *The Women*, a 1939 Oscar winner, according to the box. "Great shoes."

One by one each of the staffers and Mr. Martinez left, until it was only Duncan and me. Both Duncan and Clem had keys to Portable Five, and while I don't think school admin knew, Mr. Martinez occasionally left them to lock up the station. As for me, I didn't want to leave. For the first time in weeks the universe was in alignment.

I walked over to the control room, where Duncan was working on what looked like a CD player.

"No garbage tonight?" I asked.

"The thrift store closes at six on Fridays. I pushed it and got the trash done early."

I sat on my royal throne and kicked off my shoes. "Is it like this every Friday night at the station? I mean with everyone here?"

He nodded.

"But why? It's not like everyone's needed. Haley could have watched her old movie at home. Frack could have recorded his PSAs elsewhere, and Frick could have written his sports wrap at Extreme Bean, but everyone chose to be here together, yet apart, all of them doing their own thing."

Duncan tapped a small screwdriver on the faded denim of his thigh. "Weird, huh?"

"Like beets."

A slow smile slid across Duncan's lips and fired his eyes. He tossed the screwdriver into a small toolbox and opened his mouth, then closed it. "It's late," he said.

A nice exhaustion hung over me as I followed him out of the control room. It had been a good show and a good night, despite the havoc Brie had caused for the past two weeks.

I didn't need her, or Mercedes. I had KDRS, my show, the staff, and Duncan.

He came back from putting away his toolbox and flicked out all the lights but one over the door. I thought of the paper airplane he'd made. Duncan had reached out to me in his own quiet way.

I took a pen from a nearby desk and, before he could back away, grabbed Duncan's hand. My thumb ran across the calluses before I scribbled my phone number on his palm.

Duncan looked at his palm as if it were an alien body part, but his face softened. "There's nothing subtle about you, is there?" His voice was barely audible over the transmitter that buzzed in the corner.

No, I wasn't subtle or quiet, and I didn't like distance between me and others. "Does it bother you?" I held my breath.

He shook his head. "No, I don't mind."

Cool, wonderful air flooded my lungs, and I almost spun on my glittery toes. I refrained, instead tilting my chin toward his hand. "So you'll call me tomorrow?"

His fingers curled into his palm against his chest, and he smiled.

Stop by tuna cn. Big prob. Brng HER.
N rain b%ts.
Grams

I am a pelican. Fear me.

CHAPTER 10

IT WAS SATURDAY MORNING, THE DAY AFTER MY SUCCESSFUL
radio debut as Chloe, Queen of the Universe, and I should have
been reclining in my queenly bed and eating chocolate bonbons
iced with the royal crest. That or chatting on the phone with sexy-
eyed, scarf-wearing Duncan Moore. Or at least daydreaming
about sexy-eyed, scarf-wearing Duncan Moore.

Instead, I stood in the Tuna Can living room, opening the windows to let out clouds of smoke as an inch of water lapped at my
plain white Keds. Grams stood near me, soot on her right cheek,
her gnarled fingers wrapped around a broom handle. Mom and
Dad were outside with the ceramic squirrel and the Plumber
King. Only the squirrel grinned.

Grams shoved the broom across the floor, sending a violent
wave of water out the front door. "Piece of crap pipes."

What could I say? *There wasn't anything wrong with your pipes,
Grams, until you took a hammer to them.* Or maybe, *Be glad for those*

pipes and the sprinkler system that flooded the Tuna Can because they saved your life. You could have been killed!

"Piece of crap hammer. Piece of crap teapot . . ."

My shaking hands opened the next window. When Grams woke this morning, she put a teapot on the stove to boil and forgot about it. The water boiled away, the teapot overheated, and a roll of paper towels near the stove caught fire, along with the kitchen curtains and a stack of mail. The fire alarm didn't go off because Grams had taken out the batteries for her portable DVD player and had forgotten to replace them. Luckily, the fire sprinklers Mom insisted on having installed last year went off and put out the fire before it spread beyond the stove area. Grams, however, couldn't remember how to turn off the sprinklers, so she hammered the valves, breaking them and sending a torrent of water throughout the trailer. Even worse, Grams tried more than an hour to fix it herself before calling for help. Water now slicked the ceiling and walls and soaked every piece of furniture. Drips still echoed in the closets and cupboards.

I yanked open another window. Grams should have called someone immediately. There was nothing wrong with asking for help. For the past week I'd relied on help from the entire KDRS staff, and with them I'd pulled off a killer debut show.

With the windows open, I pulled out the trash basket and thought of Duncan, my trash-toting, fix-it guy. It would be nice to have him here this morning, but something told me not even my fix-it guy could repair this mess.

Footsteps clanked on the metal porch, and Mom waded into the living room. Her hands, the gentle ones that stitched people's broken hearts, knotted into tight balls at her hips.

Please, please, don't start yelling at Grams.

Mom stretched her neck and said in an oddly calm voice, "I paid the Plumber King."

Grams said nothing. With Mom in the doorway, Grams aimed her sweeping elsewhere, disturbing the water but sending it nowhere.

Mom looked at the ceiling, her face a blank mask. "Jack called the water-damage repair and restoration people," Mom continued in that controlled voice. "He's waiting outside for them. They should be here any minute."

Grams swished a broom full of water under the couch. Why wasn't Grams saying anything? Why wasn't Mom yelling at Grams and telling her she could have been seriously hurt? That she could have died? My Keds squished as I shifted from one foot to the other.

Grams swished another wave of water under the bookshelf that held her DVD collection. Then another. *Swish. Splatter. Swish. Splatter.*

"I also called the insurance company, and they're sending out an adjuster," Mom added.

Swish. Splatter. Swish. Splatter. SWISH. The water smacked into the bookshelf, and a stack of DVDs crashed to the floor. *Ocean's Eleven*, the 2001 Brad Pitt version, sailed past my Keds.

Now would be the time to say something witty to cheer up

Grams and ease the tension. But I couldn't. There was nothing amusing about this situation.

Grams left a teapot on the stove. It started a fire. The sprinklers went off. She caused more damage when she hammered the pipes. This mess was her fault. This mess changed everything.

The same realization must have hit Grams as she dropped her broom and slumped onto the couch. Water seeped from the cushions. Grams went to that far-off place, the one that glazed her eyes and slackened her jaw.

Mom took a seat on the soggy recliner and cleared her throat. "You can't stay here."

Grams's eyes brightened and narrowed. "Can it, Deb. I don't want to hear it right now."

"Given the current state of the Tuna Can, you don't have a choice but to hear it *right now*."

My fingers tightened around the garbage can. I wished my mom would stop using the word *choice* in that tone of voice, as if she was giving a child a choice between carrots or peas.

Grams wagged her index finger at Mom. "You are my daughter, and you will not tell me what to do."

"There are six excellent residential facilities you've previewed." Mom went on as if Grams hadn't spoken. She reached into her bag and pulled out a thick folder. "Well-maintained, exceptional staff, private rooms. All are within close proximity to quality medical care, and two are near the high school, so Chloe can easily stop in for visits and drive you on errands."

Grams had been the one who used to drive me places. Again the earth spun, sending everything all topsy-turvy.

Grams stood, turned her back on Mom, and started wringing water from a throw pillow on the sofa. Her trembling hands squeezed, and streams of water soaked the front of her bathrobe and plinked to the water lapping at her house slippers.

Mom pulled two brochures from the folder. "I seem to recall you liked this one the best. Minnie's Place."

Grams clutched another pillow and squeezed. Squeeze. *Plink.* Squeeze. *Plink.*

Mom unfolded one of the brochures with shaky fingers, hardly the steady hands of a person who spent her days mending people's hearts. "When you visited Minnie's Place, you told the woman giving you the tour you liked the pretty little swing in the butterfly garden."

With the pillows squeezed to death, Grams reached for the sofa cushions. Her hands shook so much, she couldn't get the Velcro strap undone.

"Minnie's Place also allowed you to have a microwave in your room, so you could still do some cooking," Mom went on. "And they have complimentary shuttle service to the beach."

Grams tugged and tugged, sodden locks of scraggly gray hair falling over her red face.

"It's not too far from here, so Noreen and your other neighbors can visit."

Grams pulled harder, grunting and showing teeth, but the strap wouldn't let go.

"And it's close to your neurologist and physical therapist and that new acupressure clinic and—"

"Stop it! Both of you!" The garbage can slipped from my hands and splashed onto the floor. "Mom, you can't take control of Grams's life. And you, Grams"—I pointed a shaky finger at her—"talk to her. Tell her what you want, what you *need*. You have to speak for yourself." While you can.

Grams stared at me. Did she see my worry? My fear? Did she know I wanted to throw myself into her arms like I did when I was six because the world always made sense in her arms?

At last Grams straightened her spine notch by notch. She reminded me of the matriarchs on the soaps who survived brain tumors, airplane crashes, and cheating husbands with murderous mistresses. "All right, Chloe, all right." She pushed her wet hair out of her face and turned to my mom. "The Tuna Can's shot to hell, at least for now." She strutted into the kitchen and grabbed her purse. "Get your heinies in gear. It's time to go."

Mom froze, relief battled with dread across the pale features of her face.

Holding my breath I asked, "Go where?"

Grams snatched the floating copy of *Ocean's Eleven*. "Minnie's Place." Raising the DVD like a battle flag, she waded to the front door. "They have a sixty-five-inch HDTV."

On Monday before school, I walked into the radio station and blew Clementine a kiss. She grunted in my general direction as I sashayed to my whiteboard desk.

The weekend had started out a sooty, soggy mess, and I'd been outfitted in Keds, but the tide had turned in a big way. Grams had checked herself into Minnie's Place. Although she claimed she planned to stay there only long enough to get the Tuna Can aired out and back in shape, she and Mom, for the first time in months, weren't battling.

After helping Grams set up her room at Minnie's Place, I worked my Sunday burrito shift for Dos Hermanas. The sisters slipped me a big tip for luring in a bus of beach-bound tourists from Indio. I also received two marriage proposals, including one from a guy who offered to dress up as a bowl of guacamole and be my partner for life.

"Sorry," I'd told him, "I dip with someone else." At least I thought I dipped with someone else. Duncan. I checked my phone fifty times. He hadn't called all weekend. I reminded myself he worked all day at the thrift store on Saturday and Sunday and probably used the weekend to catch up on homework.

I arrived at the radio station early this morning hoping Duncan would be there, but his beat-up bike was not leaning against the portable, nor was he standing on a ladder fixing lights or tucked under the transmitter fixing whatever he fixed there.

Inside Portable Five Frick was recording his weekly sports-wrap show, and he waved when I walked by the glass-fronted production room. Haley, sucking on a toffee sucker, was writing another movie review. I walked to her corner and peeked over her shoulder. *Goodbye, Mr. Chips*.

Reaching into my book bag I took out the DVD I'd found in Grams's collection and handed it to Haley.

She frowned.

"You already have *Stagecoach*?" I asked.

She shook her head.

"Then take it. Anyone who's a big fan of 1939 movies, arguably the best year ever in the motion picture industry, needs a copy of *Stagecoach*." When she remained still, I set the DVD on her desk. "Okay, I'll admit the shoes are a little dusty, but John Wayne kind of makes up for it, don't you think?"

She studied the DVD with a puzzled frown. "How did you know I like films from 1939?"

I pointed at her towers of DVDs. "It's kind of hard to miss."

"You noticed," she said softly. With a strange little smile, she pulled a sucker from the bag on her desk and gave it to me.

As I unwrapped the sucker, I asked, "Where's Duncan?"

Clementine squinted at me. "Are you some kind of stalker?"

Nope, she wasn't going to get me down today. Life was too good, and much of that had to do with Duncan Moore, who made my thumbs and earlobes feel crazy wonderful.

"He's busy," Clementine said.

"With . . ."

"Stuff that's none of your business."

"Will he be in today?"

Every staff member looked at Clementine, who tugged at one of her frizzy curls. "I'm not sure."

Again, I was the odd man out until Taysom pointed to Frack's computer. "Hey, Chloe, you've got mail."

With a happy squeal, I hurried to Frack's desk and looked over his shoulder at a webpage with the jagged black KDRS logo splashed on the screen. "I didn't know we had a website."

"Nothing fancy," Taysom said. "Program skeds, staff bios, and a listener mail feature. For the first time, someone e-mailed us—well, you."

"No way." I punched Frack's shoulder. "Why didn't you shout this glorious news at the top of your lungs when I walked in the door?"

Frack's face grew pink.

I grabbed a chair and planted it next to Frack. Sure enough, three brilliant minions had commented after Friday night's show. I'd heard somewhere, probably from one of the sisters, that for every person who complained about a product or a service, something like one hundred others would like to complain but didn't have the time or energy. If I had three fans who took the time to write, I could have three hundred more.

I spent the next twenty minutes crafting queenly acknowledgments to my three fans.

Clementine looked over my shoulder at my computer screen. "Don't you think 'From the Desk of Her Majesty' is a bit much?"

Panic stilled my fingers on the keyboard. "Do you?" I had three people who adored me. I didn't want to alienate them.

Clementine frowned. "I guess it kind of goes with your on-air personality."

I smiled. I had an on-air personality. As I reread my fan mail, I noticed something else. "Hey, Clem, my fans loved my jester."

"I am not *your* jester."

"Seriously, look." I pointed to the screen. "This listener wants to know what the jester and the queen are going to talk about next week."

"Snort!"

I'd enjoyed taking digs at Clementine, and she'd dug back, but in an air-wave-appropriate way. Nothing mean. Our jabs at each other and snarky banter had a higher purpose. We were trying to attract listeners, and conflict attracted people. During ratings weeks at the soaps, dead wives came back to life, secret babies were hauled out of closets, and villainesses were at their scheming best.

Brie was a master of conflict. Her lies about the Mistletoe Ball had everyone whispering about me. Her attack on the drama club sent another anti-Chloe wave across the campus. But in the end, the notoriety had been a good thing for my radio show.

"I think *we* were engaging," I told Clementine. "The phones were clogged for the last forty-five minutes of programming, which happened to be the time you and I were going at it on air. The listeners loved it. They loved us. Together."

"So?"

"So, this type of programming boosts ratings." Sometimes you had to get out of your comfort zone and try new things. Like Minnie's Place and Garbage Games. At the thought of Duncan, I wondered again where he could be. I hoped his bike hadn't blown another chain. I aimed my gaze at Clementine. "So why not join my show this week?"

"Because I don't want to." She grabbed the papers on her desk and headed for the production studio.

Following her, I planted myself in the doorway. Normally I didn't do confrontation, but today I could tackle anything and anyone. I had a great show. Grams was in a safe place, at least for now. Duncan, wherever he was, held my phone number next to his heart.

"Why don't you like me?" I asked.

Clem sat behind the mic. "Out. I have news to record."

I settled my shoulder against the door frame. I remembered the look on her face a week ago as she stared at me through the glass with a glare that mirrored Brie's. Had I done or said something to hurt her? Was she jealous?

"Leave," Clementine said.

"Not until you tell me why you hate me."

Clementine slammed her papers onto the desk. "I don't hate you, Chloe. No one can hate you. You're too"—she waved her hand at me and wrinkled her nose—"too you."

This was not what I expected. "Was that a compliment?"

She spun in the chair until she fully faced me. "Okay. Fine. You want to know why I don't find you too queenly. Here it is." She aimed her finger at the center of my chest. "You're a royal skater."

I waited for her to go on, but she remained silent. "Is this some new radio term I need to learn?"

Clementine flung her hands above her head and roared. "You're a princess on roller skates. People like you skate through life on shiny gold blades to full orchestral music with the wind at your back. Everything comes easy to skaters. You have the right friends. You wear the right clothes. You have brilliant, rich, wonderful families. Everyone loves you."

My jaw dropped. "And what planet have you been on lately?"

"Even with Brie Sonderby's smack, you're still skating. It's freakin' mind-blowing." Clementine shook her head, her frizzy hair making a soft, swishing sound. "One of the most powerful people in school smears you, but you manage to skate in here and pull off a stupid talk show that everyone loved, which is good. I can't argue that." Clementine stared out the glass at the newsroom, her wild hair settling around her face, which was pale, oddly snuffed of fiery bluster. "But you have no interest in broadcasting, and until a few weeks ago you didn't know KDRS existed. You don't care about the station. You're too wrapped up in you to have a clue what's going on with any of us."

"That's not true." I'd given Duncan a lift, helped him with his work, and showed him fun with Garbage Games. I made a sandwich for Frack. Haley gave me a sucker.

Clementine pointed to Frack, who was still on the KDRS website. "Have you ever noticed that Frack barely talks to you?"

I had noticed. He said less than ten words to me in two weeks. "Ever wonder why?" Clementine asked but didn't let me answer. "He stutters. Can't spit out more than two words without tripping over his tongue."

"Frack stutters? But he records all the PSAs." I'd heard his voice. It wasn't as deep and smooth as Taysom's or as animated as sportscaster Frick's, but clear and certainly without stutters.

"His PSAs are done on a mic in the production studio away from people. He's here because radio is giving him a voice he never had."

I knew the power of the station. It had been a haven from the sea of stinging jellyfish, and on Friday it officially became my wonderful royal castle. I'd become a part of the KDRS team, but Clem didn't see it.

Clem dipped her head toward Haley. "And Haley, she needs a place she can go where people don't treat her like she has a contagious disease. You think you've had to deal with crap the past few months? Hah. Haley's boyfriend bailed when the pink dot appeared on the stick, her supposed best friends treat her like a leper, and her dad hasn't spoken to her for four months." Clementine let loose a sigh, more heavy than fiery. "And Duncan . . . Duncan needs us." Her eyes drilled me, some of the fire back. "Come April, if we survive that long, your JISP will be over and you'll be gone."

I opened my mouth to tell her she was wrong, but for one of the few times in my life, the words wouldn't flow. Honestly, I hadn't thought that far ahead. My goal was to host a successful talk show and to JISP well enough to keep an F off my permanent record. Clementine's sigh was without fire, not even a hint of smoke. "Bottom line, Chloe, you don't need us, not like the rest of us need one another. We're not part of your world, and you're not part of ours. Hell, Chloe, we're not even in the same universe."

With a flick of her arm, she pushed me and shut the production room door. It didn't slam, but closed slowly, softly, which gave me time to stare at the ocean between us.

CRHAPPY TRAILS
TRAILER PARK

A PLACE FOR FRIENDS

Trailer Lots Available
See Manager in #11

CHAPTER 11

THE HAPPY TRAILS TRAILER PARK WAS NOT A HAPPY PLACE.
Nor was it parklike. It squatted on a tired, dry bit of earth about
twenty miles east of town and smelled of wet garbage and cat
pee. Mobile homes in faded shades of gold and avocado were
topped with rusted, sagging roofs. Spiky weeds clawed up from a
spiderweb of asphalt cracks. No smiling ceramic squirrels in this
trailer park.

But Duncan was here.

He'd called thirty minutes ago, not to chat, but for a ride. On
the phone he told me he'd ridden to the trailer park to visit a
friend but someone had stolen his bike. I drove to the common
area and spotted him next to a graffiti-covered phone booth near
a swimming pool with no water.

"Thanks," he said as he climbed into my car and tossed a wad-
ded brown-and-beige scarf in his lap. "I can't imagine who'd be
stupid enough to steal my crappy bike."

"Someone who has amorous feelings about duct tape," I said.

His broad shoulders sunk as he leaned his head against the headrest. He looked hammered—rammed, cut, and spread by the Jaws of Life. I wanted to wrap my arms around his scarf-wearing little neck and hug.

Duncan reached into his pocket and withdrew a worn wallet. "Let me give you gas money."

I waved him off. "I woke this morning and said, Hey, it's a great afternoon for a picturesque drive."

On the way out, we rolled past a dozen overflowing trash cans, where a bony, collarless dog rooted through the bags. A skanky girl smoking a cigarette on a sagging porch gave us the finger. Duncan shook his head but said nothing.

Talking always helped me to relieve stress and make sense of the world. I talked to Grams, to my brothers, to Mom and Dad when they weren't working, and to Merce and Brie. I didn't need to be a psychologist to know Duncan didn't do much talking. To anyone. If there was anyone who looked like he needed a heavy dose of talk, it was Duncan. And contrary to what Clementine said, I knew how to listen.

"You said you were visiting a friend?"

"Yeah." His fingers dug holes into his scarf.

"Everything okay?"

His jaw ticked. "No."

"I'm sorry." I shot him a sideways glance. "Want me to sic Clementine on him?"

A groaning laugh rolled from Duncan's throat. "I'm not sure

if I'm ready to unleash that beast on anyone." Duncan stopped stabbing his scarf and looped it around his neck.

On the drive into town, he refused to talk, so I filled the silence with chatter about the afternoon at the station, about my fan mail, and about dipping into the Question Bag for next week's show topic. I said nothing about Clementine calling me an outsider, because she was wrong. I belonged at KDRS. I wasn't an outsider. Proof positive: Duncan called me when he got stranded and needed help.

Once in Tierra del Rey, Duncan directed me to a single-story duplex on the south side of town. Both sides of the house had flaking stucco and faded plastic roses in sagging window planters.

Duncan's hand hesitated over the car door handle. "Are you sure I can't pay you? I got my paycheck yesterday."

"Consider it a favor from a friend." Would he call me a friend? Did he have tingly thumbs and earlobes? Did he know I wanted more?

He squinted out the front windshield at the setting sun. "How about dinner, then? Nothing fancy, but I'm pretty good with a frying pan and eggs."

I was out of my car and at Duncan's front door in half a second.

Duncan's duplex was small but homey. A worn plaid sofa and a single tweed recliner huddled in a tiny living room next to an even tinier kitchen with a plastic dining set and toasters. I blinked and counted. Fourteen toasters?

"It's not much, but it's only Mom and me," Duncan said.

"It's cozy, everything close by." I thought of Grams's beloved

Tuna Can. "It's not about the space but how you fill it." I pointed to the toasters. "So what's up with you and toast?"

A sheepish grin tugged at his mouth as he opened the refrigerator. "The toasters are thrift store rejects. No one would buy them, and I couldn't stand to see them thrown away."

"So you fixed, prettified, and gave them a loving home?"

His grin fell away, and he shrugged. "Something like that. Now, how about scrambled eggs and cheese on toast?"

A perfect comfort food, and this evening Mr. Serious needed comfort. "Sounds great."

Duncan mixed six eggs with milk and poured the mixture into a frying pan sizzling with melted butter. He handed me a loaf of bread and pointed to the toasters. "Take your pick."

Most were chrome. One was robin's-egg blue, another candy-apple red. Some had two slots, others four or six. One looked like a bird cage. "They all work?" I asked.

Duncan raised both eyebrows.

Of course they all worked. Because Duncan fixed things. I grinned and took out four slices of bread. As I slid them into the candy-apple red toaster, the windowpane over the sink shook. I jumped. A wide, lined face pressed against the glass. "Phooooone," an older woman yelled through the cracked glass. "Get your ass over here."

Duncan looked like he wanted to crawl under a heavy piece of equipment. He took the towel from his waistband. "That's Hetta. She lives next door. She lets Mom and me use her phone." His fingers dug into the dish towel. "Can you keep an eye on the eggs? I probably should take this call."

The vertical line creased the center of his forehead as he hurried out the back door. The woman at the window moved to the open doorway of Duncan's kitchen, her fleshy hands on her wide hips. She smelled like cabbage. "What are you doing here?" Hetta glared at me like I was a cockroach that had crawled through the kitchen drain.

"I'm having eggs with Duncan."

The doughy face glowered. "Why?"

"Uh . . . we're friends."

She huffed and walked toward me. "Duncan don't have no time for friends." She raised a thick finger and wagged it at me. "Now, what are you really doing here? You're looking for him, aren't you? You're one of Stu's friends."

I backed away, feeling the heat of her words. "No, I . . . I don't know anyone named Stu." And if I did, I wouldn't admit it to this woman, who clearly despised Stu.

"Well, you better not cause no trouble around here. I don't stand for trouble." She spun away on a puff of cabbage-scented air.

With Hetta and her horrendous scowl gone, I looked around the kitchen and small living area. No phone. Duncan had been uncomfortable when I first gave him my phone number. Was this why he never called?

As I studied his house, I also noticed no television, no CD player, and no computer, only a small box on a scarred end table next to the sofa. I grinned. A radio. One of Duncan's nubby scarves, this one the color of the beach, shades of brown and white and coral, rested on the sofa. Like all his other scarves, this one had a little heart knitted onto one end.

I wondered who stitched her heart into scarves for loner Duncan Moore.

I checked the eggs, which were starting to set. Opening a kitchen drawer, I looked for a spatula but found various hammers and wrenches and screwdrivers. I giggled. Duncan lived here. The next drawer held a stack of mail. On top was a bill from the utility company. I wasn't being nosy, but it was hard to miss the words *Past Due* in bright red.

"The eggs need to be stirred." Duncan was so close his words brushed the back of my neck.

I slammed the drawer. "I . . ."

"I can get it." Without meeting my gaze, he nudged me aside and pulled a spatula from the bottom drawer and stirred the eggs.

I searched his face. Was he upset over the phone call? Embarrassed about the bill? Even this close, I couldn't tell. Duncan had a way of distancing himself that I still didn't understand. When I was upset, I wanted to share my pain, to pour it in a sandbox and invite all my friends to come over and dig around in it with shovels.

"Okay, do it," he said.

"Do what?"

He poked at the eggs. "Say something funny or sweet to make me forget we're about to lose power."

"Do you want me to?"

His eyelids dipped closed as if the lids were too heavy. He nodded.

I settled my hip on the counter. "Okay, if it gets too dark and cold here, I have a Tuna Can you can move into. Rent free. Must like soggy furniture and grinning ceramic squirrels."

Like air and water, we needed laughter, and I'd never seen a person who needed to laugh as much as Duncan Moore. He didn't burst out in a guffaw, but the heaviness lifted from his eyes as a chuckle rumbled. "Tuna can?"

"One bedroom, one bath, six-hundred-square-foot mobile home in a lovely shade of tuna can silver."

"Soggy?"

My face grew serious. "Slight mechanical malfunction."

His eyes sparked, and I laughed out loud. Dunc loved a good mechanical malfunction. He also needed a distraction from the Happy Trails Trailer Park and the past-due notice in the drawer. Enter Grams and her hammer. I kept the story lighthearted, not mentioning the war and shaky truce between Grams and Mom or Grams's vow to leave Minnie's Place when the Tuna Can was made inhabitable. By the time I reached the part about Grams setting up Brad Pitt Movie Mania night at Minnie's Place, Dunc was laughing out loud and scooping eggs onto two slices of toast, which he topped with cheese. I set the plates on the table while he held out a chair. "Has anyone ever told you you're wonderful?" Dunc said.

"Yes, but feel free to continue with that and other similar adjectives."

The table was so small, my toes brushed against his, and a hot spark ignited. I swear, even my toes reacted to Dunc's touch.

"Exactly where is this sorry, soggy piece of real estate you call the Tuna Can?"

"Fifty yards from the beach," I told Duncan. "Grams loves the ocean."

Grams and I had spent most of our summers on the shores of the Pacific Ocean building sand castles, boogie-boarding in the cold waters, and collecting shells.

"Look at this beauty, Poppy," Grams had announced one summer as she unearthed a shiny, spiraling conch. It was bigger than my sand bucket, the swirling inside as bright and shiny as a new copper penny. It smelled of salt and sea. I still remember the glorious swooshing sound it made as Grams held the conch to my ear. "Listen, do you hear it? Do you hear the heartbeat of the ocean?"

"You love it, too," Duncan said, pulling me back to the tiny kitchen and comforting smell of steamy eggs on golden toast.

"Love what?"

"The ocean."

"How do you know?"

He reached over and slid a single finger along my upper arm. "You wear your heart on your sleeve." He pressed his finger against my skin. "Right here for all to see. Everyone knows when you're happy or sad, fighting mad, or ready to take on dragons."

I stared at my arm and his finger creating a firestorm along my skin. "And that's wrong?"

"No. I think it's good not to let things bottle up inside." He reached for his sandwich. "It's healthier that way."

As far as I could tell, Duncan didn't open his heart to anyone. He kept everything close to his chest, which by his account made him unhealthy.

At school he was a loner. I hadn't seen his mother, nor did he tell me where she was. If she was anything like Duncan, she probably worked two or three jobs. He never talked of a father or brothers or sisters. Duncan was all alone, except for Hetta, the grumpy neighbor who smelled like cooked cabbage.

"Everything okay next door with the phone call?" I asked. Now that he was more relaxed, maybe he'd download some of the heavy stuff he carried on those broad shoulders.

Duncan paused, then shook his head, but he didn't frown, nor did that line crease his forehead. Instead, he lifted his sandwich. "But that's okay. Tonight I have eggs and cheese on toast and"—he tipped the sandwich toward me—"a pretty girl with a big heart on her sleeve."

That big heart did a big jump. With a laugh I lifted my right foot and waggled it to the side. "And great shoes. You can't forget the great shoes."

Duncan slipped his fingers around my ankle and critically eyed my styling cork wedge. "Yeah, a girl with great shoes," he proclaimed as a crazy tingle raced across my ankle.

Ankle: Check. Another wonky erogenous body part.

SUBJ: I <3 Jester Clem
FROM: pj.rodriguez@gmail.com
TO: kdrs@delreyhs.edu

Hey Clementine,

Thanks for being the voice of reason in an insane universe.

Your #1 fan!
Sam Littlefield

The life which is unexamined is not worth living—Socrates

CHAPTER 12

FRIDAY NIGHT, THE ON AIR SIGN BRIGHTENED AT EXACTLY EIGHT.

"Welcome, minions, this is Chloe, your queen. Glad to have you in the realm for another program of royally rousing talk radio. Tonight we'll talk, we'll laugh, and talk some more. Back by popular demand is *Jester* Clem." I smiled at Clementine, who once again was sitting in the production studio. Her nostrils flared, and she looked ready to singe the curls off my head.

I pointed to Duncan, who was sitting next to me in the control room. He cued a hand-to-head-slap stinger.

"Oops, I forgot," I went on with a wink at Clementine. "Clementine said she'd have me overthrown if I continued to call her Jester. Can you believe that? She got her little sparkly jester tights all in a wad over a nickname, which, by the way, is our first topic of discussion tonight." *Wham!* A perfect segue into tonight's show. I bowed to Clem, who shook her head, but I saw the small dragon smile.

Earlier in the week Clementine had agreed to be part of the show, and not because I bribed her with beets. Her fans demanded it. Yes, Dragon Clementine had fans. She received a half-dozen e-mails hailing "Jester Clem." I think the adoration shocked Clementine more than anyone else, and perhaps it was in that stunned state she agreed to join my *Chloe, Queen of the Universe* show. Our format would be similar to the first week. Hour two Clementine would pop in, but hour one was all about me and nicknames.

"Most nicknames are usually terms of endearment, given to us by our loved ones," I said into the mic. "You can call me Queenie, but my family nicknamed me Poppy. Yep, minions, you heard right, Poppy, as in floppy, orange flowers." Duncan cued a mass groan. "I know. I, too, wondered if my family had been taking opium hits when they came up with it."

I went on to dish about my wavy orange-red hair, then nicknames for famous people like Charlie "the Little Tramp" Chaplin, Michael "King of Pop" Jackson, and Eldrick "Tiger" Woods. "Now it's time to open the lines. Grab your phones, minions, and let's talk nicknames."

Clementine cleared the first caller and patched the call through to the control room.

"I can't believe I'm going to admit this in public, but my family calls me Pee-Bug," the first caller said. "I wet the bed until I was, like, seven or eight."

The next caller admitted to being called Scooter, because until age two he refused to walk and scooted around on his butt. "Love your show, Chloe. Too bad you're not on every night."

Pretty soon the phone bank was solid. When Bubba hung up, Punkin Seed, Kater-Tater, and Fitter Cat took his place. Through it all Duncan sat next to me, cueing sound effects and loading news and PSAs. During one of my breaks Duncan admitted his mom called him "Dunkeroo." Every once in a while our knees touched, and tingly sparks fired my leg.

We cruised toward the end of hour one as I took the final caller Clementine cleared.

"Welcome, caller, this is Poppy. At my side is Dunkeroo and Don't-Call-Me-Jester-Clem. What nickname should we call you?"

A slight pause stretched over the airwaves. "Cheese Girl."

My heart skipped. Brie? "That's . . . uh . . . different. How did you get a name like that?"

"A former friend who thought she was funny but wasn't started calling me that in seventh grade." Definitely Brie.

Don't panic. This was my universe. Here I ruled, I was the queen, and I had the Great Silencer. If Brie Sonderby said anything stupid or inappropriate, Duncan had seven seconds to kill the comment before it got on air.

"At first I thought the nickname was kind of cute," Brie went on. "But now I find it incredibly annoying."

I licked my lips. "You make a good point," I said. "People outgrow nicknames, just like they outgrow many things in life, such as shoes or a great pair of jeans."

"And friends."

Dead air crept onto the air waves. Was Brie about to hammer me?

Duncan placed his hand on my knee and squeezed. That touch snapped me away from the drama growing in my head. "Another good point," I added. "People change and grow, and as they do, their interests and the people they hang out with are likely to change, too."

"Yes." Brie hung up.

I breathed. It must have been loud, because Clem gave me an odd look. "Uh, that's a wrap for hour one, minions. Next up, we'll address the million-dollar question. Literally. Exactly what would you do for a million dollars? It's an hour you won't want to miss. Thanks for tuning in to one station, one queen, one Chloe. KDRS 88.8 The Edge."

Duncan cued my theme music and on the On Air sign darkened.

"That was that Brie chick, wasn't it?" Clementine asked over the speaker.

"Yes."

"She didn't sound too cutting."

"No." Which made no sense, because these days Brie was a shark with razor-sharp teeth.

By the end of my third week on the air, I was a Radio Rock Star.

The school newspaper ran an article on my show with the rock star headline, and the local daily picked up the story and ran a front-page feature on the plight of the beleaguered and under-funded student-run radio station. That got Clementine's dragon nostrils flaring, but in a good way. After all, publicity on a grand scale was what my live call-in show was all about. More publicity meant more listeners. More listeners meant underwriter dollars. Clementine and I had been delivering the sales kits I'd made, and after almost fifty sales calls to local business and community groups, we had five maybes.

"If the money comes through, we have enough to cover basic expenses for the rest of the semester and to pay for the mobile storage units admin is so keen on getting rid of to save money," Clementine admitted at Monday's after-school staff meeting. "But we still don't have enough for next year."

Haley took the apple-caramel pop out of her mouth. "Chloe could always do another live show."

"Ha-ha," Clementine said.

"What's wrong with another live show?" Frick asked. "We have that hole on Monday afternoon we're trying to fill."

"I think the universe has enough Chloe," Clementine said.

"Do we?" Duncan asked. He stood near Haley's desk, attaching a pair of shelves to the wall. The shelves were bench seats from a broken lunch table, and while they couldn't hold butts anymore, they would work well for Haley's DVD collection, which was expanding as fast as her stomach. Duncan, screwdriver in hand, looked over his shoulder at me with a half smile.

My heartbeat sped up.

"Of course we have enough Chloe." Clementine snorted.

"The b-b-blog commenters think otherwise," Frack said.

Clementine squirmed. Grams had helped me set up a blog, and for the past two weeks, visitors had been stopping by to discuss my talk show topics. One commenter suggested I expand my show, and at last count, more than 150 people had weighed in, all asking for more Chloe.

Taysom twined his earbuds around his finger. "Seriously, Clem, everyone loves her. Another Chloe show couldn't hurt."

It took every ounce of willpower I had to keep my mouth shut. How I wanted to chime in and say, *Yes! The world needs more Chloe,* but I was having too much fun watching the other staffers do it for me.

"She could do a sports talk show," Frick suggested.

"Or something on p-p-politics," Frack added.

"No, that's not Chloe," Haley said.

Everyone knew me because I wore my heart on my sleeve. They knew when I was sad, determined, and deliriously happy.

"Why not a love-and-relationship-type show?" Haley said.

Every staffer grew still except for Clementine, whose nose ring twitched.

"Seriously, she gets the whole people thing," Duncan said.

"I could see Chloe doing a show where people can call in and share their love stories and broken-heart woes," Haley added.

Frick nodded. "With Valentine's Day a few weeks off, the timing is perfect."

Clementine shook her crinkly black hair. "A love-relationship show is way too dangerous. Too many VSPs could get too agitated and say too many stupid things."

"Or n-n-not," Frack said.

I could see the gears in everyone's minds turning. Another live show would mean more listeners; more listeners would mean we'd be that much more attractive to underwriters with bulging wallets.

"We could have some killer ratings," Taysom said.

We. In three weeks I'd become a part of the station.

"Look at D-D-Dr. Phil," Frack said.

"Chloe is no Dr. Phil," Clementine argued.

"No, but she has a proven track record of handling callers in an effective and sensitive manner," Haley said. All duly noted in my bright blue JISP progress report notebook. My primary goal was still to crank out a shiny JISP that would wow my counselor and not disgrace my brilliant family, but now I had a dedicated group of listeners to hang on to.

"No," Clementine said.

Clementine was a control freak. Was she worried I'd take over *her* radio station? My toes twitched. "It's because you don't like me, isn't it?"

Clementine looked at her knitted fingers. "This isn't personal, Chloe."

"Then what is it?" The entire staff wanted me to take on another show. They were behind me. I was tired of Clementine's attitude, tired of her trying to close me out.

Tiny lines ringed Clementine's mouth. "Honestly, everyone's

right. This type of show could probably help our ratings. But we have a responsibility that has nothing to do with ratings. We may only be a rinky-dink high school radio station, but we have a journalistic responsibility to our listeners. My problem is you're in no position to give advice. You're not a psychologist or a counselor. What you say could hurt someone."

Words hurt, whether whispered in hallways, written in frosty pink lipstick on your locker, or keyed in over pictures on Our-World pages. They knocked you over, pummeled you, and left you with a bleeding heart. Thanks to Brie, I knew all about hurt, and that would make me an even better host. "You're right," I told Clem, "words hurt, so I'll be extra-mindful of what I say and where on-air discussions go. You've heard me handle callers. You know I can do this. "

"But you're not a relationship expert."

"So before taking calls, I'll feature some tips from the experts," I added with a huff. Clementine was being ridiculous. "My mom's a heart surgeon, so she knows plenty of doctor types, and I'm sure my dad has some colleagues at the university who I could interview."

Taysom nodded. Frick and Frack joined in.

Clem's nose ring stilled. The idea of giving more airtime to a "skater" like me killed her. "We would need to talk with Mr. Martinez," Clementine said. "He has to sign off on all programming changes."

"Fine. I'll crank out program notes and get adviser approval," I said. "So if Mr. Martinez agrees, we're on?"

Clem shook her head. "You still have to address the VSP element. Love is a powerful topic. Things could get messy. What if some wounded heart wants to crucify his ex over the airwaves? And it's not just wounded people who do or say stupid things. Lonely people, too. I can see some desperate lonely heart using the show to fish for a date. Then he gets together with someone via the show, and the date turns out to be some psycho."

"Not a problem," Duncan said from where he hung the last of Haley's shelves. "We have the Great Silencer."

Clem threw her hands in the air in surrender. She couldn't win, not when the entire KDRS staff was on my side. The newspaper had labeled me a radio rock star, but I was something more. I may no longer be welcome at lunch table fourteen or at the ficus tree in the quad, but that was okay. I had a wobbly chair and dented whiteboard desk in Portable Five, a place of honor with my KDRS clan.

Beeeeep.

Okay, JISP Girl, Mr. Martinez gave us the green light for *Heartbeats*. He also said to tell you thank you for the chicken enchiladas. I can't believe you freakin' bribed him (*grrrrr*). And I can't believe it freakin' worked (*grrrrr-grrrrr*). Anyway, you're on for next Monday. And . . . (looooong pause) and we got those five underwriters signed up. Admin was impressed. Bottom line. We're on the air until the end of May, but I swear, if you screw up my station with your new program, I will personally throw you and every pair of shoes you own into the Pacific Ocean.

Beeeeep.

End of messages.

CHAPTER 13

AFTER THE FINAL BELL ON THURSDAY, I RAN TO PORTABLE FIVE
and put on a set of glittery gold wings, a perfect match for my
strappy metallic Candies stilettos, circa 1980. All week I'd been
donning my cupid outfit after school and handing out flyers for
Heartbeats, my new love-and-relationship show, which would
debut this Monday.

I reached for my quiver, and my ear-to-ear grin fell off. "What
happened to my flyers?"

Haley reached under her desk, making a *DUNT-da-da-daaaa*
sound. She handed me a crinkly bag. I pulled out a red heart-
shaped sucker. On one side was a sticker that read: *Heartbeats*,
4–6 p.m. Mondays KDRS 88.8.

"Frack's idea," Haley said. "He made five hundred and
forty-four."

"L-l-let me know if you need more," Frack added with a shy
smile.

"And let me know what you think of this," Taysom, who was in the production room, said over the speaker.

Before I could say anything, I heard a faint *thudda-thud*, followed by more *thuds*. The heartbeats gave way to soft music, a lone flute-y sound. A syrupy voice said, *"Heartbeats* with Chloe Camden . . . Mondays from four to six . . . KDRS Radio . . . where love is on the air."

Taysom poked his head out of the production room. "Well?"

I tossed him a sucker. "Sa-weeeeet!" I loved the teaser. I loved Frack's promo suckers. I loved everyone at KDRS 88.8 The Edge.

Clementine walked over and jerked my left wing.

Maybe not everyone. "Hey!"

"You were crooked." Clementine eyed the other wing and whooshed me away with her fingers. "Now go away and don't act too stupid."

"I'm feeling the love, Clem, I'm feeling the love." With the adoration of my dysfunctional but wonderful radio family, I hurried outside to the bus loop, which at this time of day had the highest density of students. All week I'd paid attention to student density and traffic patterns in my effort to improve my promotional efforts. My JISP notebook was full of dandy notes and numbers and graphs and grids. I was pouring my big heart into my new show. A. Lungren should have been purring.

After I handed out my suckers at the bus loop, I hit the bike compound and student parking lot, a winged promo wonder. When traffic let up, I checked my watch. Perfect timing. The track meet would start in five minutes. I could pass out suckers to people in the bleachers, and maybe I could get the announcer to talk up my show.

As I hurried across the quad, my feet slowed for the first time in an hour. I'd reached Our Tree. Brie stood surrounded by clansmen. Over the past few weeks, more and more people gathered about Brie. She led them around with a royal flick of her wrist, and they obeyed. For a moment I wanted to rush off in the other direction.

Then I thought of the KDRS staff. They liked me, believed in me, made me promotional lollipops, and straightened my cupid wings. Brie was talking on her cell and didn't seem to notice me. Out of habit I looked for Merce, listened for her seal-like laugh, but she wasn't there. The other girls noticed me, and a hiss of whispers snaked through the air. I pulled my quiver close to my chest and quickened my step. As I reached the end of the grassy area, my wing jerked, and I heard a soft pop.

"Nice wings."

I turned. Brie held one of my feathers in her hand. She looked Brie beautiful with hair in a golden knot near the top of her head, frosty pink lipstick, green eyes lined and powdered with carefully applied makeup, and her two-carat diamond studs glinting in her ears. She was obviously not wallowing in misery over our snapped BF thread.

"What do you want?" I asked.

She turned the feather over, as if fascinated with it. "To wish you luck with your new show, of course. *Heartbeats*, isn't it? And you're . . ." She waved the feather at me. ". . . Cupid. Hmmmm . . . a show about love. And you know about love, don't you, Chloe? Because everyone loves Chloe." Her words should have been blistering. But they weren't. They were oddly flat.

"Your listeners love you," Brie went on, her voice singsongy but without emotion. "The entire student body loves you. Teachers love you. Your big, *happy* family loves you."

This was getting creepy. "What do you want? I need to go."

"Hmmmmm . . . what do *I* want?" She tapped the feather against her cheek. "I want an end to global warming. I want shoes for every barefoot child in Ethiopia. I want world peace. You hear that, Chloe?" Brie took a step toward me, her serene smile at odds with the feather that she jabbed at my chest like a dagger. "I want peace, and since you're queen, maybe you can arrange it." With a hollow laugh, she crushed the feather in her fist, snapping it in two, and dropped it on my Candies.

The hair at the back of my neck stood upright as I hurried away.

While I drove from school to Minnie's Place early that evening, Brie's words echoed through my head. *I want peace.*

Welcome to my world, Brie.

Ever since winter break, I'd been seeking peace—with my BFs, with A. Lungren, with the KDRS staff, and with Mom and Grams. I got out of my car and headed up the front steps of Minnie's Place. Thankfully, the Tuna Can was still drying out and the peace accord between those with whom I shared DNA was still holding.

Grams had promised to help me brainstorm topics for my

Heartbeats show, and I'd promised her we'd do it over green chili burros at Dos Hermanas.

After signing in, I checked Grams's room. Not there. Nor was she in the media room with the monster HDTV or dining room. I checked the butterfly garden—the one with the swing. No Grams, but I found the swing, or at least what was left of it. Both chains were snapped in two, and jagged splinters of wood that had once been a seat were scattered on the ground.

A blue-haired woman on a bench nearby aimed her three-legged cane at the broken swing. "The new girl broke it. Got swinging too high, and the whole thing came crashing down."

Was Grams the new girl? "Did she get hurt? Did she have to go to the ER?"

"Heavens no. She said she'd have a sore heinie for a day or two, but she thought the whole thing was a hoot. Practically bust a gut, she got to laughing so hard."

Definitely Grams. "Do you know where she is?"

The woman shook her head. "Check with the office. They keep a close eye on everyone coming and going." Good. After high-flying on the swing, Grams clearly needed someone to watch over her.

In the office, a clerk checked the logbook. "Looks like she checked out at three this afternoon. She went to Dos Hermanas with her granddaughter."

I double-checked the entry. "I'm the granddaughter, and she's obviously not with me." I jammed a finger at Grams's uneven handwriting. "Why didn't someone stop her?"

"This isn't a jail, dear."

The clock on the wall read after six. She'd been gone more than three hours. "But she has Parkinson's, and sometimes she gets lost." I remembered the police bringing Grams home the night she spent on the near-freezing beach. She was missing a shoe, the wind had knotted her hair, and her bone-white limbs wouldn't stop shaking. I stabbed a finger at the clerk. "Why aren't you keeping better track of her?"

The clerk closed the book with a polite smile. "At this point, your grandmother is still in charge of keeping track of herself. She can check herself in and out anytime she likes. Our job is to make sure it's documented. Now, I suggest you go to Dos Hermanas and join her."

A sharp tapping beat at my temples as I rushed from Minnie's Place. I'd been so focused on myself, on promo for *Heartbeats*, I wasn't there for Grams.

Just like I wasn't there for Brie and Merce the night of the Mistletoe Ball.

No, I couldn't forget that one, either, could I? I rubbed at the sides of my head.

Once at my car, I called Dos Hermanas, but Grams hadn't stopped by. I checked with Noreen, but she hadn't seen Grams either. I wiped my palms on my thighs. Maybe Grams had a doctor's appointment or lab work. Maybe she went to the movies to see the new Brad Pitt flick but got lost.

Maybe she's bleeding, hurt, dying.

I snagged a deep breath. Maybe I needed to chill on the drama and get a grip. I drove the short route from Minnie's Place to Dos Hermanas and didn't see her along the way. I wound through the side streets. No Grams.

Finally, I called Mom.

"How long has she been gone?" Mom asked.

"She checked herself out at three."

"What! That was three hours ago."

"I know."

"She had her physical therapy appointment today, which always puts her in a bad mood. Your grandmother needed you today."

"I know."

"You were supposed to go out to Dos Hermanas together."

"I know."

"And on Thursdays Dos Hermanas has that green chili burro special she loves so much."

"I know!" The roar tore from my chest. "I screwed up. Care to pound me any harder?"

Mom said nothing, or if she did, I couldn't hear her because someone was pounding on the big bass drum that was my skull. I rubbed at the center of my forehead. Grams was missing, and it was my fault.

"Chloe, now is not the time to argue," Mom finally said. "We need to find your grandmother." She spoke in her doctor voice, the one she used to calm relatives after quadruple bypass surgeries. "Where do you think she could have gone?"

Deep breath in. Deep breath out. "No vehicles have been reported stolen from Minnie's Place, so she can't be far."

Mom puffed out a half laugh, which we both needed. "Okay, Poppy, you know her better than anyone. Think. Where could she be?"

Think. Don't feel. Just think. Head stuff. But it was hard with the steady pounding at my temples. "Tuna Can is the obvious, but Noreen hasn't seen her," I said. "Maybe the boardwalk off Calle del Mar. Maybe the movies."

"Good. You check those places. I'll check her church and dash home to see if she went there looking for you. If we don't find her within an hour, I'm calling the police."

The pounding rhythm in my head now had lyrics. *Find Grams. Find Grams. FINDGRAMS.*

Grams wasn't at the movie theater. She wasn't at the Tuna Can or on the boardwalk. Dark crept in, and the breeze off the ocean blew cool and damp. Had Grams remembered to put on her coat? Was she cold? Shivering? As I continued to drive through the neighborhood, the charcoal sky gave way to black, but I wouldn't stop looking. I knew this neighborhood well. So did Grams. She'd been such a huge part of my early years. She took me everywhere. To the beach. To playdates. To school.

I slowed my car. I pictured the splintered pieces of wood in the butterfly garden and whipped my car in a U-turn. Within three minutes I was at my old elementary school, more specifically at the playground next to it. The big bass drum silenced.

Grams swayed on the tire swing.

My legs were boneless, like Twizzlers left in the sun too long.

When Grams saw me walking toward her, she waved. "There you are, Poppy. I was getting worried about you."

"You were worried about me?" I studied her body for bumps, bruises, and blood. None. Thank gawwwwwd.

"You didn't call," Grams said.

Yeah. Another less-than-brilliant move on my part.

Grams's hand settled on my arm. Did she know she was touching my heart? "It's okay, Poppy. You're here now. Let's go get a green chili burro. I'm starving, and we still need to go over those topics for *Heartbeats*. Valentine's Day is around the corner and I have this great idea for a . . ."

Grams talked, but I didn't hear her. I was too busy hammering myself over the head.

SECOND-CHANCE THRIFT STORE

Because everything deserves a second chance

HOURS:

Monday—Thursday 10 a.m. to 9 p.m.

Friday—Sunday 10 a.m. to 6 p.m.

CLOSED

CHAPTER 14

IT WAS AFTER NINE BY THE TIME I GOT TO THE THRIFT STORE,
and I found Duncan walking his bike out the back door. His new
secondhand bike had duct tape on the seat and mismatched
pedals. Tonight his broad shoulders were uncharacteristically
slumped. I thought about not asking for his help, but I pictured
that broken swing. The big bass drum in my head started booming again. Guilt made way too much noise. I pulled up next to him
and lowered the passenger-side window. "Hey."

His gray eyes brightened as he straddled his bike and placed
his palms on the roof of my car. Tonight he smelled of an ocean
breeze and just enough sweat to remind me he was a guy who
knew how to work. "Hey."

"Going to play Trash Man?" I asked.

That incredible half smile curved his lips. When I was with
Duncan, the entire universe was in order. "Someone's gotta keep
the evil garbage of this world in its place. So what's up?"

Even though he looked exhausted, I reached across my car and opened the passenger door. "I need a hammer."

When we reached the Tuna Can, I pointed to the porch. "There it is. Do you think it will fit in the trunk?"

Duncan grabbed his toolbox from the backseat. "We'll make it fit."

As Duncan's broad back bent over Grams's porch swing, the pounding in my head disappeared. A part of Grams's world was broken, and Duncan would fix it. More than a month ago, he posted the flyer to get promo help to fix the station, and last week he'd been the one to convince Clementine that with the seven-second delay, VSPs wouldn't be a problem for *Heartbeats*. He fixed clocks and toasters and me.

He must have sensed me smiling at him. He looked up. Nice eyes. Nice face. I took in a wonderful cool breath of ocean air. Duncan was a genuinely nice guy.

After we got to Minnie's Place and I explained to Grams and the manager on duty what I wanted to do, Grams whooped, wrapped Duncan in a wobbly hug, then motioned to his toolbox, "You don't have Brad Pitt in there, do you?" Duncan looked at me with half-terrified eyes but smiled. At least he knew where I got my dramatic flair.

Duncan was quieter than normal as we took the swing parts to the butterfly garden and started assembly. Maybe because my mom, who'd learned about the broken swing when I called her and told her I'd be late, had arrived and wouldn't shut up.

"Make sure the arms are securely attached to the chains," Mom warned Duncan. "We don't want her to fall again. Doesn't the back look like it's leaning too far? Are you sure the chains will hold? Have you had any experience in putting a swing together?"

I wanted to boot my mom from the butterfly garden. World War III was brewing again, and Duncan, who needed more fun in his life, didn't need to be in the middle of missile volleys.

Grams folded her arms across her chest. "He's doing fine, Deb. Leave him alone."

"How do you know it will be fine?" Mom asked, her voice rising.

Grams rubbed at her forehead as if the bass drum player had set up shop in her skull.

"How do you know it won't come apart like the other one? You could fall and suffer a concussion or a displaced hip or—"

"Holy hell, Deb, would you just shut up!"

The lines around Mom's eyes narrowed as if she'd been pummeled in the gut. That's how I must have looked when Brie told me to shut up. But Mom didn't offer Twizzlers and search for nice words to make everything peaceful. "I'm keeping you safe."

Grams's hands started to shake, then her arms, chest, and legs. Her whole body was a quivering, angry mass. "I'm not a child."

"Then stop acting like one!"

I dropped the hammer I'd been holding for Duncan. He stopped turning the screwdriver. The night silenced. Only the ocean whispered in the distance.

Grams was the first to recover. She stopped shaking and picked up the hammer and handed it to Duncan with an apologetic smile. With weary but wise eyes, she turned to my mom. "If you're worried about the swing, you can try it first, okay?"

That seemed to calm Mom, but I couldn't shake the antsy feeling. It was as if we were all walking through a minefield, not sure who and what would be set off where. As soon as Duncan locked the swing chain in place, he stood and gave Mom and Grams a nod, then gathered his tools.

"Sorry about them," I said as I followed him through the garden to the exit. He probably thought I descended from a family of wack jobs, and he probably wanted to get as far away from the whole gang as possible. "They're both normally pretty sane, but it's been a . . . um . . . difficult past few months." We walked in silence but for the clank of the tools in Duncan's toolbox. When we reached my car, I tried to stick my keys in the trunk lock, but my hands were shaking. The keys clattered to the ground. I ignored them, instead closing my eyes and dropping my chin to my chest. The war was clearly not over, and a girl who wore her heart on her sleeve couldn't deny it or the sadness that came with the prospect of more battles. "Grams's Parkinson's is progressing, and Mom . . . she doesn't quite know how to handle it. They fight, and more often than not, I have to dive into the middle of it with a white flag." I opened my eyes and stared directly at Duncan. "And for the record, Dunc, there's nothing fun about any of it." I tried to smile, but my lips refused to curve.

Duncan shifted his toolbox to his other hand, bent over, and picked up my keys. After opening the trunk and storing his tools, he uncurled my fist and placed the keys on my palm. "People worry about people they love." His fingers tapped the keys. "They love each other, and love"—the line creased his forehead—"it's pretty messy sometimes."

My fingers curled over his, and relief flooded my chest. Duncan understood. He didn't think my family was wacked, although that shouldn't have come as a surprise. He got along with all the wacked radio staffers.

As we got into my car, I pulled out my cell phone and called up my photo gallery, the one I hadn't looked at since August, when my youngest brother, Zach, left for med school. Looking at the smiling faces of my family reminded me of everyone leaving me. Duncan clicked his seat belt. I wasn't entirely alone.

"Meet the whole crazy gang." I handed him my phone.

He let out a low whistle. "Five brothers?"

"Yep. All in med school or doing residencies now. Absolutely brilliant." I clicked my heels. "But they have lousy taste in shoes."

Duncan smiled, and a warm sizzle raced through my 1970s pink espadrilles with hemp trim. He took his time scrolling through the photos, laughing out loud at a picture of my brother Jeremy playing a piano while I stood on a coffee table singing into an eggbeater I was pretending was a microphone. "Your brothers adore you."

"I don't think they're too bad, either."

Duncan continued to flip through the photos.

"What about you?" I asked. "Any brothers or sisters?"

He shook his head.

"Just you and your mom?"

His smile faded. "Usually."

"She's gone?"

"She was. She's back now."

I was surprised he answered. Duncan rarely spoke about his personal life, but something was clearly happening between us. I reached for his hand, and he didn't pull away. "Where was she?"

"Staying with a *friend*." His lips curled as they did when he talked about the *friend* he visited at the Happy Trails Trailer Park.

"I take it you don't like this *friend*?"

"There's nothing to like about Stu."

Stu was the name Duncan's neighbor Hetta had spit out. "A loser?" I asked.

"Loser. User. Abuser. Take your pick. Unfortunately, those are the guys my mom's drawn to. Stu got out of jail a few months ago, and my mom went to live with him in that hellhole of a trailer park." He handed me my cell phone. "Not all of us have picture-perfect families."

"Um, Dunc, did you or did you not just witness Grams and my mom almost come to blows?"

"That's nothing." He rolled his head along his tensed shoulders, as if trying to shrug off the thoughts in his head. At last one shoulder slumped, then the other. "Hey, I need to get back to the thrift store and my bike." His volume had softened, but his words still had a sharp edge. "I have garbage to haul."

I remembered the first time I noticed those shoulders,

thinking they could carry the weight of the world. Tonight they slumped because of a mother who made bad choices and her jailbird boyfriend who made even worse. Dunc looked like he'd been slammed by a convoy of garbage trucks. I didn't have a toolbox to fix Duncan's family, but I knew how to lighten the load.

"Simple rules," I said. "Five paper balls. Five lines at various distances. Five shots. The closest line is worth one point; the farthest line is worth five. Player with the most points after the final shot wins, so strategy is key. Got it?"

Duncan ran his hand along the front of his face, trying to hide a smile. "I'll *get* it all right if the property manager comes in and finds me playing games."

"So we'll invite her to play." Because everyone needs fun, especially Duncan. Especially tonight. On the drive from Minnie's Place, he said nothing more about his mom and Stu. He shut up, shut down, and closed me out. Dunc shook his head. "No games for me. I can't afford to lose this job."

Because most likely his mom couldn't keep one. I hadn't met her, but I was having a serious case of dislike. "When's the last time the property manager checked in on you?"

He scratched absently at the side of his neck before putting on a sheepish smile. "Never."

"And what are the chances she'll show tonight?"

"About zero."

I crushed a final piece of paper into a ball and tossed it at

Dunc, who caught it. "So the only one holding you back from a little fun," I said, "is you."

He balanced the trash ball on the palm of his hand and shook his head. "Does anyone ever say no to you?"

With five older brothers and a doting grandmother, the truth was, not often.

Sometimes you're so self-centered I can't stand it. Brie's biting words ricocheted through my head, and I winced. The thread may have snapped, but that didn't change the fact that best friends knew you at a soul-deep level. They knew what made you tick and why. Tonight I'd set up trash ball for Duncan, to make him laugh and forget about his mom and a loser named Stu. But that wasn't the only reason.

Okay, Brie. I'm not a liar. I'll admit I also set up trash ball for me.

I liked how Duncan looked at me. I liked how strange and varied body parts sparked when they brushed against him. Was I selfish? Did I expect the universe to revolve around me?

I'd been so focused on *Heartbeats*, I forgot my own grandmother. And I'd abandoned Brie the night of the Mistletoe Ball. *Wham-wham.*

"Hey." With a crooked grin, Duncan wagged the paper ball in my face. "Looks like we both need some fun tonight."

The grin, the barest tug on a mouth that rarely smiled, pulled me in and pushed everything else away. The universe consisted of only us and ten crinkly trash balls. "Before we start," I said as I grabbed a wad of paper, "let's talk about what we're playing for."

"This isn't about bragging rights, like in the paper airplane contest?"

"Nope. Time to raise the stakes." I stroked my chin, loving the way Duncan's gray eyes lightened to shimmery silver. "You start. If you win . . ."

Duncan looked puzzled until a slow smile spread across his lips. "If I win, you'll help me with the econ essay that's due next week."

Econ was cake for me, and if I recall, our next essay was on the fantabulous topic of supply-side economics. "You're on." I tilted my head to the side. "And if I win . . ." *You'll look at me in a way that makes me forget about mean, lying best friends and broken swings.* "You'll handle the boards for my new *Heartbeats* show."

"I'd do that anyway." His soft gaze melted me. I wanted to ooze to the ground in a warm, bubbly puddle at his feet. Nope, no oozing puddles allowed. It would ruin my espadrilles and this wonderful moment with the most wonderful Duncan Moore.

"Okay, if I win"—I flexed the fingers of my shooting hand and thought of tingling thumbs and ankles—"you'll come to the Tardeada this Saturday with me." I stood at the two-point line and took a shot. Score.

He walked to the five-point line but didn't shoot. "Like a date?"

"Yes. You, me, and some activity that involves copious amounts of fun." But the look on Duncan's faced mirrored nothing close to fun. "Hey, it's not like I'm asking you to stick your finger in a toaster."

He shot from the five-point line. Miss. Red crawled up Duncan's cheeks. "No . . . it's . . ."

I took my second shot and scored another two points. "The Tardeada's a blast." I tried to keep my voice casual. It was a huge party on the beach with Hispanic crafts, music, and vendors. I'd be there, dressed in my burrito costume for Dos Hermanas, who had a food booth.

Duncan took his second shot, another five-pointer. Another miss. He squeezed the bridge of his nose as if he had a headache. "I'm working at the thrift store on Saturday."

"Not at night." I tried not to rush my words, but nervousness chased them off my tongue. "You can get to the beach by seven, which is when I'll be done working for Dos Hermanas. We can check out the bonfires." I shot my third ball, a rim shot that bounced to the floor. "So, how 'bout it? You, me, and roasted corn on a stick."

He took another five-point shot. Miss. His eyes didn't meet mine. "I'm sorry, Chloe, I can't."

I picked up my fourth ball. *Squeeze. Crackle. Crumple.* For weeks Duncan and I had sparking thumb and ankle encounters. We worked together and laughed together. Tonight he helped me repair a tiny corner of Grams's world and helped me relieve some of my guilt for totally forgetting about my dinner date with Grams. Didn't I mean anything to him? Or was it something else?

"Do you have a girlfriend?" *One who knits her heart into your scraggly scarves?* I shot. Another miss.

His head shook. "Definitely not."

I shifted from one foot to the other. I didn't understand why Duncan wasn't in the arms of some girl. He was sweet and nice and had incredible stormy eyes that glinted with silver when he smiled. "Do you have other plans Saturday night?"

He flinched before his gaze flicked to the ground. "I don't have time."

"You could make time." Just like we were making *fun*. A person made time for people and things they cared about.

His knuckles grew white as his fingers wrapped tighter around a trash ball. "Forget it," I said around the lump in my throat. Duncan didn't need any more angst in his life coming from my corner of the universe. I asked him out. He shot me down. I had to move on. It's not the end of the world. I'd lost my brothers. I'd lost my best friends. Hey, what was another—

"Chloe." Duncan's fingers caught me under the chin. My chin—my stupid, traitorous chin—tingled at the brush of his touch. Surely he felt it. Surely this thing wasn't that one-sided. "I . . . I . . ."

I waited. It was so hard not to scream, *I want to be with you, walking on the beach or sharing eggs and cheese on toast.*

"You. You're nice . . . and funny . . . and . . ."

This would be the part in the soap opera where Mr. Hunka-Hunka bends over his ladylove, pulls her to his chest, and whispers, *And I need you more than air.*

"And . . ." My voice sounded squeaky, like the wheel on the trash cart.

He opened his mouth, then closed it, like he was in pain.

Without looking at me, he tossed the trash ball from the farthest line. The ball clanked the rim, then fell in, and he muttered something that sounded like, "God, I suck at this."

He walked away, the trash cart wheels shrieking.

I took my final shot. Miss.

Final score. Five to four. Duncan won.

Tierra del Rey
Tardeada

SATURDAY, 10 A.M. TO 10 P.M.
¡MÚSICA Y BAILE PARA TODOS!

- Ballet Folklórico
- Mariachi Corazón
- Del Rey High Latin Show Dance Team
- Zumba with Anita y Amigos
- Children's Booths with Make-and-Take Crafts
- Face Painting & Balloon Animals
- Authentic Mexican Food
- Beach Bonfires

CHAPTER 15

JOSIE CRANKED THE ROASTING TUMBLER AND SNIFFED THE AIR.

"Rojita, get bags, *pronto!*"

I set ten brown paper bags on the prep table. Josie turned off the propane tank and plopped a scoop of charred, stiff chilies into each bag. I quickly folded the top, creating a tight seal. The bags puffed, dampened, and darkened as they filled with steam.

Ana waved a bag and called out, "Buck a bag! Fresh roasted chilies! Buck a bag."

All afternoon Ana and Josie manned a booth at the Tardeada, selling fresh roasted chilies for a smokin' hot deal of a buck a bag. They also sold six different kinds of burritos with all the toppings. The chilies, Josie said, were their secret promo weapon. "People smell the chilies," she explained. "They come and buy. Then they see burritos and buy them, too."

People at the Tardeada bought plenty. We'd sold hundreds of

burritos and bags of chilies. Now it was after seven, and we were closing the booth.

With the last tumbler of chilies roasted, I slipped out of my burrito shell and started to clean the salsa bar. Josie opened a paper bag of roasted chilies she'd set aside earlier and poured the still charred but now limp mass onto a cutting board.

"You too quiet." Josie scraped the blackened, papery skins from the chilies. "Why you no talk? You always talk."

I snapped lids on the guacamole, green salsa, pico de gallo, habanero salsa, onions, jalapeños, sour cream, and cilantro sprigs. "I've been thinking."

"About?" With a sharp knife, Josie slit a chili down the middle and slid the blade along the flesh, scraping away the membrane and seeds. Using the knife in a rocking motion, she chopped the veggie into small pieces.

"Chilies." I stacked the toppings and put them in the insulated cooler. All the while, an ache throbbed in the center of my chest, keeping time with the crashing waves on the beach below. For the last few weeks I'd been roasted like a chili thanks to Brie, and a few days ago I'd been sliced and diced by Duncan, who didn't want to come to the Tardeada with me and who'd been avoiding me since trash ball. "Things haven't been too good lately in my universe." I pointed to the cutting board. "I've been tumbled and roasted, then steamed and scraped and chopped."

Ana squeezed my shoulder. "That good, *Rojita*."

"Good?" Did Ana need more English lessons?

"*Sí*, good." Josie picked up a raw green chili. It was long and lime green, smooth and shiny. "This chili okay. Good for pico de gallo. But"—she pointed her knife at the soft, smoky, roasted chilies—"better with fire. Better for salsas, pollo deshebrado, calabacitas, todos. Fire is—how you say—flavor."

"I could do with a little less flavor," I said under my breath as I packed the rest of the salsa bar and checked my watch. Flavor or no flavor, I had two live shows now to deal with, and I needed to get home and review my research material for *Heartbeats*, check in on the blog, and call Clementine to see if she had reviewed my format clock for the second hour of my *Chloe, Queen of the Universe* show.

I pictured my shows. My growing fans. Me reaching out to them. Them reaching out to me. Connecting across invisible air-waves. Life wasn't all burned chilies. I did have something good in my life. KDRS was good.

Holding on to that bit of good, I said good-bye to the sisters and headed toward the parking lot. Bonfires glowed on the beach as noisy groups of people strolled the brightly lit walk. Couples holding hands. Young families wheeling strollers. Clans from schools talking and laughing.

Slipping off my plain black Vans, I left the crowded beach walk and slinked into the cold, dry sand above the path. Here sand dunes rolled and sea grass whispered in the night, masking the laughter of the clans at the bonfires below.

My fingers flitted over the tops of the grass blades, and I real-ized Brie, Merce, and I hadn't done much laughing the past few months, and the sadness had sunk in well before the Mistletoe

Ball. If I had to pinpoint a date, I'd say it all started on the beach at our end-of-summer sleepover. Every August Brie, Merce, and I dragged loungers and a cooler full of snacks to the private beach behind Brie's house. We'd light a beach fire and talk until the sun rose. We'd talk about crushes and classes and clans. We'd talk about our dreams and deepest fears. Every year we'd start the summer sleepover an hour earlier, but our talk and laughter always outlasted the night. Until this year.

This past August we fell asleep before midnight. I figured it was because Merce was still struggling with her mom's death and Brie had come back from a hellacious summer cruise with her warring parents. I hadn't said anything to Brie and Merce about the lack of laughter that night or the lack of whispers and wonderings. A part of me didn't want to recognize it, to name it, because then it would be real. I think that night on the beach was the night the threads started to unravel.

I strolled through the dunes, watching the smiling, laughing, cuddling, singing, chatting people at the bonfires, all silhouettes outlined by flames. Here in the light of the fire, lines separating clansmen blurred.

As I headed past the next bonfire, an achingly familiar seal-like sound barked on the air, and my body stiffened. Because where there was Mercedes, there was Brie. The last time I'd seen Brie, she'd plucked a feather from my cupid wing and crushed it with a hollow laugh that raised the hair along my arms.

I turned, catching sight of Merce. She stood shoulder to shoulder not with Brie but with a pair of girls from the brainiac clan. She talked and waved her arms. The girls tossed their hair and laughed. When their laughter died, Merce started talking again. It was strange, seeing Merce so animated.

Seconds later Merce raised her head and looked across the fire. Our eyes met, and her face grew serious. We stared at each other for the longest time, separated by flames and two different worlds. Should I close the distance and ask her about her new world and tell her about mine? Should I ask why she wasn't with Brie? One of the girls tugged her arm. Without another look at me, Merce said something to her friends, eliciting peals of laughter.

Again, the world went all topsy-turvy. Merce wasn't the jokester. She was the smart one.

The night grew blacker and cooler as I passed the final bonfire, my arms wrapped around my waist. Here the crash of waves and rush of wind pounded the night. As I crested a dune, I saw two figures sitting on a piece of driftwood and staring at the ocean. The moonlight silhouetted their bodies. The boy's hand rested on the girl's back and his broad shoulders tilted toward her, two people so close, they looked like one. At one point the boy cradled the girl's hands and brought them to his lips.

My feet stilled. I didn't want to go any closer. I didn't want to be reminded of what I didn't have with Duncan.

A gust of wind off the ocean rushed the beach. The girl shivered, and the boy reached for something around his neck. A scarf.

My toes dug into the frigid sand.

But it was early February, chilly, especially here on the beach. Lots of people wore scarves. Anyway, it couldn't be Duncan. He said he definitely didn't have a girlfriend. But those shoulders were broad and strong, the hair dark and wonderfully wind-blown, and scraggly bits of yarn dangled from that scarf.

The chill in my feet climbed my legs.

Another gust of wind kicked up sand. The boy shielded the girl with his body, and when the worst was over, he stood, pulling her with him.

My knees refused to work as the couple walked up the beach, his arm around her shoulder, bodies so close you couldn't tell where hers ended and his began. When he raised his face, there was no mistaking those silvery eyes.

Duncan froze mid-step when he spotted me. The girl leaned into him, her cheeks flushed. Was it from the cold or from the excitement of being in Duncan's arms, a place I longed to be? The muscles along my neck tightened, refusing to let loose the words racing up my throat. Another gust of wind peppered us with sand. The girl shivered, and Duncan drew her into the wall of his chest.

Okay, Dunc, why don't you turn up the chili roaster another notch or two? What's a few more blisters and some scorched skin?

Still Duncan said nothing. Tears blurred my vision, and I told myself it was the gritty sand. So Duncan and I had played Garbage Games and ate eggs and cheese on toast. So what? We were noth-ing to each other. At least I was nothing to him. I was too loud, too self-centered, too controlling. And he was too nice to point that out.

"Gotta go. You know. Stuff." I needed to put an ocean of space between me and Duncan and that quiet waif of a girl he couldn't keep his hands and lips off of. I rushed past them.

"Wait!"

Dunc had said the same thing on the day admin announced they were shutting down the station because of my survey. Back then I'd wanted to run from Portable Five, to get far away from the radio staffers, who had every reason to hate me. But Duncan's next words, *We need her*, kept me at the station, at his side. I needed to be needed now.

My feet stilled in the ice-cold sand. I crammed my fists against my watery eyes. Damn! Why did I have to be so needy?

Duncan bent and whispered something against the girl's hair. She looked like a beach mouse, frightened and small and jittery. Duncan rested his hand on her shoulder and gave a soft squeeze. She rubbed her cheek against that hand and left, making her way through the dunes to the parking lot.

Duncan stuffed his hands in his pockets and stared at the ocean. A full minute ticked by, my booming heart counting the seconds.

"Okay, let me start," I said around the hard, scratchy lump gathering in my throat. "Who is she?"

Duncan rolled his head along his shoulders. "It's complicated."

"Seems to be a common theme with you." Another whip of wind stung me, and I hugged my shoes to my chest.

A low growl thrummed in his throat. "She's not my girlfriend." He jammed his hands through his wind tossed hair. "She's not even a friend. She needs me."

"Hmmmmm. She *needs* you. Care to elaborate?"

He raised his face to the moon and stars as if seeking their help. "I can't."

"You can't or you won't. There's a big difference, Dunc." I threw my shoes to the ground. Time to bare my heart. "I like you, Duncan, *really* like you, and at times I think you feel the same way, but you won't let me get close. You won't let anyone get close, and it's probably because of all your family . . . stuff. But that's okay. I can deal with crazy family stuff, and we can ease into a relationship. What I can't deal with is the silence. I need to know how you feel about me. I need to know what you want from me. I need you to talk to me." Wind and sand swirled, stinging my hands and face.

I wanted to say more. I wanted to fill the silence with words that made sense and lessened the ache in the middle of my chest. Because words, whether given on a late-night radio show or whispered between BFs at end-of-summer sleepovers, soothed. But the next words needed to be Duncan's.

A seagull squawked, and somewhere on the black sea a buoy clanked.

Dunc knifed his fingers through his hair and ran them down the length of his corded neck. Seconds ticked by, then eons, and Duncan remained silent.

And there it was. My answer.

I grabbed my shoes—black Vans the color of chilies left too long in the roasting tumbler—from the sand, spun, and ran to my car before Duncan could see the tears rushing down my cheeks.

• • •

On Monday after school Clementine sat across from me in the production studio holding her thumb and fingers in the letter *C*. Thirty seconds to the debut of *Heartbeats*, my new call-in show, which focused on love and relationships.

Meet my new BF, Irony.

Here I was, a total fail at the vast majority of relationships in my life, hosting a show about relationships. Were the airwaves ready for this? Was I?

"On the beam." Clementine's voice came through my headphones.

I flicked on my mic. I was going solo in the control room this afternoon. Duncan, even though he'd promised to work the boards, had failed to show. While I didn't expect him to contact me, not after our one-sided heart-to-heart on the beach Saturday night, he should have warned Clementine, who now had to juggle assignments so she could engineer my program. Clem raised her right hand, then one by one lowered her fingers. Five, four, three, two, one . . . She cued my theme music.

Thudda-thud. Thudda-thud. Heartbeats pulsed over the airwaves and gave way to a flute that spoke of love and longing. I closed my eyes. Deep breath in. Deep breath out.

The control room door clicked. My eyes flew open. Duncan, winded and red faced, unwound his scarf and tossed it in the corner. He took the seat next to me and started adjusting dials and knobs. He said nothing, didn't even try to meet my gaze.

Across the glass Clementine mouthed, *Dead air!*

I gave my head a shake and grabbed the mic as if it were a life preserver. "Greetings, listeners and lovers. This is Chloe Camden, and I'd like to welcome you to *Heartbeats*, where love is on the air. You heard right, friends, this is your queen, but you can call me the Queen of Hearts, because this afternoon we'll talk about . . ." I pointed at Duncan, who cued the first stinger, a slurpy kissing sound. We both looked straight ahead. ". . . love and relationships."

For the first ten minutes I talked about the physical responses to love and attraction, things like why your heart rate increased and pulse pounded, why your hands grew sweaty or you forgot to eat. All the while Duncan dropped in bites from interviews with my heart surgeon mother and a psychologist specializing in relationships. We worked side by side, close, but not touching, which was fine. My heart was safer this way.

Within fifteen minutes, the phone bank was full. Clementine prepped our first caller and wrote a name on a sheet of paper and flashed it at me.

I did a double take, at first thinking Clementine had written *Brie*. A few weeks ago, Brie was everywhere, spewing lies, circling me like a shark, and wreaking havoc in my life, but I hadn't seen her since the day she plucked a feather from my cupid wing. She wasn't at the Tardeada with Merce, and I hadn't seen her at school the past few days. I wasn't sure if I should be concerned or relieved.

Years ago when I was swimming in the ocean with Grams, I refused to paddle in the deep water. "I'm afraid of what's under there," I'd said as I clung to Grams and pointed to the black, bottomless section of the ocean, where I was sure hundred-foot sharks and mutant sixteen-armed octopuses roamed.

As Grams treaded water, she tapped my forehead. "What's in here, Poppy, is scarier than anything you'll encounter in the depths of the ocean. An imagination is a powerful thing."

I refused to imagine the damage Brie with her twisted mind could do if she called in. Thankfully, the name Clementine displayed wasn't Brie's.

"Our first caller is Brad. Welcome, caller, this is Chloe. What's on your heart today?"

"Man, you described me to a tee," Brad said. "Fast heart rate, sweaty palms, shortness of breath. Hard time concentrating on anything but her. I failed an econ test today." He groaned.

I couldn't help but shoot a look at Duncan, who looked pained at the mention of econ. Or maybe it was because he was pained to be sitting within twelve inches of me.

I cleared my throat. "Sounds like you have a pretty bad case of the love bug, Brad. Tell us about your lucky girl."

"She's not exactly mine. I haven't told her how I feel about her yet."

"Not a word?"

A nervous chuckle sounded on the other end. "Not to her face."

"More info."

"I've . . . uh . . . written her poems."

I crinkled a piece of paper in front of the mic. "Ooo . . . we have a love scribe. Tell our listeners, what did the recipient of your love poems think of them?"

"I haven't sent them to her."

"Brad, Brad, Brad." I banged my forehead against the mic. "What are you thinking? Seriously, listen to me. You sound like a nice guy. You need to give her one of your poems. We girls love pretty words that make our hearts go pitter-patter."

Silence.

"Brad . . . ," I said. "This is a talk show. You need to talk."

Next to me Duncan let out one of his rare laughs.

Brad. I needed to focus on Brad. "Brad, you still there?" I asked. "Why haven't you given your ladylove one of your poems?"

"She might turn me down."

"And she might not. She might adore your poems and you."

"You think so?"

"I have no idea, but I do know absolutely nothing will happen if you don't try. You'll be in the dark until you jump into the fire."

"That's the problem, Chloe. I might get burned."

"Brad, my friend, let's talk about green chilies." I shared with Brad and my audience Josie's take on fire adding flavor. Out of the corner of my eye, I noticed Duncan nodding slowly. "So you have a choice, Brad, you can stand outside the fire or jump in for a little spice. It's up to you, but be sure to call in next Monday and let us know."

"Okay. I will," Brad said. "I'll do both. I'll give her a poem and call next week."

As Brad hung up, everyone in the newsroom gave me a

thumbs-up. A most wonderful first call. Before I could bask in the success, Clementine patched in caller number two, Vanessa, who had a different take on the love bug.

"When I'm in love, I cry," Vanessa said. "I'm like this faucet that can't be turned off. Of course, they're happy tears. Oh, and another thing—I start playing sappy love songs. All the time."

This led to twenty minutes of banter on the subject of "Our Songs." As one caller got into a long-winded gush about old Journey songs, I thought about Duncan. If we had a song, which we didn't and never would, it would be the squeaking trash cart's wheels.

At the top of the second hour, I moved on to the next topic: creative ways to show your love. "Everyone knows about balloons and chocolates," I said. "But they're not for everybody. Good ol' Clementine, she'd probably love to receive a handful of beets tied with a bright red ribbon."

Clementine switched on her mic. "Purple ribbon. A better match for the beets."

I blew her a kiss. Clem wrinkled her dragon snout but smiled.

"So, listeners, I'm asking all of you to call in with how you show you love someone."

Ideas zipped across the airwaves.

"One time I filled my boyfriend's locker with balloons."

"I left a trail of chocolate kisses at the beach for my girlfriend to follow."

"I made a mix of her favorite songs and snuck it into her car so when she turned on the CD player, it started to play."

All went smoothly until the final segment when Clementine showed me a piece of paper identifying my next caller. *Brie.*

The single name grew and pulsed.

Hang up? Clementine mouthed.

For the first time, Duncan edged closer to me, his knee nudging mine, but I scooted away. I could handle my callers, including possible VSPs who were once BFs. This might not even be my former friend, and if it was, she couldn't do anything to damage me or KDRS. I had the seven-second delay switch. Anyway, the last time she called, she hadn't pulled anything, so maybe it was safe.

Deep breath in. Deep breath out. "Welcome, caller, this is Chloe. How do you show someone you care?"

"Actually, this is something someone did for me." It sounded like Brie, but not. There was something different about the voice. It had a tinny ring to it. "For Valentine's Day last year, a guy who had a crush on me bought me a white guinea pig with a little pink nose. He named him Cupid and tied a big pink bow around his neck."

My heart took off, but not in a good way. I vaguely remembered the guinea pig. This was *my* Brie. "A guinea pig named Cupid. How cute," I said.

"No, not really. He kept escaping his cage and pooping all over the house and chewing on electrical cords. My mom went ballistic. She doesn't like it when things get messy."

"Bummer." I checked the time. A few more questions and I could go to break. But something about that guinea pig was raising a red flag. "Did you get little Cupid some piggy chew toys?"

"No. He escaped his cage, chewed on the cord to the dryer, and got electrocuted. Saddest thing, the smoke coming from his fried little whiskers."

Clementine looked at me, her mouth open in horror. In the newsroom where my show was broadcasting, the staff stilled. Dead air.

Duncan nudged me.

"Oh." I cleared my throat. "I'm sorry."

"It's okay. I didn't like the guy." Brie let out a laugh that sounded distorted, as if Taysom had twisted it with his sound editor, and hung up.

I ignored the shiver sliding down my spine and leaned into the mic. "Oooookay, listeners, we'll take a break, and when we come back, we'll lighten things up as I share some fun Valentine's Day events going on in Tierra del Rey this month. This is Chloe Camden of KDRS 88.8 The Edge, and you're listening to *Heartbeats*, where love is on the air."

Duncan broke to one of Frack's PSAs.

"That bitch," Clem said when the On Air sign went dark.

"But Chloe handled the whole thing pretty well," Duncan said. "We didn't need to use the seven-second delay."

Clem nodded. "True, but I'm not letting her on the air anymore. She's psycho."

I didn't argue. I didn't know this version of the person who used to be my best friend, and I didn't want to.

The remainder of my *Heartbeats* debut remained wonderfully Brie-free, although occasionally her empty laugh found its way into my head. At those times I quickly pushed it aside. This was my world, not Brie's.

When I signed off the air, Duncan switched the station over to the automated programming that would run for the next twenty-one hours. I took off my headset, wrapped the cord, and put it away. I refused to look at him, even when he said, "Great show."

"Mmmmmm-hmmmmm." I gathered my notes and put them in my bag.

"I, uh, liked how you handled the guy with the poems. You made him feel comfortable and, by the end, confident."

"Mmmmmm-hmmmmm." See, I could do this. I could work with Duncan and not let my bruised heart get in the way. I stood and pushed in my chair.

Next to me Duncan stood. "Are you okay? I mean with that whole Brie thing, she didn't get to you, did she?" He settled his fingers on my arm.

My elbow sparked with a gush of heat. Anger at Duncan and anger at the dancing sparks on my stupid elbow flared. How was I supposed to safeguard my heart if he wouldn't stay away? I yanked my arm from his touch. "Like you care."

The vertical line creased his forehead. "Okay, I deserve that. My life's been pretty messed up lately."

"Well, let's buy matching T-shirts and start a club."

He jammed his hands in his back pockets. "Listen, Chloe—"

"To what? To things you won't or can't say?" Dunc's life was messed up, and I didn't need any more messes, but I took a few deep breaths and waited for him to go on.

He craned his neck as if making space for words. None came. When it came to anything personal, he shut down and shut me out.

Enough. Dead-Guinea-Pig Girl put me over the edge today. "Fine, I'll say the words for you. You don't want to date me. You prefer machines to people. And you suck at self-expression. I accept that." I yanked my bag over my shoulder and left the control room.

He followed. He shouldn't be following me. Duncan may be good at keeping things close to the chest, but I wasn't.

"But that doesn't mean it doesn't hurt," I said. For the past two hours I'd talked about love and relationships, and I'd given out comfort and advice. I'd gone deep into my heart, and maybe a part of me was still there, because I turned to Duncan and for once forgot he was a nice guy who worked too hard and didn't have time for fun. "Now, if I were the kind of girl who hid her emotions, I wouldn't tell you you're so caught up with your *stuff* that you neglect to see other people's *stuff*. I wouldn't tell you that picture-perfect families have heart-shredding problems that can't be fixed with a hammer and duct tape. I wouldn't tell you that silence can hurt worse than mean words. And I wouldn't tell you that you can be a first-class jerk. But I'm not someone to keep things bottled up, am I?"

I bulldozed past him and out the door, but not before I heard Clementine's voice. "Man, Dunc, you freakin' screwed that up."

TODAY AT
MINNIE'S PLACE!

7 a.m. Sit and Fit Exercise Class!

9 a.m. String Art in the Butterfly Garden!

10 a.m. Watercolor Workshop!

1 p.m. Quilting: Advanced Squares!

3 p.m. Pole Dancing!

7 p.m. Bunco with Sue!

CHAPTER 16

WELCOME TO SWEEPS WEEK AT THE SOAPS, WHERE VILLAINOUS vixens are at their most vile. They steal triplet newborns from their half sisters who've been fighting infertility for seventeen years, and they sleep with their best friend's husband, son, *and* therapist.

Last summer during sweeps on *Passion Bay*, wicked Valerie Westcott, disguised as a priest, visited the hospital room of the long-suffering but much-loved Loretta Hooper Chesterfield Hayes, who had brain surgery. Val injected an evil yellow liquid into Loretta's IV, and dear Lottie immediately went into cardiac arrest. Despite the beeping and spastic machines, the two nurses on duty didn't come to her rescue. Val had bound and gagged one nurse and locked the other, along with her doctor lover, in the cleaning closet where they had their nightly trysts.

"Loretta's never going to get herself out of this," I'd told Grams.

"Of course she is, Poppy. Good always conquers evil. Everything will be hunky-dory."

I needed Grams right now. I needed to hear her say that despite all the chaos and conflict, everything would be hunky-dory, because I didn't feel hunky-dory. Brie's twisted laugh about her dead guinea pig still echoed in my head, and the look on Duncan's face when I stormed past him in Portable Five still haunted me. Duncan, who kept his emotions locked away and tied with a scraggly scarf, looked like I'd clouted him with a giant conch shell.

When I got to Minnie's Place, Grams wasn't in her room, the butterfly garden, or in any of the communal areas. I immediately checked the logbook, but she hadn't checked herself out.

"My grandmother's missing." I tried to keep my voice calm as I spoke to the attendant on duty, because everything would be *hunky-dory*.

"Did you check the movie room?" the attendant asked.

"Yes."

"The butterfly garden?"

"Yes."

The woman with blue hair and a three-pronged cane hobbled over. "Did you say you're looking for the new girl again? The one who has the life-size picture of Brad Pitt in her room?"

"Yes. That's Grams. Have you seen her?"

"Try the laundry room. She seems rather attached to dryer number seven. That new girl hangs out in the strangest places."

Grams was not in the laundry room, so the blue-haired woman

took me to the maintenance closet, then to the shed that held a pair of three-wheeled bicycles. Eventually, we found Grams in the food pantry sitting on a supersize can of peaches reading an entertainment magazine with Brad Pitt on the cover.

"See"—the blue-haired woman pointed her cane at Grams—"she's always hiding, like she doesn't like us."

"Nothing personal, Aggie." Grams handed the woman a giant box of Fig Newtons. "Just needed a little private time with Brad."

After the blue-haired woman left, I pulled up a five-gallon bucket of oatmeal and sat next to Grams. For a moment I pushed aside the chaos of my world to figure out why my grandmother was sitting in a pantry on a giant can of peaches. "What are you doing?"

"Checking Brad's marital status." She winked, but I didn't smile.

The ridge of the oatmeal bucket dug into my butt. I shifted, but I couldn't get comfortable. "Grams, why are you reading in the food pantry?"

"Because today is laundry day."

"And . . ."

"And someone is sitting on the bench near dryer seven." She delivered the line with no trace of humor, like she was announcing, *The sky is blue.*

I rubbed at my head where an insistent tapping had started somewhere between Brie talking about dead guinea pigs and Duncan reaching for my elbow. "What does that mean?"

"There aren't many places you can be alone here, and, Poppy, there are times when this old girl needs to be alone."

I didn't miss that irony, either. For the past few months, Grams had been chasing solitude, while I'd been running from it. I massaged my temples.

"But the good news is"—Grams closed the gossip magazine with a gleeful clap—"in less than twenty-four hours, I'm outta here."

"What?"

"Tomorrow I'm headed back to the Tuna Can." Grams tucked the magazine under her arm. "I talked to the restoration boys this morning, and they said the whole place is dried out and painted. New carpet is down. They're airing it out tonight, so tomorrow Brad and I are going home."

And World War III would start again. The tapping at my temples morphed into cannon booms. "Does Mom know?"

Grams hopped up from the peach can. "Don't know. Don't care."

"Well, maybe you should." My words were soft. If we weren't in a food pantry the size of a refrigerator, Grams wouldn't have heard me.

But she did. Her knees creaked as she squatted so we were eye to eye. "This has been hard on you, hasn't it, Poppy?" Grams ran a hand along my rumpled hair. "I hate that you've been put in the middle of this. I hate seeing you hurt."

"So talk with Mom," I said. "You're good with people. Surely you can talk with her and find a living arrangement that is okay with both of you. Because she's not going to give up. You realize that, right? She's not going to stop worrying." I grabbed her hand, pulling her close. "Do something, Grams, for me. If I'm that important, do it for me."

Grams squeezed my hand before she pulled away and stood. "No, Poppy. I can't give in."

I stood so fast, the bucket tipped over, and a hill of papery oats spilled onto the floor. I didn't care. "You wouldn't be giving in, you'd be working things out."

"No, Poppy, I'd be giving in, and once I start giving, they'll start taking more." Grams took two steps, then turned. Another two steps. Turn. Oatmeal whirled around our feet.

"What are you talking about? What are they taking?" Sometimes Grams didn't make sense.

"First they took my car. Now they want my home." Grams paced faster, her steps growing more unsteady. Was it anger, fear, the Parkinson's? "Then they'll take my phone, saying I can't push the buttons. They'll take my magazines and movies, saying I can no longer see them. They'll take my computer, saying I no longer know how to use it. And you know what, Poppy? They'll be right. Because by then they'll have taken my hands, my eyes, and my mind. Pretty soon there will be nothing left of me." Grams stilled, the oatmeal now powder beneath her feet. "So, you see, Chloe. I have to keep holding on to the Tuna Can as long as I can."

I found Mom at home in the backyard sitting on one of the swings of my old play gym. She wore her scrubs—a bad sign. It meant she was too busy or too upset to change into normal clothes at the hospital.

"Do you know that scientific teams throughout the world have studied the act of swinging?" Mom said. "Studies have shown that repetitive self-stimulatory behavior such as rocking or swaying releases endorphins, which reduce the sensation of pain and have the ability to block pain."

I sat on the swing next to her and made a *hmmmmm* sound.

"It's why mothers rock fussy babies," Mom went on, "why couples swaying to music fall deeper into a blissful state, and why junior high girls spend hours on end talking and swinging on old swing sets."

I'd forgotten that. Brie and Merce and I would swing and talk. Talk and swing. But we hadn't since . . . since before summer.

As Mom gave a hefty pull on the swing chains, I kicked off and started to pump. "So what's on your heart?" I asked.

Mom's mouth curved in a weary smile. "On the drive from Minnie's Place, I heard part of your show. You sounded great. I'm so proud of you."

I ignored the compliment and focused on the bombshell. Mom had been to Minnie's Place. This afternoon. "You talked to Grams?"

"She's determined to live in the Tuna Can. Alone. And she can't. She's a danger to herself and others." Mom bit her lower lip. "I started to fill out the paperwork today to have guardianship of Grams transferred to me."

I sucked in a gasp of air. "Mom, she needs to make this choice on where to live on her own. You said I know Grams better than anyone. I do, and if we force her out of the Tuna Can, she'll be miserable for the rest of her life."

"You think I don't know that?"

"She's losing control, and she's scared," I said. I needed to help Mom understand what I saw in the pantry amid oatmeal dust. "She's grabbing whatever she can to keep from being swept away by a disease she can't control, and in this case it's the Tuna Can. We need to give her a little more time."

"We've given her time. It's been more than six months since the doctors first recommended she find new living arrangements. Since then she's crashed her car into an ATM. She spent a near-freezing night wandering the beach. She almost sliced off her thumb doing yard work. And she set fire to her home, then flooded it. What's next, Chloe? Will she seriously hurt herself or someone else?" Mom's voice cracked.

I pictured Grams's Jeep folded around that ATM, her blue-white lips, her bloody hand, her soot-covered face. Old fears and worries danced with new ones.

"Do you think I like taking away her independence?" Mom pumped higher in the swing. "Do you think I want to take control from a woman who raised me? Who cared for my children? Who gave them her time and wisdom and heart?" A tear leaked from the corner of Mom's eye. "It's going to kill me to force her from the Tuna Can. Absolutely kill me."

"Me, too," I said, but I don't think Mom heard because she was swinging too high.

• • •

When I got to school the next morning, A. Lungren slinked down the hall and crooked a kitty claw at me. "In my office, Chloe. Now."

I didn't want to deal with my guidance counselor, not when my head was too busy trying to figure out how to make one final bid for peace between Grams and Mom. I understood Grams's need to hang on to her independence, to control her own life, but I also understood my mom's need to keep Grams and others safe. As I told Mom last night, the key was for Grams to choose to give up the Tuna Can. But where was the freakin' key?

"I don't approve of this *Heartbeats* program, Chloe," A. Lungren said as I took a seat across from her desk. Her sharp kitty nail stabbed my JISP progress report notebook. "It's not the best use of your JISP time. You have a twenty-page report and fifteen-minute oral presentation due in less than two months. You should be analyzing your empirical data, gathering supporting research, and getting ready to pre-write."

I should be getting to econ. I sank deeper into the chair because in econ I'd have to deal with Duncan. The whole I-kind-of-like-you-but-I-can't-be-your-boyfriend-because-I-have-stuff was not okay. His inability to share a piece of his heart with me was not okay. The way he closed me out was not okay.

A. Lungren made her hacking fur-ball noise. "Plus, it's the spring semester of your junior year, and you should be seriously looking into colleges, but you haven't even created your online college prep account yet."

Maybe if I sunk deep enough into the chair, I'd disappear. And college would disappear. And World War III. And dead guinea pigs. And boys with silver eyes and scraggly scarves.

"Chloe, I want you to cancel the *Heartbeats* program."

And evil-kitty school guidance counselors.

I rotated one ankle, then the other, but the glint of light off my shiny 1944 two-tone red-and-black patent-leather pumps didn't cheer me. "I can't cancel *Heartbeats*. It's part of my JISP."

"No, your JISP is about you taking on a clearly defined project, following through, and reporting on it. With this *Heartbeats* program, I think you're taking on too much."

A. Lungren's words were too loud, too wrong. The walls of the office closed in on me. Was this how Grams felt, people telling her what to do when she knew what was best for her?

I settled both pumps firmly on the floor. "I'm perfectly capable of handling a second show."

"I'm sure you are. But it serves no purpose."

"Of course it does. *Heartbeats* will help increase Monday's audience, making us a better value to potential underwriters."

"Your report last week indicated that Clementine already secured eight companies and organizations willing to support the station."

"True, but what's wrong with getting more?"

My counselor folded her arms and leaned toward me, inviting a confidence I didn't want, didn't need. "Chloe, why are you really doing this second show?"

Like Brie, I could lie. I could make up a cockamamie story

about wanting to be a counselor and say the whole *Heartbeats* thing gives me an up-close-and-personal look at people and their problems. However, I wasn't a liar.

Like Duncan, I could be silent. I could walk around with the weight of the world on my shoulders in quiet misery. But I was a gal who wore her heart on her sleeve for the entire world to see.

"Because it's fun."

My counselor studied me. Did she know how much I needed fun? Did she realize how important it was for me to succeed at something because I had failed Brie and Merce? I abandoned them when they needed me. I'd failed to smooth things between Grams and Mom. I'd even failed Duncan, messed-up Duncan, who wanted to talk to me but couldn't figure out how.

Man, I needed a new pair of old shoes.

A. Lungren whisked her kitty paws together. "Okay, I'm going on record that I'm concerned about the widening scope of your project, but I know whatever you take on, you'll give it your all. So let's go ahead and schedule the time for your JISP oral." She scrolled through her calendar and jotted a date and time on a notepad and slid it toward me.

April first. No joke. I'd be giving my JISP oral presentation on April Fool's Day.

After school I went straight to my car. I probably should have gone to the station to give Mr. Martinez my notes for Friday's show, but I had to get to the Tuna Can.

Grams had moved into her trailer this morning, and I'd

promised Mom I'd check on her. I also didn't want to run into Duncan. I needed to be focusing on Grams, making sure she was all right.

When I got to the Tuna Can, Grams was standing in the kitchen microwaving a plate of twice-baked potatoes. On the counter sat bowls with neatly chopped chives and beautifully browned bacon bits. Knives in their place. Stove off.

Like the ceramic squirrel perched on her front porch, Grams grinned from ear to ear. "You know, this old place needed a little sprucing up. I don't think she's ever looked better."

With the new paint and carpet and the furniture cleaned and polished, the Tuna Can looked great, and so did Grams. The fiery twinkle that never sparked at Minnie's Place lit her eyes. Her steps were steady and even, and her hands didn't shake when she took out plates and handed them to me. This did not look like a woman who needed a guardian.

While Grams didn't have any advanced degrees, she wasn't dumb. A smart woman would realize when she needed a little help. Somehow I needed to make Mom realize that. I set the plates on the table and noticed Grams got out three, not two.

As I reached for the cupboard to put away the extra plate, Grams grabbed it. "What are you doing?"

"You got out one too many."

"Oh, no. That's for our guest." She tilted her chin toward the front porch.

For the first time I noticed noise outside, a sharp tapping, like a hammer. "Our *guest*?"

Before she could answer I ran out the front door and found Duncan kneeling on the front porch as he attached one of the armrests to the swing bench and back.

"Hey," he said as if it were the most natural thing in the world to be working on my grandmother's porch next to the grinning squirrel.

But he didn't belong here. We weren't even friends. I'd let him know that clearly after my *Heartbeats* show when I gave him a little piece of my heart and mind. I fingered the pin curl along my cheek. Was it his turn to take a jab at me? Like Brie, would he lob a dead guinea pig my way?

My toe tapped the porch, the sound sharp and metallic. "What are you doing here?"

"Calm down, Chloe," Grams said as she joined us on the porch. "Duncan graciously offered to hang the porch swing when he learned I'd moved back."

"And how did he learn *that*?"

Grams patted my shoulder. "Perhaps you and Duncan should talk about that."

Duncan moved to the other end of the swing and positioned the other armrest and started to hammer. The muscles on his forearm bunched and stretched as he worked.

My toe continued to beat a tattoo on the porch. If I waited for him to talk, we'd be here until Halloween. "So you just happened to be walking by the Tuna Can and offered to help hang a swing?" I asked.

Whack. "No." *Whack.* "I stopped by Minnie's Place this

afternoon, and they told me your grandmother moved out. I figured she'd want her swing."

"And of course you stopped by Minnie's Place to see if they had some toasters that needed to be fixed."

Whack. "No, I stopped by Minnie's Place because Clem told me to."

"Clementine? What does *she* have to do with anything?"

Whack. Whack. Whack. A line of sweat trickled along the dark waves of his rumpled hair. "Clem—hell, the whole radio staff— told me to stop being a first-class jerk."

A nice, non-dragon-like heat settled over me. My radio family was in my corner.

Still avoiding my gaze, Duncan put down the hammer and picked up a screwdriver and a handful of screws. One by one he twisted the screws into place. With the last one in, he tugged and yanked at the joints. "Clem told me I needed to talk to your grandmother." He hoisted the swing on his shoulder. His shirt came untucked, showing a sliver of hard, strained back muscle. "About you. About us." The swing wobbled, dipped, and almost crashed to the floor.

Part of me wanted to stay away, to watch him sweat and strain under this heavy load, but I couldn't. When someone needed help, I was there.

I crossed the porch and steadied the swing. Duncan didn't push me away. "Did you talk to Grams?" I asked.

He hooked one chain to the armrest, the line dividing his forehead. "Yes."

"And?"

His entire face, not just his forehead, folded in a frown. "She told me to get you a pair of size seven red platform shoes with laces and a tassel, preferably in the original 1940s box."

I laughed. I knew Grams, and she knew me. She also must have figured out that Duncan wasn't good at the whole people thing. Or talking thing. "Did you find the shoes?" I asked, keeping my tone flat, almost uninterested.

Duncan went to the other side of the swing and hooked on the other chain, his face serious. "No, but Rhonda, who runs the shoe department at the thrift store, is keeping her eyes open for me." He tugged on the chains and turned to me. "This stuff is hard for me."

When he didn't elaborate, I prompted, "Stuff?"

"You. Me." He shoved the hammer and screwdriver into his toolbox. "This week I got some stuff settled with my mom— good stuff. She's away from Stu and at home, and with that out of the way I've been thinking about you." His cheeks flushed. "A lot." Another long silence settled over us as he rearranged his tools.

Quiet. Must. Keep. Quiet.

He clicked close the toolbox lid, cupped his hands around the back of his neck, and looked at me. "I'm not like other guys. I don't have the luxury of taking girls out on dates. I work all the time, and even then I don't have enough money to take you to a movie or even to a beach fair. Hell, Chloe, I don't have a stupid

TV, so I can't ask you over to watch one of Haley's DVDs. Plus I'm not good with people. With relationships. With words. I have a hard time saying what I mean." His shoulders bunched, then fell. "I guess what I'm trying to say is I'd make a crappy boyfriend."

A little part of my heart softened. Duncan cared. And while I wanted to grin like the ceramic squirrel and throw myself into his arms, I needed to ask the question. "What about the girl on the beach? You seemed to be getting along just fine with her."

"It's a long story."

I crossed my arms over my chest.

He unclenched his hands from his neck and tugged on the swing chains again and again. Mom would be thrilled with his triple safety check. "Okay. I was with her that night because she needed someone, anyone, to hold her and help her deal with some . . . some bad stuff."

"But you won't tell me the whole story?"

A shadow crossed his face. "It's not my story to tell."

I threw my hands in the air. "Aaaaargh!"

A surprised Duncan reached for me, but I sidestepped his hand and positioned myself behind the squirrel.

"What is it? What did I do?" he asked.

"It's what you're not doing. You're not telling me how you *feel*."

"Feel?"

"About *her*?"

He looked at me as if I were a talking squirrel. "I don't have any feelings for her. Well, maybe concerned and kind of obligated." He shucked a hand through his hair. "Nothing like what I feel for you."

I grabbed the porch railing to steady myself. "What did you just say?"

"About what?"

This should not be so difficult. Deep breath in. Deep breath out. "Dunc, do you like me?"

"More than any girl I've ever met." The words were so fast and unfiltered, I knew they came straight from his heart. I also knew Duncan was a guy with baggage.

But he had broad shoulders.

He had serious communication issues.

But he was here at least trying to talk.

Duncan's watch beeped, and I bit back a groan.

He also had two jobs and no time for fun. No time for me.

He jabbed at his watch until it stopped beeping and rolled his head along his shoulders. "I need to go to work," he said, the words dull and heavy.

"I know."

"But I don't want to."

The porch door flew open, and Grams waved us over. "Get inside, Dunc. Got us some hot potatoes. And after you eat, I need you to hang those shelves and move the bookcase. The movers put it in the wrong place. And I need you to check the washing machine. I'm not sure they hooked it up right. I sure as hell don't want another flood."

I almost snorted at Grams's sudden neediness. If I didn't adore her so much, I'd call her a master manipulator.

"I'd have to call the thrift store and tell them I'll be late," Duncan said, fiddling with the strap on his watch.

"I'm sure the toasters won't be too upset," I added with a smile. Duncan was confused and confusing to talk to, but he was still nice, the kind of guy who'd be late for work just to help out my eighty-two-year-old grandmother.

"Get your heinies in gear," Grams said. "We have a lot of work to do."

Relief washed over Duncan's face at the word *work*. He ushered me into the Tuna Can, where we ate twice-baked potatoes and worked side by side, neither of us mentioning stuff or feelings or relationships as we tackled Grams's ever-growing fix-it list. He stayed long past dark until another beep sounded.

We were alphabetizing Grams's DVD collection—seriously, Grams would make the best evil villainess if she ever chose to switch to the dark side—when I pulled my phone from my purse and frowned at the display.

"What's wrong?" Dunc asked.

"I don't recognize the number, but it's flagged *Urgent*." I showed him the display.

Duncan sighed. "I know who it is."

URGENT
Come home. Now!
Hetta

CHAPTER 17

I HEARD THE MUSIC WELL BEFORE DUNCAN AND I PULLED INTO the duplex driveway. Loud and metallic, it cut the night and pulsed from Duncan's house, which was ablaze with light and filled with people.

"She promised," Duncan said on a half whisper. "And I believed her." He glowered at an old Chevy Camaro parked in the driveway next to Hetta's Oldsmobile. "She's partying again. That's Stu's car."

"Stu. That would be Mr. Loser-User-and-Abuser? I thought she left him, that everything was good."

"This morning when I left for school, it was." The words came out in a growl. "But this is how things work with Mom. She makes promises and gets clean. Sometimes she goes for days, sometimes weeks or months, but it never lasts. She always goes back to him. To it."

"It?" I forced myself to ask.

"Meth." The single word came from a dark, ugly place Duncan clearly despised. His wide shoulders trembled.

I settled my hand on his knee. "I'm sorry, Duncan." Sorry he didn't have a cell phone gallery full of happy family pictures. Sorry he didn't have any brothers to teach him to play Garbage Games. Sorry he didn't have a grandma to make him twice-baked potatoes.

He slipped his hand over mine. "Me, too." His jaw tightened as his gaze moved to the house.

"What are you going to do?"

"Depends."

"On?"

"On how far she's cranked." He let go of my hand and reached for the door handle. "Why don't you stay here?"

"Why don't I not?"

"Sometimes it's . . . uh . . . not very nice. Stu can get pretty ugly."

"All the more reason for you not to go alone."

I watched the battle in his head. He wanted me with him, but he didn't want me exposed to this "not nice" world. But he didn't have a choice. With a queenly tilt of my head, I got out of the car.

Despite the chilly night, the air inside the duplex was hot and steamy and smelled of too many bodies and a strange, tangy smoke. The heavy metal music shook the walls.

Duncan tucked me under his arm as we weaved through the bodies in the kitchen toward the living room, where a thin woman with dark hair and huge gray eyes called out, "Dunkeroo!" She flapped her arms like an agitated sparrow.

"She's gone," Duncan said between clenched teeth. "There's no use talking to her tonight."

His mom flittered toward us with open arms, her hands gesturing wildly. "Hey, folks, this is my son, Dunkeroo."

Duncan hauled me down a short hall. "Let me get my stuff."

His mom followed, digging her birdlike hand into his arm. "Aren't you happy to see me?"

In this heat, Duncan had taken the scarf from his neck, and I saw his pulse quicken. "You promised. You promised this time you'd stay away from him, that you'd stay clean. For me."

She looked at him with a perplexed frown, then she laughed, a high-pitched cackle that hurt my ears. Her hands fluttered, and an angry, red hole in her forearm oozed a foul-smelling yellow pus. "But it's all for you, Dunkeroo. Everything's for you. Whatever you want, it's yours. We can do anything. Absolutely anything. Stu and I rule the world."

A man in tight blue jeans and a silky shirt open to the waist slung an arm around Duncan's mom. Slime. The guy was pure slime. Slicked-back hair, practiced smile, and unlike most people in the room, he had a clear, steady gaze. "Hey, son," he said.

"I'm not your son." Duncan's mouth barely moved. "My last name sure as hell isn't Drug-Dealing-Scum."

The petite gray-eyed woman on Stu's arm hurtled her body at Duncan, her bony hands pummeled him, one flailing fist after another, like a windmill. "You will not talk to Stu that way. Not now. Not ever!" Her hand connected with Duncan's mouth, and blood spurted from his lip. The blood oozed down Duncan's chin, a single drop falling to the floor.

Dizziness grabbed me, but I didn't let it take hold.

He wiped the trickle of blood from his mouth. Without a word, he guided me into a small bedroom with a mattress on the floor and a bookshelf that served as a dresser. He moved quickly, tossing clothes into a small garbage can next to his bed. He ducked into the hallway and came back with a toothbrush and other toiletries, which he tossed into the trash can. My heart twisted as I realized this wasn't the first time Duncan Moore packed his things in a garbage can to leave his mom and this place.

He hoisted the trash can under one arm. With his free hand, he took mine and dragged me out of the room past the crush of bodies and his wild-eyed mom. In the kitchen I stumbled to a halt when I saw the girl from the beach, the one Duncan had held in his arms. There was nothing frail or mouselike about her tonight. She danced on one of the chairs, her hands pumping above her, her lanky hair flailing wildly.

"She's gone, too." Dunc dragged me out of the room so fast faces and bodies blurred.

In the driveway we slowed enough for me to spot Hetta, his cabbage-scented neighbor. "I'm going to have to call the cops," she said. "I told you last time, no more."

Duncan waved at the old woman. "Do what you need to do, Hetta. When she clears out, you know where to find me."

Duncan tucked me into the passenger seat of my car and took the keys. It was only then I realized my knees were shaking so much they knocked together. Duncan was right. That hadn't been nice. Is this what Duncan had to live with every day of his life? No wonder he thought the radio station was fun. No wonder he didn't get close to people. People close to him kept letting him down. Just this morning Dunc's mom had promised to stop partying.

Duncan drove from the duplex, and I quieted my booming heart so I could hear myself think. He needed a place to go, somewhere far from those people. "If you want, you can stay at my house. We have tons of room, and I'm sure my parents wouldn't mind after they heard about the circumstances."

Duncan shook his head. "It's okay. I have a place."

"Are you sure that will hold you?" I asked as Duncan unfolded an old, rickety nurse's cot in the corner of the KDRS storeroom.

An hour ago he'd been helping me alphabetize Brad Pitt movies. Now he was escaping his meth-addict mother and her drug-dealing boyfriend and sleeping in a storeroom.

Can you say, *Wrong*?

"It's not as bad as it looks, especially with this." Duncan reached under his workbench and pulled out a sleeping bag with the Boy Scout logo.

"You were a Boy Scout?" Duncan had a be-prepared air about him, and I could see him earning badges and shiny things to put on a shirt that told the world he was good and nice and hardworking.

"No, Frack was a Boy Scout," Duncan said. "Pillow's from Frick."

"This isn't the first time you've stayed here?"

"No." He missiled the pillow at the cot. "Probably won't be the last."

Duncan had strong shoulders, offering support to everyone on the staff. He fixed the lights, made Haley shelves for her DVDs, and ran the boards for me. He was a pillar of strength, but tonight in the dusty, crowded storeroom, I saw a crack.

"There are places that can help people like your mom," I said. "I can talk to my parents and get some referrals."

"Did you see her arm?" His jaw trembled, and I remembered the angry, oozing hole in his mother's forearm. "She had an abscess in her vein, and she had surgery to remove it, but get this. She had so many staph infections the doctors couldn't stitch the incision. Do you understand that, Chloe? The doctors couldn't fix a stupid hole in her arm." He slumped onto the cot, the metal legs creaking. "No one can fix her. I've been trying for years. Stupid, huh?"

"You worry about people you love," I reminded him. "And you never give up hope. You can't, because you love her."

"Because I love her." The words were whisper soft, but they were there. "Why are you always right?"

I tossed my hand in a royal wave. "Because I am the queen."

"Yes. The queen of the universe. The queen of hearts. The queen of . . ."

Your heart, Duncan? But I didn't say the words. Words were important, but as I was learning, so was silence.

"Are you sure you're going to be okay?" I asked. "Can I get you anything before I leave? Something to eat or drink?"

He pointed to a box near a small microwave on the workbench. "Clem's got it covered."

I spotted cans of soup and listened to the silence between his words. "But?"

"It's hard." He shrugged. "Being alone."

Puzzlement wrinkled my forehead. "Alone? You're not alone. You have Frick's pillow, Frack's cot, and comfort food from Clem. If you need entertainment, you have Taysom's music mixes or Haley's DVDs. Your family's here. They care."

Duncan looked confused. And exhausted.

I gave him a quick hug. "Sleep on it, Dunc. Maybe it'll make more sense in the morning."

As I drove home from the station I couldn't stop thinking about how the radio staff had turned a storeroom into a safe, loving place for one of their own. Only one thing was missing. Nowhere in that storeroom was a piece of my heart, something to show Duncan I cared.

"Loved the new show, Chloe. I've got this great idea for . . ."

"Hey, Chloe, nice shoes! Maybe you can show me where you go thrifting someday."

As I hurried to Portable Five the next morning, I heard the words but didn't listen. I was too worried about Duncan. The security guard or custodians may have discovered him. He may need toothpaste or breakfast. I clutched a steaming brown-paper bag in my hand. A breakfast burrito from Dos Hermanas, the Mexican equivalent of eggs and cheese on toast.

When I walked into Portable Five, Duncan stood on a ladder in the middle of the newsroom changing the batteries in the smoke alarm. Just looking at him, no one could have guessed he'd been slugged by his meth-addict mother; had a close encounter of the ugly kind with her scumbag, drug-dealing boyfriend; and slept the night on a Boy Scout cot in a dirty storeroom. Only the damp bottom layers of Duncan's hair and faint smell of the pink soap used in the gym locker room hinted at anything out of the ordinary.

Not surprisingly, Duncan didn't mention last night, nor did any of the staff as they trickled in. It was business as usual as Clem prepared the morning news, Taysom and Haley recorded something in the production studio, and Frick and Frack sat at a computer going through KDRS e-mail, which, after my *Heartbeats* show, had quadrupled.

Despite Brie and her dead-guinea-pig story, *Heartbeats* was a hit.

Throughout the week, dozens of people stopped me in the hallway or in class to tell me they loved the new show. A local television station called for an interview. My celebrity status reached all-new heavenly heights. Yet I didn't hear the chorus of angels or feel light-headed from being on top of the world. I was too busy worrying about people I cared about.

All week Duncan continued to sleep in the storeroom at the radio station. To their credit, Duncan and the KDRS staffers were discreet. At night Duncan kept off all lights, and whenever he needed food or clean laundry, the staffers carried things in their backpacks.

As for Grams, she was back in the Tuna Can and acting as if the fire and flood had never happened. Mom was gathering medical records and talking to an attorney in hush-hush tones about things like "self-determination," "incompetence," and "conservatorship."

And then there was Merce. On Wednesday morning, I walked through the school parking lot when my former best friend, her arms loaded with books, cornered me. "Have you seen Brie?" Merce asked with a tremor in her voice.

"Uh, no. In case you forgot, we're not exactly besties these days."

"She isn't returning my calls, and this morning when I went to her house, she wouldn't answer the door even though her car was still in the driveway. Do you know what's going on with her?"

"Merce, seriously, the last discussion Brie and I had was about a dead guinea pig."

"But she's been gone all week. All week." The top two books fell from the stack in Merce's trembling arms.

I stooped to pick them up but didn't place them on the load in her arms. As a rule, Merce was no drama queen, but she was clearly upset. Unfortunately for her, Brie and I no longer breathed air from the same planet. "And you want me to do what? Put out an all-points bulletin on the radio?"

Merce shifted her books to her other arm, and her mouth quirked as she must have realized the ridiculousness of asking me to help track down Brie. "I . . . I'm sorry, Chloe. I shouldn't be coming to you with this. But these days when it comes to Brie, I'm lost. She's not making sense."

And Merce, with her logical, analytical mind, struggled with things that didn't make sense. Of course, I owed Merce nothing. She'd sided with Brie, bailed on me, and never once tried to stop the lies or mean gossip. But old habits, and maybe old friend-ships, died hard. "You okay?" I asked.

A deep sigh rocked her chest and she shook her head. "But I'll get through it." She grabbed her books from me, two fat SAT guides, and walked away.

Without consciously deciding to, I looked for Brie all day. I found myself searching through the bodies near the ficus tree, in the hallway outside Brie's locker, and at lunch table fourteen.

At the end of lunch period I spotted a blond-haired girl sit-ting on a bench at the far end of the drop-off/pick-up loop, but I figured it couldn't be Brie. Like me, Brie didn't do "alone." But as I drew closer, I got a better look at the solitary figure.

She wore no makeup, no signature diamond earrings, but it was Brie. Oddly enough, even without her frosty pink lips and chunks of ice in her ears, she looked ice-cold as she glared at me.

I hurried away, shivering.

Program Name: *Chloe, Queen of the Universe*
On Air: Chloe
Boards: Duncan
Friday

HOUR ONE

00 Underwriter Spot
01 Legal ID, Sweep, Banter with Clem, Parkinson's Disease Intro
05 PD fast facts
10 Event Cal, Weather
15 Sweep, PD calls
20 PD calls
25 PD calls
30 News
35 Sweep, Substance Abuse/Addiction opening
40 PSA
42 SA/A fast facts
50 SA/A counselor interview
55 SA/A calls (flow into hour two)
59 Underwriter Spot

CHAPTER 18

"ABSOLUTELY, POSITIVELY NO!" CLEMENTINE DROPPED THE notebook with my format clock on my desk with a loud splat.

I shoved my notes at her. "It's *my* show. I get to do what *I* want." Even to my own ears, I sounded bratty, but I didn't care.

She waved at the sheets of paper as if she were fanning the stink off old garbage. "But this kind of show isn't you."

"How do you know who I am?" I grabbed the last Twizzler in the bag on my desk and tried to find a peaceful, happy place, because tomorrow I had another live Queen Chloe show and the kingdom was in chaos.

Clementine let out a dragon sigh. "I know who Queen Chloe is. She's funny, at times irreverent, and more than mildly entertaining." She pointed at my format clock, which detailed in five-minute increments what I'd cover on my upcoming show. "Parkinson's disease isn't entertaining, and topic number two isn't much better. Substance abuse and addiction? My gawwwwwd, Chloe, what the hell are you thinking?"

Exactly. I *was* thinking. I rubbed at the thoughts hammering my skull. I was thinking about Parkinson's and meth and upended worlds.

Clem dragged a chair to my desk and sat in front of me. "What's going on?" She stared at me with a gaze that didn't waver. She was observant and not afraid to dig deep for the truth, which would make her a great journalist. "You are not going on the air until you talk." Her dragon snout barely twitched.

I rubbed at my head, then finally said, "I'm worried. I'm worried about the giant shoe that's about to stomp Grams and the Tuna Can, and I'm worried that the guy I'm starting to care for is up against a monster." I motioned to my format clock. "I've been researching meth. It's a huge, loud, destructive beast. When it's in a room, there's no space for anything else, no people or feelings or words. No wonder Duncan's so disconnected. And he's getting worse. Have you noticed he hasn't laughed all week? Not once."

"We can't laugh all the time," Clem said. "We have to experience sad times, too. They make us appreciate the good times. And Duncan's strong. He'll get through this."

"You sound like a Hallmark card."

Clementine grabbed both sides of her hair. "Shoot me and put me out of my misery."

I aimed my Twizzler at her and made a gunshot sound that would have done Haley proud.

"Seriously," Clem went on, "do you want to spend an hour talking about Parkinson's and Alzheimer's? Do you think that kind of stuff will be of genuine interest to the audience you've built? And do you *really* want your callers phoning in to talk about substance abuse and addiction?" Clem shuddered. "Duncan, for one, doesn't need to hear that."

I stuffed the entire Twizzler into my mouth and chewed thoughtfully. "You're right."

"What?" Clem thwacked her ear, vaudeville style. "What did you say?"

I let out a sound that was part groan, part laugh. "Clementine Radmore is one hundred percent, unequivocally right. Do you want me to get on the air and issue a royal proclamation?"

"Can you?"

I ignored the grin on her face. I was a talk show host, and tomorrow I was expected to talk. "Ideas, please."

Clementine leaned back in a chair and crossed her ankles. "You mentioned your JISP a few times on air. Have you ever thought about a show on the whole JISP thing? It's timely. I finished my literacy program at the school for kids of migrant workers, and Haley's almost done with her diaper drive. Beyond the human interest stuff, there are some classically hilarious JISP stories out there, like Lizzy Delgado, who organized that Girl Scout lock-in last year and accidentally booked a male stripper as entertainment. Plus, JISPs give us plenty of options for sidebar discussions. We can talk about the causes people work for and are passionate about. We can put together a list of local nonprofits and their most pressing needs. You could even interview Ms. Lungren."

"I'd never get her to shut up. JISPs are her life."

"Honestly, she'd be good."

On Friday, I learned Clem was right. Again.

For *Chloe, Queen of the Universe*, I interviewed A. Lungren live. My counselor was an articulate and enthusiastic speaker about the subject of community service, and she even managed to ditch her annoying kitty purr. After the interview, Duncan broke to the news and Ms. Lungren took off her headphones.

"I'm so proud of you, Chloe, for all you've done for the radio station," she said. "KDRS does so much good for the school and our community. I'd hate to see it taken off the air."

What did a do-gooder like Ms. Lungren see? Did she see Frack, a boy who stutters, find his voice? Did she see Haley wrapped in a cocoon of people who accepted her and the child growing in her belly? Did she see this building as Duncan's refuge? And mine?

"Funding-wise, we're good through May," I said. "But I'm not sure about next year. We're going to need not just operating expenses but big bucks for new equipment. There's only so much Duncan can do with duct tape."

Ms. Lungren made a soft, purring noise. "Hmmm ... a capital-improvement-campaign proposal." Her kitty nose twitched, like a cat eyeing a new mouse squeak toy. "Might be a wonderful JISP project for someone next year. It wouldn't have to be someone as outgoing as you, Chloe, but someone good at mobilizing people and money. Someone who excels at organization ..."

I wanted to laugh. I was in the presence of a guidance counselor who still thought she could make a difference. A rare species. I slipped on my headphones for the next segment of my show.

During the next hour, we talked about superheroes, including those on Saturday morning cartoons and real-life heroes. No one seemed to notice that I talked less and took more calls than usual. Tonight the minions had run of the castle.

On Monday, the second official installment of *Heartbeats*, I figured I'd also be able to lie low because we'd have plenty of calls, given Valentine's Day was coming up. Everyone wanted to talk about love.

Right before *Heartbeats* kicked off, Clementine gave me the thirty-second hand signal and said over the mic, "If Guinea Pig Girl calls, she's not getting through."

I wondered what was going on with Brie and if she'd call the station again with something more appalling than dead guinea pigs. Not knowing what was going on behind Brie's beautiful face was worse than her rumors, because rumors, even those based on lies, were known. Like Grams had said, an active imagination made the unknown a frightening place.

I kicked off the first hour of *Heartbeats* talking about the most romantic movies of all times. Haley put together her top five: *Titanic*, *Casablanca*, Zefferelli's *Romeo and Juliet*, Cocteau's haunting black-and-white *Beauty and the Beast*, and another 1939 fave, *Gone with the Wind*.

"My vote goes to *Casablanca*," I said. "Gotta love Ingrid Bergman's shoes."

The calls poured in.

"*Ghost*, that old eighties movie where the guy dies but can't leave his love, is sooooo romantic."

Another caller loved *West Side Story*. "I think what makes it so incredibly romantic is they can't have each other, and so many times we want what we can't have."

I let the callers have free will, and we moved from movies about romantic love to movies about other kinds of love.

"*Schindler's List*. A man who loves humanity."

"*Dr. Doolittle*. A man who loves animals."

Animals. Guinea pigs. Would Brie call? Would the hammer come down tonight? By the end of the hour, still no Brie.

At the break for news, Duncan said, "You're pretty quiet tonight." He sat in the chair next to me folding a piece of paper. If he was trying to make a paper airplane, it was looking pretty bleak. Too round. Too lopsided. Maybe I wasn't the only one having a bad night.

"Got a thing against quiet girls?" I picked at a hole in the chair armrest.

He chuckled. "No." His fingers continued to fold and tear. "I was wondering if you had plans for Valentine's Day. I have this idea . . ."

When he looked up, all thoughts of Brie fled. The silver of his eyes sparked with something that lit a fire in the center of my chest. He handed me the paper, which I now recognized as an origami heart.

"It's nothing fancy, and you might not even want to do it."

Duncan shucked his hand through his hair. "But if you're free and you don't have anyone else to hang out with on Valentine's Day, then maybe you—"

"Duncan . . ." I grabbed him by the scarf and pulled him toward me.

"What?"

"Shut up." Over the past month I'd changed. I left my old clan. I joined the radio staff. I was listening more. But some things about me would never change. I still loved spicy salsa bars, I still had orange-red curls, and I was still bold, still Chloe.

I raised my face to his. The spark as our lips met was a thousand snapping bonfires.

From the look on his face, Duncan felt it, too. He snagged in a few deep breaths. "I guess that means you'll go out with me on Valentine's Day?"

"I'll be there. With bells on my toes."

His gaze shot to my feet, where I wore a pair of sixties sequined platform wedges.

I swatted him on the arm. "It's an expression, Dunc."

With my mind on all things Duncan and Valentine's Day, I took a greater interest in the second hour of my show, during which we talked about Valentine's Day food. One caller explained how to make a chocolate fondue spread. Another caller said she put together a picnic one year with all red and white and pink foods. I looked at Duncan and thought of eggs and cheese on toast.

It was the bottom of the hour and Brie—Cheese Girl, Dead-Guinea-Pig Caller, whatever you wanted to call her—hadn't dialed in. There was something creepy about her silence. Like me, Brie needed to be noticed.

About five minutes before signing off, Clementine flashed the name of my next caller, and I smiled.

"Hey, callers, Brad's back," I said as Duncan patched the call through. "Remember him? He's our silent, suffering poet with a major crush. Well, Brad, how'd it go with your ladylove?"

A nice, dramatic beat of silence filled the air before Brad said, "She hated it."

"What?"

"My poem. I took my favorite poem, wrote it on fancy paper, and put it in her locker. She read it"—a choky sound waffled over the line—"and shoved it at me, like she was embarrassed or afraid of it. Of me."

Some people were mean. Time for a bit of Chloe cheer. "This girl, who obviously doesn't have good taste in poetry or guys, made a whopper of a mistake, and that's her problem, not yours. Now, what I want you to do is write a—"

"But that's not all," Brad went on, as if I said nothing, "her friends found me after school in the parking lot, three of them. They told me to stay away from her."

"Ahhhhh, Brad—"

"They said not to come within three feet of her or I'd be sorry." His voice cracked.

Brad was hurting. I didn't want to use the Great Silencer on him, but I needed to end the call. Clementine gave me a wrist twirl, the signal to wrap up things. "So let's talk about how—"

"I went home," Brad barreled on. "At first I cried so hard I couldn't breathe. It was as if my heart had been ripped from my chest, and not only that, someone had thrown it in the middle of the lunchroom, and everyone stomped all over it. Blood was everywhere."

I fought a wave of wooziness. "Brad, we need—"

"Then I stopped crying. Maybe I ran out of tears or maybe there was no more blood to pour out of the huge hole in my chest."

Duncan placed his hand on my arm. Duncan. Always at my side.

Brad must have arrived at a more peaceful place, because when he talked next, his words were steadier. "I took all the poems I'd written to her, more than twenty, and I burned them one after another, lots of hot flames and curling, snapping paper. Now I have a pile of ashes."

Time to take control of the airwaves. "Okay, that's not a bad thing, Brad. You crushed hard, she didn't crush back, but you're not hanging on to her. This is good."

"No, Chloe, it's not good." Brad hung up.

The entire staff gave me a What now? look. No problem. I'd been bayoneted lately; I knew how to handle this. "Brad, I feel your pain, we all do. It's hard to put yourself out there, to make yourself vulnerable, and, yeah, sometimes you get hurt. Maybe that's what we need to talk about next week, how to pick up and move on, but for now, Brad, I send you healing thoughts over the airwaves. We all do. I also send good thoughts that love—the right love for you, one that loves your poems—will find you, because it will all work out in the end. The person you think you can't live without, who you think is your perfect match, might not be it.

"On that note, listeners, it's time to sign off. This is 88.8 The Edge, and this has been *Heartbeats* with Chloe Camden, where love is on the air."

Duncan cued my theme music, and the On Air sign went dark.

"Good job, Dr. Phil," Clementine said. "That had VSP written all over it."

"Not VSP, VHP." I slipped off my headphones. "Very hurting person." Because when you cared about people, you handed them a little piece of your heart, and with those hands, they had the power to cause pain.

**SAY NO TO DRUGS
SAY YES TO TACOS!**

CHAPTER 19

"HEY, GRAMS!" I PUSHED OPEN THE FRONT DOOR OF THE TUNA
Can. "The radio staff stopped by Dos Hermanas after my *Heartbeats* show, and I brought you a green chili burro."

The living room was bottom-of-the-ocean black, as was the kitchen behind it. I fumbled for the light switch, but when I flicked it, the room remained dark. I flicked three more times. No light.

"Grams? Are you home?"

Silence.

My arms outstretched, I walked into the living room. My shin slammed against something cold and hard in the middle of the floor. A box of some kind.

"Grams?" I called again. A sliver of panic tinged my words. "Where are you? What's going on?" Something crunched and snapped beneath my feet. The sliver turned into a full wedge. "Graaaaams!"

"Can it, Poppy, or we'll have nosy Noreen over here."

My heart, which had reached breakneck speed, slowed. "Grams? What happened to the light?"

"I threw a shoe at it."

"Why would you do that?"

"Because I didn't want to see them anymore." A chill hung on each word.

"Grams, you're starting to freak me out." I set her green chili burro on the boxlike thing and fumbled through the dark to the kitchen, where I switched on the light over the dining table.

"What the . . ." Not one, but two boxes sat in the middle of the living room, and Grams sat between them, her lap piled high with hundreds of glossy bits of paper. Photos? It was hard to tell. Some were warped, others torn.

"What happened?"

Grams lifted the bits of paper over her head, and they tumbled to the ground. "Eighty years of living. Gone." Her voice was cold, dead.

Rushing to the living room, I dropped to her side. "Grams, what's going on?"

Grams's hands slid through the heap of photos on her lap. "The company that oversaw the restoration work of the Tuna Can dropped off my photo albums this afternoon. They spent some extra time on them, trying to salvage what they could, because they knew what's important to an old girl living in a Tuna Can." Her hands and bottom lip shook. "A stupid old girl living on her own."

I grabbed photos from a heap on the coffee table. Mickey Mouse and three of my brothers without heads. Half of the Grand Canyon and my father's right ear. "Surely some of them weren't damaged by the water."

"A few survived." Reaching into her pocket, she showed me pictures of Zach on the beach, Sam and Max playing basketball, Jeremy and Dad riding a tandem bike, and Luke on his graduation from med school. "But none . . ." Her hands slid over the mutilated photos in her lap. This close I could see orange hair the color and curl of poppy petals. "But none of you, Poppy. Not one of you survived." The first tear fell. Then another.

I sat on my heels. I'd never seen Grams cry. Not at weddings or graduations. Not when the tow truck took away her ruined Jeep after she slammed into the ATM. Not even when Gramps died five years ago. My world was upside down, inside out, and wrong.

"I'm a stupid old woman."

And Grams was wrong. "You're not stupid. You're brilliant when it comes to dealing with people. You know how to make people happy and tamales de dulce. And you—"

"Chloe?"

"—know how to create blogs, and you can name every role Brad Pitt played, and you—"

"Chloe!"

"Yeah, Grams?"

"Shut. Up."

"I . . ."

Grams cocked an eyebrow.

Deep breath in. Deep breath out. "I guess I need to work on my listening skills."

A choky laugh tumbled over her lips. The laugh shook her mouth, her face, her chest.

I hadn't meant it as a joke. It was true. While gabbing away on the airwaves, I'd learned the importance of listening. Heedless of the photos, I scooted next to her. Her laughter rumbled along her legs and through her arms. She got to laughing so hard, she fell over. Me, too. We rolled on the floor of the Tuna Can, letting laughter work its healing magic.

"What now?" I asked when I caught my breath and struggled upright. Between the photos and the broken glass of the light, the floor was a mess.

"It's time for a little change before I ruin anything else." Grams steadied her hands on the coffee table. "You better give Dunc a call. He's going to need to move my porch swing again."

I held my breath. Grams needed to make this decision, one that made sense to both her head and heart. "Where?"

She stood, her legs steady. "The black hole. I'm moving in."

TAMALES DE DULCE

* 2 cups masa harina
* $\frac{1}{2}$ cup sugar
* $\frac{1}{4}$ t. salt
* 1 $\frac{1}{2}$ t. cinnamon
* 1 $\frac{1}{2}$ t. baking powder
* $\frac{1}{4}$ cup margarine
* $\frac{1}{4}$ cup lard
* 1 $\frac{1}{2}$ cups chicken stock
* 1 cup walnuts, chopped
* 1 cup raisins
* About 24 dried corn husks, soaked in hot water to
  soften

Stir together masa harina, sugar, salt, cinnamon, and baking powder. Cream margarine and lard until fluffy. Gradually beat masa harina mixture and broth into the lard mixture. Beat for 5 minutes. Stir in walnuts and raisins.

Shake excess water from the softened corn husks. Spread 2 T dough down center of each husk. Roll, turning under ends. If needed, roll in an additional husk to secure. Pack tamales into steamer and steam for 1 $\frac{1}{2}$ to 2 hours.

Makes about 12 tamales.

CHAPTER 20

I SLIPPED ON MY PLAIN WHITE KEDS.

The sneakers weren't fashionable and they didn't make a statement as I walked to school the next morning. With their quiet rubber soles, these shoes were made for walking. And listening.

Like spinning the knob of an old-fashioned radio dial, I tuned in to the beautiful morning: squawking seagulls, the tapping ocean, a babbling toddler being pushed by his mother in a stroller with a squeaky wheel, and somewhere far away the whisper of a siren's wail. As the siren faded, I couldn't help but think somewhere something had gone wrong, and someone's life would probably change forever.

Change.

Change was inevitable, and it wore many faces. Some life-altering changes came fast and hard, like secret babies or revenge-seeking ex-wives who hit the screen during sweeps weeks. The whole thing with Brie slammed me like a Category 5 hurricane. One moment I had two of the world's bestest friends and a fungus crown. The next I was alone. Then there were the life-altering changes that occurred with less fanfare, the ones that had been transforming quietly as the minutes ticked into hours and days and years. Over the past year, Parkinson's nibbled away at Grams, taking away her car, her ability to open a DVD case, and ultimately the Tuna Can.

Mom and Dad had been shocked when I brought Grams home last night. Shocked, but relieved and clearly happy, even when Grams hung her life-size picture of Brad Pitt at the head of the stairs. In the morning, a group of Dad's students from the university started packing the Tuna Can and moved Grams into the second floor of my home.

Not all changes were bad, I thought, as I continued my silent walk to school. Joining KDRS was good. Making friends with the staff, even dragon Clem, was good. And kissing Duncan? That was beyond good. My lips tingled at the memory.

Lost in my thoughts of Duncan, I forgot about the siren until I got to school. Once there I saw a fire truck pulling out of the parking lot. Wispy clouds of gray hovered over the east side of the campus, and a breath of acrid air snagged in my throat. "Smoke?"

I ran across campus to where the portables sat. My practical tennis shoes skidded to a stop in a puddle of ashy mud in front of Portable Five. Before me sat the black, smoking, hissing shell of a building that had once been the home of KDRS 88.8 The Edge.

"Duncan!" The word hitched in my throat. He'd been

sleeping in the storeroom under Frack's Boy Scout sleeping bag with Frick's pillow.

I scanned the crowd and at the front spotted Clementine. Elbowing my way through the press of bodies, I grabbed Clem's arm and spun her toward me. Her nose ring was gone.

"Duncan." I tried to keep my voice low, but I wanted to scream. "Where is he?"

"We don't know," someone other than Clementine said. I blinked. Next to her stood Haley and Taysom.

"Is—was—he in there?" I refused to look at the charred shell.

Taysom shook his head. "Clem got here first. She told the fire captain right away about Duncan. The firefighters checked the rubble and didn't find anyone anywhere in the portable."

"They're sure?"

Haley rested her hand on my shoulder. "Positive. The fire chief told Clem he'd send the police to check Duncan's duplex and the places where he worked."

Duncan wasn't in the portable when it caught fire. Good. That was good. But where was he?

"Chloe, I'm sure Duncan's safe," Taysom said as he unclamped my fingers from his arm. "We would have heard by now if something bad happened."

"But his mom's with Stu again. He has nowhere to go." I was blathering.

Haley looped her arm around my waist. "He has us."

Yes, he has *us*. I leaned into her, letting her warmth and strength rush through me. You needed one person in your corner to lift you when you fell, to hold your hand when you were scared, and to open a few doors when your home burned to the ground. Duncan didn't have just one person; he had all of us at KDRS.

With my heart back in my chest, I watched the firefighters poking around the building. "How do you think it started?" I asked.

"The investigators aren't done," Taysom said. "It's such an old building, and we told them about the wiring issues. They're starting there."

When the first-period bell rang, we all turned to leave—except for Clementine. I literally had to drag her away from the charred ruins. I tried to put myself in her shoes, because somewhere while JISPing along, I'd tried to start looking at others. Did Clementine think her radio dream died in those flames? Did she feel like she was floating in turbulent seas without a life preserver? I would eventually ask, but as we walked through the hallways to first period, I respected the quiet she seemed to need. Like I respected beets. My lips twitched, but I refrained from any comments about purple, bulbous vegetables. The jokes would come later, because laughter was a great healer. I helped Merce laugh again after her mother's death. I helped Brie laugh through her parents' ugly battles. And I helped Grams laugh her way out of the Tuna Can.

Clementine had Ancient History first hour, and I delivered her directly to her desk. "You going to be okay?"

She said nothing.

What could I say? *Of course you're going to be okay. This isn't the end of your world. This isn't the end of your radio dreams.* I knew from experience words wouldn't help. Time would. "I need to go, Clem. I want to see if Duncan comes to first period. I'll meet you for lunch at your locker."

With a final shoulder squeeze, I hurried toward my first-period classroom. I pictured Duncan sitting at his desk, a soft scarf around his neck, his fingers folding a paper airplane or maybe an origami heart. I walked faster, almost running by the time I reached econ, and when I burst through the doorway, I saw his seat. Empty.

Don't think about it, I warned myself. Because if I thought, I'd devise a hundred different horrible scenarios with drama and intrigue and horrible villains and villainesses.

I focused on my classes until the middle of fourth period, when Ms. Lungren called me to the guidance center. My JISP. I hadn't thought of how the fire would affect my project.

When I got to the guidance center, Ms. Lungren led me into a small room used for parent-student-counselor meetings. However, neither my parents nor Ms. Lungren sat at the table. A man with a navy blazer, light blue shirt, and a black smudge on his forehead motioned for me to take a seat across from him.

"Chloe, this is Sergeant Cargill," Ms. Lungren said. "He's an investigator with the Tierra del Rey Fire Department, and he wants to talk to you about the radio station."

The question rushed over my lips before my butt hit the chair. "Duncan, he wasn't in the fire, was he?"

"No," the fire investigator said. "We've completed our search, and I assure you, your friend was not in the building, and the police are currently trying to find him."

"Try his neighbor, Hetta, and the thrift store where he works and the office buildings where he empties trash. He has a bike. It has mismatched pedals, and the seat's covered in duct tape. The front wheel makes a squeaking sound, kind of like the squeaky wheel on a trash cart. You got all that?"

He gave me the kind of smile Mom gives her patients as they come out from anesthesia. "Is there anything else you need to say?"

"The Happy Trails Trailer Park. Sometimes his mom stays there with a friend named Stu. Stu. Just Stu. I don't have a last name, but he drives a maroon Camaro. Duncan doesn't like him, but . . . I . . . I sound like an idiot."

"Don't worry, Chloe, we'll find your friend."

My friend. And Valentine's date. And the boy who makes my thumbs and ankles and lips and other body parts tingle.

"Chloe, I need you to focus on me," Mr. Fire Guy said. My frenzied brain couldn't remember his name. "Are you focusing on me?"

I nodded.

"Good. We discovered the fire started not because of faulty wiring but a liquid accelerant. We believe someone purposefully started the fire."

A heavy sensation settled in my chest. I couldn't believe anyone would want to burn down the station. Record numbers of listeners were tuning in. We were airing engaging, enlightening, fun programming. Fun. Duncan. The boulder in my chest plummeted to the pit of my stomach. Fire Guy said the police were looking for Duncan. "Duncan didn't start the fire. He wouldn't do that kind of thing. I know him. He's nice and—"

"Whoa, there. From what we learned from the other radio staff members and Mr. Martinez, we don't think he started the fire, but we're trying to find him and see if he saw anything or anyone." Fire Guy glanced at the notepad on the table in front of him. "Last night when you left the station with the radio staff to go to Dos Hermanas, did you see anything or anyone near Portable Five?"

I still couldn't get my head around the idea that someone would purposefully torch the station. KDRS had become a second home to me. Who could hate a home that much?

"Chloe?" Fire Guy prompted. "Did you see anyone near the radio station when you left?"

I tamped down my panic and tried to recall last night. "No, I don't remember anyone near the building."

"And when you left Dos Hermanas, where did Duncan go?"

Duncan had kissed me good-bye. The kiss had been longer than the peck in the radio control room, deeper, and had left me a little fuzzy brained. "I think he went in the direction of the thrift store. He works there until nine most weeknights."

"Did you go by the school after leaving Dos Hermanas?"

"No, I went to the Tuna Can—that's my grandmother's trailer— and ended up helping her pack her DVD collection. She's moving in with us."

The Fire Guy made notes on the pad. "Now, I want you to tell me about Brad."

A manic giggle stuck in my throat. Was Fire Guy concerned about his smokin' hot heinie? But I wasn't asking the questions today, I was answering them. "He was on *Another World* a long time ago, a small acting part. I don't know what his first movie was, but I think he got a few Oscar nominations."

Fire Guy's forehead furrowed. "Who are you talking about?"

"Brad Pitt. Didn't you ask me what I knew about Brad Pitt?"

He cleared his throat. "Brad, your caller, the one who burned all his love poems, the one who broke down on your show yesterday afternoon."

Brad, the VHP. I could still hear the pain in his voice, the hurt fueling his words. "Oh God, he's not behind the fire, is he?"

"We don't know, but we're looking into anyone who may have a grudge against the station or any of its staff members."

Unfortunately, I was no help to the fire investigator. I didn't know Brad's last name, grade, or where he went to school. Heck, I didn't even know if Brad was his real name.

"Do you personally know any Brads here at school?" Fire Guy asked.

Off the top of my head, I named two Brads and a Bradley. I tried to blot out their faces and focused on their voices, but nothing clicked. I could not positively ID any of these Brads as my distraught caller.

By the time Fire Guy finished the interview, the lunch bell had rung. I found the KDRS staffers in the lunchroom, even Frick and

Frack, who had a different lunch period. They sat at table nine, scrunched tightly together. They were still, as if posing for a family portrait, but they didn't smile. They weren't talking when I sat next to Haley and took out my lunch bag, which held a dozen tamales de dulce Grams and I made last night to celebrate a new life in the black hole.

My throat convulsed. "Any news on Duncan?"

Haley and Taysom shook their heads. Frick and Frack joined them. I pushed the bag of tamales into the center of the table. "How about some comfort food?" I asked with half a smile, all I could muster today.

Clementine snapped her head my way, her crinkly hair whipping like hundreds of spikes on a dragon tail.

"Clem . . . ," Haley warned.

"What? You want me to play nice?" Clementine asked with her fiery dragon snarl. "Well, I won't. I'm mad as hell, and it's *her* fault."

Her was a bad word. Like *mean* and *Parkinson's* and *meth*.

"*You* told that idiot to send that girl one of his love poems. *You* told him to open his heart and jump into the fire. *You* had no freakin' idea who he was or who she was. *You* torched the station. *You*." Each time she said *you*, her finger dug into my shoulder.

Frick and Frack each picked at a tamale. Taysom fiddled with his iPod. Haley stared at her stomach.

Clementine gave me one final push. "Get the hell out of here."

Dead air settled around us, but not just radio dead air. This was black-hole dead air, cold and without life. I could hardly breathe.

Frack spoke up. "It's p-p-probably best if you g-g-go."

Best for whom? For Clementine, who was about to explode? For Duncan, who was missing? For me, who couldn't breathe?

I stumbled out of the lunchroom, the different clans blurring as the tears gathered in my eyes. Clementine was right. They were all right. I wanted more listeners, more fans, more adulation. It was my fault KDRS was now silent.

Wanting comes from the head and heart. Your heart whispers you want that shiny pair of black-and-red 1934 ankle-strap stilettos. Your brain hears and sets in motion a plan to add a new hot pair of heels to the shoe tree.

Need is an entirely different beast. It still involves the head and heart, but it goes deeper, to a primal place without a name. Let's say you're swimming and a riptide grabs you by the ankles and sucks you under. The primal place, the one that deals with life and death, tells you that you *need* air. *Without air*, it screams, *you will die.*

As I walked away from the lunchroom, I *needed* someone. Three months ago that would have been Brie and Mercedes. Three weeks ago it would have been Duncan or Haley or even Clementine.

Now I had no one.

I walked through the quad, past Our Tree, and toward the auto-shop building. Behind an old Ford truck was a small hole in the fence stoners used to get off and on campus so they could do what they do. I slipped through the hole in the fence.

For a while I thought my Keds would take me to Dos Hermanas, where I could sit under the shadow of Larry, Moe, and Rizado and listen to the wisdom of two women who decades ago walked barefoot across the Sonoran Desert and now owned one of the most successful small businesses in town. I also thought they'd take me to Grams to celebrate the demise of the black hole.

They did neither. My dorky tennis shoes headed east toward Duncan's duplex because I needed Duncan, but not just for me. Even though I'd been cast out by a bunch of outsiders, I needed to know he was safe.

When I reached the duplex, I saw his bike, his wonderful duct-tape-covered bike, leaning against the house. Running to the door, I knocked.

Surely Duncan was home. He rode his bike everywhere. When he didn't answer my fifth knock, I turned the door handle. Inching the door a crack, I called, "Duncan, are you here?"

An image of too-slick Stu flashed through my head, but my need was greater than my fear. I pushed open the door. "Duncan? It's me, Chloe." Not queen of the universe. Not the queen of hearts. Queen only of her screwed-up life.

I'd been to Duncan's house twice. The first time it smelled of eggs and cheese and buttery toast. The next time a strange metallic smoke hung on the air. Today it smelled of stale air and neglect.

"Duncan?" I called louder. "Are you here?"

A soft clicking sound, one decibel above silence, came from the back of the house. My rubber-soled shoes silent, I followed the noise. The clicking didn't come from Duncan's room but from the other bedroom, where the door was open a crack.

"Hello?" I tapped on the door. "Duncan, are you in there?"

The clicking sped up, like a ticking clock on speed. Meth. My blood froze. Was snake-eyed Stu behind the door? Could it be Duncan's mom? Was she hurt? Dying? Did she need help?

I pushed open the door and thankfully didn't find Stu, but a woman.

"Mrs. Moore?" I asked. Was this Duncan's mom? Hard to tell. She sat on the floor in the corner of a messy bedroom. She wore an oversize men's T-shirt, and greasy black hair hung over her face. Her bird-thin hands and arms moved at a frantic pace as she dipped and clicked a pair of worn knitting needles. The bizarre thing was, she had no yarn. She was knitting air.

"Have you seen Duncan?" I asked.

Clickclackclickclackclickclack.

"Mrs. Moore, please listen to me. There was a fire at the school. In the radio station. Duncan was the last one there. We're all looking for him."

Clickclackclickclackclickclack. "I know. Cops came by."

"And did you tell them where Duncan was? Do you know?"

Clickclackclickclackclickclack. A line of yellow rot streamed from the open sore on her arm. "I'm out of yarn." She jerked her head, whipping the greasy hair from her face. "I *need* some yarn."

"Where's Duncan?" I kept my voice calm. One of us needed to stay calm.

"Where's my yarn?"

Clickclackclickclackclickclackclickclackclickclackclickclacklick.

"Where's my god-damned yarn!"

Beeeeep.

Hey, Mom, it's Chloe. Give me a call. I need a ride. I'm okay, but a friend of mine, well, a friend of a friend needs some help.

Beeeeep.

Beeeeep.

Dad, it's me. Are you there? Call me.

Beeeeep.

Beeeeep.

Uh, Ms. Lungren, this is Chloe Camden. I need some help. ASAP.

CHAPTER 21

TWENTY MINUTES LATER MS. LUNGREN, WHO STILL THOUGHT she could make a difference in my life, did. After picking me up from Duncan's duplex, she dropped me off at home. She didn't ask how I got off campus in the middle of the day, although as I hurried out of her car, she strongly suggested my mom or dad call the school ASAP.

I agreed.

When I reached my house, I grabbed the handle of my front door and burst into the entryway, the rubber soles of my shoes squealing across the marble. Strangely enough, that was the only sound. Unlike this morning when I left, there were no student movers hauling in furniture and boxes of DVDs, no Grams giving orders, no Mom running around and replacing batteries in smoke alarms and installing bathroom railings.

"Grams?" I called. "Mom?"

No signs of life. I rushed up the stairs. Had something happened to Grams? Did she fall down the stairs? Did she and Mom exchange nuclear missiles?

I calmed my heart. Now was not the time for drama. If something had happened to Grams, Mom or Dad would have let me know.

That's when I heard the steady squeak, familiar and strangely comforting, coming from the backyard.

On the porch I found Grams, swaying on the swing, her arms crossed over her chest as she watched something on her portable DVD player. I peeked over her shoulder and smiled. It must have been an ugly morning with Mom, because she'd pulled out the big guns, Brad Pitt with a bare chest.

"Everything okay?" I asked.

"We haven't killed each other. Yet."

"Hmmmmm."

Beyond the fountain, pool, and terraced flower beds on the side of the house I found Mom pumping away on my old swing. "How's your endorphin level?" I asked.

"Not quite high enough. Yet."

I gave her a push. "Keep swinging."

With Grams and Moms moving forward, albeit slowly, I headed for the garage and my car.

I'd never been in a craft store before. Mom and Dad weren't crafty types. Ditto for my five brothers. And Grams, she was born without the bread-baking-sewing grandma gene. The famous

Question Bag was a brown-paper lunch sack. But I figured a craft store would have yarn.

"Can I help you find something?" the clerk asked.

One Duncan would be nice. You wouldn't happen to have any in aisle fourteen, would you?

According to Mrs. Moore's muddied memory, Duncan had stopped by the duplex early that morning to check on her. "Or maybe not," Mrs. Moore had said as she gripped the sides of her head as if trying to hold her brains in place. "Maybe it was yesterday or the day before. Hell, it was probably last week. God, I'm a mess."

And because Mrs. Moore was a mess and Duncan was still missing, I nodded at the craft store clerk. "Yarn, please."

The clerk led me to the back wall, where tubes of soft, lumpy yarn lined five rows of shelves. My fingers slid over the brilliant chili greens, orangey reds the color of poppy petals, and blues and yellows like the feathers of Larry, Moe, and Rizado hanging over the salsa bar.

So bright, so bold, so Chloe.

But they'd probably hurt Mrs. Moore's bloodshot eyes.

I reached for a soft black and gray tube shot with silver, like Duncan's eyes. I picked two, frowned, and grabbed another four. I had no idea how many tubes of yarn it would take to knit Duncan a new scarf, but I wanted to make sure Mrs. Moore had enough. She'd explained that when coming down off the meth, she knitted like a maniac. "Keeps my hands busy and my mind off what I really want."

I was no doctor, but something told me Mrs. Moore was going to need more than yarn and knitting needles to get straight. Again I wondered where Duncan was. Was he so disgusted with his mom that he wanted, no *needed*, to get far away? Or would he dig deep past all his disappointment and anger and fear and decide to stick by her side?

Over the past two months I'd discovered Duncan was a lousy communicator and not in touch with his emotions, but I also learned he was loyal to those he cared about. He took care of the KDRS staffers, his mom, even that girl on the beach, who was probably coming down off a major high that night and needed Duncan to keep her feet on the ground.

By the time I left the craft store, the sun had begun to set, and I wasn't sure what I'd find lurking behind the dark eyes of the closed windows of Duncan's duplex. No light shone. This was a smaller version of the black hole.

I knocked on the door.

"Come in," a voice croaked.

In the kitchen I switched on the light and found Mrs. Moore at the tiny table. She'd taken a shower. Her dark hair was combed back from her pinched face, and the musty, sour smell was gone. Despite her baggy blue jeans and oversize sweatshirt, she was shaking. In one hand she held a half-crushed cigarette, and in the other a lighter that refused to light.

"Let me help." I took the lighter and lit the end of the cigarette, which flared, then dulled to a crackly red.

She took a long, shaky draw. "Thanks."

I set the yarn bag on the counter. "Are you hungry?"

She pointed a trembling finger at the refrigerator. "Not for anything in there."

I knew little about withdrawal, but logic and my recent painful experience told me if you can't have what you want, you need to focus on something else. "Well, I am. How about eggs and cheese on toast?"

Mrs. Moore's upper body convulsed, as if she were trying to keep from throwing up. "Yeah, fine."

Recalling Duncan's movements from a few weeks ago, I took out the frying pan and spatula, then started digging ingredients out of the refrigerator. Had it been only a few weeks since Duncan started wreaking havoc with weird body parts, including my heart?

Mrs. Moore shot a crooked stream of smoke toward the ceiling. "Do you know where he is?"

I dropped a pat of butter in the frying pan, where it sizzled and popped. "No, I was hoping you would."

She'd smoked the cigarette to the filter, which she dropped onto the table, missing the small glass plate I'd set in front of her to use as an ashtray. She reached for another cigarette and this time managed to light it on her own. "Is it true?" she asked with trembling, puffing lips. "Did he sleep in that storeroom when things got out of control around here?"

"Yeah." I cracked an egg and dropped it into a bowl. "The staff made it kind of homey. He didn't seem to mind."

"Duncan's a great kid." She puffed and puffed, and the line

of ash on the end of her cigarette grew into a long, gray, powdery worm. "He makes do with so little. Always has. He was always thankful for everything. One Christmas all he got was this red butt-ugly plastic bear I think I got from the dollar store. You know what he did? He hugged me and said it was perfect, that he always wanted a red butt-ugly plastic bear." She looked at her cigarette with loathing and smashed it in the dish. "Duncan had nothing to do with the fire. He wouldn't hurt the radio station. He loved that place."

"I know. The police aren't looking for him because they think he started the fire. They're more worried about his safety."

My vivid imagination kicked into high gear: Brad the love scribe storming into the station seething with anger at me. Duncan trying to calm him, to fix the mess I made. Brad hurting Duncan.

I cracked three more eggs, then whipped. With the eggs officially dead, I poured them into the sizzling butter and made toast.

"You need to eat," I said when I set the sandwich before Duncan's mom.

Her mouth quirked in an attempt at a smile. "You sound like Duncan." Her trembling fingers clutched the sandwich. Clumps of eggs spilled onto her lap. Cheese oozed onto the table. She clutched the sandwich tighter. The toast crumbled, egg clumps falling onto the ash worm. "I can't stop." She glared at her hands. "Dammit! I can't stop."

I took the remnants of her sandwich from her shaking hands and set them on the plate. "You don't need to." I knelt next to her and put my arms around her shoulders and started to rock. Back and forth. Together.

Sometime later the back door swung open. I turned, expecting Hetta.

"Chloe?" Duncan walked through the door, that deep vertical line bisecting his forehead as he set a bunch of bags on the kitchen counter. "What are you doing here?"

A happy cry clogged my throat. This was my nice, sexy, broad-shouldered Duncan, who was clearly safe. As I rocked with his mom, lyrics joined our rhythmic swaying. *Dunc's okay. Dunc's okay. Dunc's okay.* I gave him a smile meant to outshine any sun in any universe. I'd changed, but not entirely. Need a friend? Call Chloe. How about a laugh? Enter Chloe with joke book in hand.

"I'm talking with your mom," I said.

Mrs. Moore looked up. Her eyes didn't meet his but strayed to the bags on the counter. She pressed her bird-thin body into mine, then pushed off. "You up to trying again?" Her reedy voice quaked.

Duncan swallowed. Three times. "Yes."

She stood. "Okay. Let me get my stuff together."

With Duncan's mom shuffling down the hallway, I threw myself across the kitchen and into Duncan's arms. I ran my hands over his beautiful face and broad shoulders and strong back. "You're okay? Brad didn't hurt you? You escaped the fire?"

"I'm fine." He cupped my face with his hands, my cheeks heating in a warm-sizzling-butter kind of way. "What's going on? Who's Brad, and what's this about a fire?"

"You don't know?"

"Know what?"

"About the station." He shook his head, and I told him about the fire, the investigation, and the suspicions about Brad.

"The poet guy?" Duncan asked. "They're blaming him for the fire?"

"Technically, everyone on the staff is blaming *me*." I unwound myself from his arms, picked up the frying pan, and took it to the sink. "And you know what? They're right. It's my fault. I invited Brad to share a piece of his heart. I encouraged him to give his crush the poem. I—"

"Shut up." Dunc snatched the frying pan from me and tossed it in the sink. "Am I to blame for my mom's addiction?"

"Of course not."

"Then why would you blame yourself for Brad's actions?"

"It was my show, my stupid advice—"

"You didn't tell him to burn down the station." Duncan placed both hands on my shoulders. "You may be the queen of the universe, but you can't control the way the minions act. If Brad really did burn down the station, then it's his fault, not yours. Just like it's not Clem's fault because she's the GM or Mr. Martinez's fault because he's the sponsor or the underwriters' fault because they've kept the station on the air the past month. Got it?"

I breathed in his words, took comfort from him just being close. "You know, Dunc, for someone who doesn't know how to communicate, you're doing a lot of talking."

With a grin, he pulled me into his arms, and I rested my cheek on his chest and matched my breathing with his. I thought about his words, and, yes, he was probably right. I wasn't to blame for Brad's actions, but I would have a hard time living with myself until the rest of the staff accepted that, too.

"The fire investigators need to talk with you," I told Duncan when I finally pulled away. "They want to know if you saw Brad that night near Portable Five."

"No. After we kissed and you drove off"—his finger slid along my lips—"I couldn't make myself go to work. I didn't want to be alone with my toasters or garbage, so I decided to check on Mom. I found Stu in the driveway, and he was mad as hell, because Mom had thrown him out and threatened to call the cops. And you know why? Get this. Stu broke one of the toasters on the kitchen counter. He got pissed off and chucked it across the room. Hetta said Mom came unglued. Anyway, last night Mom said she was ready for rehab. So Hetta and I spent all day checking into in-patient rehab facilities, and we found one in San Diego."

Duncan looked so little-boy hopeful.

"You believe this time it will work?"

"I have to."

Duncan's soul was way too old. It had seen too much, but I couldn't undo it. Instead, I wrapped him in my arms and let him feel the pounding of my heart.

A few minutes later Mrs. Moore walked in with a plastic grocery bag filled with clothes. On top sat a picture of Duncan hugging a red butt-ugly bear. "Did you get enough?" she asked Duncan.

He shifted me to his side and looped his arm around my waist. Perfect fit. He pointed to the five bags he'd set on the counter. "Hetta said you could make at least five scarves."

"Five?" She raised her hands, the trembling so bad I could hear her bones clacking. "I think I may need a few more skeins of yarn."

I pointed to my own little pathetic bag of yarn I'd left near the kitchen table. "I got six and an extra set of needles."

Duncan looked like he wanted to kiss me and never stop, but that wasn't an option. Mrs. Moore picked at the oozing sore on her arm.

"You ready?" Duncan asked his mom.

"You . . . you found a place?"

"Yeah. In San Diego. Supposed to be a good one."

"And we can afford it?"

"They'll work with us."

Hetta, who'd been standing in the kitchen doorway the whole time, walked in and took Mrs. Moore by the arm. "I'll get her in my car." Hetta stared at me hard. "You take care of things in here."

Duncan brought me into his arms and rested his chin on my head.

"What about you?" I asked. "Where are you going to go?" Duncan couldn't stay at the radio station anymore. He was seventeen, a minor, and the police knew about his situation.

"I'm taking the bus to San Diego with Mom. I'll stick around for a few weeks until I'm sure she's not going to run off to Stu.

Friends and family aren't part of early in-house rehab, but I want to be close by."

"To make sure she doesn't run?"

"Yes. No. Maybe. I don't know. I need to be there for her. For me. Does that make sense?"

When people you cared about needed fixing, you wanted to be close by. I thought of Grams on the porch swing and Mom on my old play gym. At least they were on the same property now. "Yeah, it makes sense, but that doesn't mean I like it." I stood on tiptoe and brushed a kiss on his lips. "I'll miss you."

His face fell.

"What?"

"Valentine's Day. Our date. I'll miss it."

"We can celebrate when you get back." Go with the flow. Keep rocking.

He didn't look reassured, but his gaze softened. "At least I can give you your Valentine's Day present before I go."

That melted butter feeling zinged through my veins again. Duncan was beyond nice, and he was mine.

He ran down the hall and came back with a small box covered in wrapping paper with pink cabbage roses and tied with pink yarn. "I borrowed the wrapping stuff from Hetta."

"I can tell." I slipped off the yarn and pictured Duncan's grumpy, frumpy neighbor. "She's the one who taught your mom to knit?"

"Yeah, she's kind of been there for both of us." Someone in his corner.

With the yarn off, I tore the wrapping paper and found a Velveeta Cheese box. "In case I need some eggs and cheese on toast while you're gone?" I asked.

"Ha-ha."

I took off the lid, and my teeth caught my bottom lip. Duncan had given me one of his treasures. "I love it," I said when my mouth agreed to work. "Let's plug it in and give it a try."

He dug through a kitchen drawer, bowed, and handed me a pencil stub as if it were a royal scepter. I stuck it into the best Valentine's Day present in the universe, a pencil sharpener painted with a glittery crown, one fit for a queen.

As it whirred, I pictured his hands taking the broken sharpener out of the garbage, those same hands fixing it and carefully painting it with gold and red glitter paint. Duncan did the best with what he had. He went with the flow. He rocked with life's punches.

"She's ready," Hetta said from the doorway. "You better get going before she changes her mind."

In the driveway Mrs. Moore sat in the front seat of Hetta's old car. She looked like she wanted to jump out of her skin. Something told me it was going to get worse before it got better.

"You going to be okay?" I asked Duncan.

Duncan paused before he nodded. "I already talked to my first-period teacher, and she's going to make sure I get my assignments and talk to Lungren about doing my JISP when I get back."

I nodded. "She likes to help."

"Yeah." He reached for his scarf, but it wasn't there. "Tell everyone at the station I'm okay."

Nod.

"Man, Chloe, I'm going to miss you." He grabbed my hands, holding tightly as if we were standing in crashing waves. He studied our intertwined fingers, and I knew what he was thinking. Getting close to someone and giving them a piece of your heart made letting go that much harder. Each time one of my brothers left for college, I had another gaping hole. As our hands melted together, I realized the perfect gift to give Duncan, something to show I cared. The first day of kindergarten Grams had given it to me, and this past August, I'd given it to my brother Zach when he left for med school.

I raised Duncan's hands to my lips. First I kissed one palm, then the other. "When you feel lonely, I'll be there."

Duncan stared at his palms and wrapped his fingers around my kisses.

Send Chloe Camden to the
school office immediately.

A. Lungren

CHAPTER 22

THE DEL REY SCHOOL'S STUDENT POPULATION INCLUDED TWO
Brads, fourteen Bradleys, two Bradfords, and one Bradshaw, and
according to the fire investigator, each claimed to know nothing
of the fire that raged through the radio station. What's more, the
investigator had made samples of all of their voices, and when he
played them for me, I shook my head.

"None of them sounded like my Brad," I told him. *My* Brad.
The love scribe. The VHP. The possible firebug. "I'm sorry."

The fire investigator straightened the edges of the stack of
papers that had grown over the past two weeks since the fire.
"That's okay, Chloe." He pointed to the digital recorder. "This
isn't the end of things, we'll keep looking and keep making voice
recordings, and eventually we'll find him. This is a serious crime,
and the person behind it won't go unpunished."

Fire Guy escorted me out of the guidance-center meeting
room, and in the lobby I ran into Clementine, who was obviously

waiting to listen to Fire Guy's Brad "bites." The former GM of KDRS 88.8 The Edge looked at me in a way that screamed, *Criminal!*

For the past two weeks, she'd glared at me and whispered snide things when I walked by. Picture Brie with a nose ring. And as with Brie and the stupid Mistletoe Ball thing, I felt horrible. No, I hadn't personally torched the radio station, but one of my callers, a brokenhearted boy named Brad, may have.

As I passed Clementine in the guidance center lobby, I wanted to grab her hands and apologize for the 751st time, but it wouldn't help. All of my apologies had gone unheard. I'd e-mailed Clem, called her, and even left a basket of beets tied with a purple bow in front of her locker. No joke. I spotted them later, basket and all, in a hallway trash can.

Grams said I needed to do a better job of listening. I heard loud and clear. Duncan may not blame me, but Clem and the rest of the radio staff held me responsible for the death of KDRS. They still wanted nothing to do with me. The next step, the conscientious act of internalizing and acting on what I heard, was much more difficult. Every hair on my head stood upright at the thought of sitting by quietly and allowing the radio staff to shun me. I wanted to joke and smile my way back into their hearts. But like Grams, I needed to accept that there were times when I needed to give up control, to let go. Holding on could be dangerous for me and those around me.

That afternoon I walked into the lunchroom with a heavy heart. Mercedes sat at table fourteen with a few of her brainiac friends. Brie was, as usual, MIA. Last week I heard the first wave of Brie whispers, something about my former BF wigging out and seeing a therapist during her lunch break, but I didn't join the sea of jellyfish. I'd been on the stinging end far too long.

Taking a seat at table three, I took out my lunch. I ate slowly, listening to the burrs of various clans. I had nowhere to go, no people to talk to, not even Duncan. The calm mask of my face almost split. I hadn't heard from him since he took his mom to the drug rehab place two weeks ago. I figured he was worried about his mom, trying to keep up with school work, and didn't have money for a long-distance call.

But he could have charged the call to me. If he cared?

No. I wasn't going to hammer my heart. I was going to be patient, to trust that Duncan was going to take care of what he needed to take care of. Then he'd come home to Tierra del Rey and me.

The days dragged and built up like sluggish clumps of seaweed in a slimy inlet.

Another week went by. And another. They were quiet weeks, weeks when I listened to my heart. It told me I missed Duncan, horribly, but unlike the old Chloe, I didn't hop in my car and hunt him down because I needed reassurance. He needed to be there for his mom. I accepted that, although it didn't stop me from going to his duplex every day after school to see if he'd arrived home. Hetta, the cabbage-scented neighbor, would stand in the driveway scowling at me.

Until today. When she found me knocking on Duncan's door, she popped her head out her living room window.

"I heard from him yesterday," she said, and my heart zigged, then zagged. "He wired me money to pay the rent on this old dive." Hetta rested her thick arms on the windowsill. "Looks like our boy's coming home soon."

Soon. What a wonderful four-letter word. "Did he say how his mom was doing?"

"Nah. You know Dunc. He doesn't talk much."

Yes, I knew Dunc, and I missed Dunc, and I couldn't wait until Dunc came home. I lingered on the doorstep as if my presence would hasten his return. This is what my caller had been talking about all those weeks ago. When you cared for someone, you wanted to be with that person all the time.

Hetta scratched at her double chins. "Hey, you got a minute?"

I have 10,242. "Sure, why?"

"I got a knot in a skein of yarn, and with these old fingers, I can't get the damn thing out. Got myself a big mess."

Did I know about messes. When Hetta left the window and opened the front door, I didn't hesitate.

Space-wise, Hetta's house mirrored Duncan's, only it was stuffed with stuff: lumpy furniture, wall hangings, fringed lamps, and baskets of yarn. She pointed to a basket near the sofa. On top sat a messy wad of blue yarn. One slow knot at a time, I started to untangle the mess.

Within an hour, I had the string untangled, and with the ends free, I started rolling the yarn into a tight, neat ball. How nice if

I could do the same thing with all the loose ends floating in my life: Duncan, the fire, Brad, the radio staffers, my JISP, Grams and Mom, and Brie.

Hetta looked up from a recliner, where she sat knitting something that looked like a sweater for an octopus. *Clicketyclick-etyclickety.* "Ever knit?" Hetta asked.

I shook my head. Mom stitched hearts, and Dad stitched feet. Grams? Hah.

Clicketyclicketyclickety. "Wanna learn?"

From the overflowing yarn baskets I picked out Converse orange and white. After one hour, I'd knitted two uneven inches.

Hetta stroked her chins. "A little rough around the edges, but you'll find your rhythm. You'll get faster, and your stitches will even out."

My stitches evened out, and life moved on. A cleanup crew removed the blackened shell of Portable Five, but there was no talk of erecting a new portable in its place. According to Ms. Lungren, who I talked to last week when I handed in my weekly JISP report, the future of 88.8 The Edge was in limbo. Grams settled into our house, but it was far from peaceful. Last week Grams bought a three-wheeled bike to ride to and from her old trailer park to visit Noreen, and the next day, the front tire had gone mysteriously flat and the tire pump was "missing." Mom looked suspiciously guilty. However, yesterday I caught Grams and Mom heading out the door to go to Brad Pitt's new release.

One Sunday in late March the doorbell rang. Of course it

wasn't for me. No one stopped by to chat these days. Some days the lack of anyone remotely resembling a friend was tortuous, other days it was only mildly excruciating.

A few minutes later, Grams popped her head through my bedroom doorway. "For you." The blue in Grams's eyes twinkled like the sun on the Pacific Ocean at sunset. "Someone with a smokin' hot heinie."

I tossed my knitting needles on the bed and tore out of my room. Was Duncan back from San Diego? Was his mom okay? Did Grams think Duncan had a nice butt? Did it bother me that my eighty-two-year-old grandmother was still looking at guys' butts? I laughed as I raced down the stairs, then skidded to a stop.

"Hi, Chloe." The fire investigator waved his digital recorder. "More Brads."

We sat at the kitchen table, and he set the recorder between us. "We extended the search to neighboring high schools, and we may have a lead," he said. "I want you to listen to four voices, and let me know if any sound like the caller you know as Brad."

When he played number two, my blood stilled. "That's him."

He replayed the voice. "Are you sure?"

"I'm positive. Ask Clementine. I'm sure she'll back me up."

He nodded. "She already IDed number two as the caller known as Brad."

I leaned forward. This was the first good news I'd heard in weeks. "So go talk to him."

Fire Guy took a notebook from his file. "We have talked to him. He admits he's the Brad who called."

I jabbed my finger at the digital recorder. "So arrest him."

"We can't. On the night the radio station burned down, Brad was with his school's chess club at an out-of-town tournament. There's no way he could have placed and ignited the liquid accelerant used to torch the station." He opened his notebook and sighed. "So, Chloe, if the other voices don't sound familiar, I need to know: Are there are any other people who may have a grudge against you or KDRS?"

I hadn't been to Brie Sonderby's house since last December, before she started the horrible, ugly rumor about me and my retired guidance counselor and a fungus crown. To my shock, her house had undergone a massive makeover, and not a glamorous one. Weeds choked the circular drive, and a fine, gritty layer of beach sand covered the front entryway. But the real shocker: a For Sale sign hung in the front yard.

When I knocked, Brie's mother answered the door.

"Why, Chloe, it's been ages!" Mrs. Sonderby said as she hugged me. Like her home, she looked drastically different. Brie's mom had always been model thin and impeccably dressed. Today she wore rumpled sweats and an extra thirty pounds. "We've missed you. How are you?"

I was rocking when life hammered me, but not totally down. "Okay."

"And Mercedes, we haven't seen her, either. How's she?"

"I'm not sure. I haven't talked to her lately."

"It's sad, isn't it? Growing up? Changing?" Mrs. Sonderby's lips curved in a nostalgic smile. "You three used to be thick as thieves. Gosh, remember shopping for prom dresses last year? You had everyone in stitches with that neon-orange number." Her eyes grew unnaturally bright, and she turned away. "But that was a long time ago, huh? I'm sure you're here for Brie. Let me go get her."

"Yes, please."

Brie's mom hesitated in the hallway. "Is this about the fire at the radio station?"

I shook my head. That was between Brie and the fire investigator. Brie and I had something else we needed to talk about. Technically I needed to talk. She needed to listen.

"The fire investigator was here yesterday and talked to us." Mrs. Sonderby rolled the hem of her sweatshirt. "Just so you know, Chloe, there's no way Brie could have started that fire. She was with me that night."

"I didn't think she did it," I said. Brie wasn't a villainess. She might be hurting or angry, and that might cause her to do bad things, but she wasn't evil. I could never have been best friends with an evil person.

"And you know what else, Chloe?" Mrs. Sonderby continued, her smile growing. "I'm glad you're here. You could always make her laugh."

Operative word. *Could.* I wasn't exactly a walking laugh machine these days, but I had brought a little Chloe cheer in the recent past. I remembered the times I'd made the staffers laugh: Duncan in the storeroom, Clementine over beets, stuttering Frack, quiet Haley.

As for Brie, I couldn't remember the last time I heard her laugh. Not a real laugh, one that came from a sunny place in her heart. When I looked back on it, the weeks leading to the Mistletoe Ball were low on the laughter scale for my trio. I figured it was because of midterm exams and the hustle of the holidays and winter-break trips. But the shift had already taken place. I hadn't been able to make Brie laugh much then, and I wasn't sure if I could make her laugh now. Honestly, I wasn't sure if I wanted to. It wasn't my job to make sure the whole universe kept smiling.

Today I wanted to say something, and I needed to make sure Brie didn't just hear my words, but listened.

When Brie walked in, she looked like a ghost: chalky skin, pale hair unbound around her face, soundless feet, and thin, so thin she looked as if a morning breeze off the ocean would whisk her away. This was a shadow of my best friend.

"Um, hi." I tried to catch her gaze, but she stared out the window. "Looks like you're moving."

Brie nodded.

"If you need extra hands, my dad has some students at the university who could help. They helped Grams move. Did a great job. They even set up all her electronic stuff. You know how uptight she gets about her screens."

Another nod.

"And if you need boxes for packing, Grams still has quite a

few. I could bring them over, but I'm not sure if they'd fit in my car. Maybe I could borrow my mom's van."

This time Brie shrugged.

Fine. This was not the time for useless chatter. I had things I needed to say to Brie, but not here in this ghost house, quiet and empty, soulless. "Can we go outside?"

On phantom feet, Brie turned and headed for the back door. We walked onto the deck and down the steps to the Sonderbys' crescent moon beach. I looked at the sand, making sure ghosty Brie left footprints. Fiddling with a curl at my cheek I wondered how to talk to a ghost. How could I make her understand the things I needed to say?

To my surprise, Brie spoke first. "I didn't start the fire."

I slipped off my sandals and dug my toes into the sand. This was probably a good place to start. "I didn't think you did, but I gave your name to the fire investigator because he asked if I had any people who may have been mad at me. There was that whole guinea pig thing and the Mistletoe Ball and—"

"Chloe?"

I clamped my lips together.

"Shut up." She held her hands over her ears, then gave her head a shake. "Man, I forgot how much you talk."

Sure I talked, but now I listened, and as we walked through the cool, powdery sand, I listened to the seagulls and rush of water, and I listened to my heart. I could never go back to who I was. I'd changed too much, and something told me Brie had, too.

Deep breath in. Deep breath out.

"I came by to apologize," I said. "For the whole Mistletoe Ball thing. For being so caught up in me, for not being there for you. Honestly, I didn't even notice you were hurting so bad that night. I'm sorry, Brie, and I'm sorry I was too consumed with family stuff over winter break to check in with you. I said it before, but I need to make sure you know that."

We walked along the water's edge. The waves barely rippled this part of beach. No squawking seagulls. No motorboats. Quiet enough to hear yourself think. Brie seemed to be thinking. Her teeth gnawed at her lower lip.

"Three words, Brie, that's all I need. I need you to say, *I forgive you*. Work with me, okay?"

A rusty rumble that might have been a laugh teetered on her lips. "I forgive you."

I breathed in the words, let them swirl through my lungs and brush past my heart. They were three simple words so easily given and received. I couldn't imagine where I'd be today if Brie and I had had this exchange in January.

We reached the small dock where Brie's dad's boat used to be tethered. Today the dock was empty. The winds of change were storming in a big way in the Sonderby universe.

"When are you moving?" I asked.

"Next weekend." Brie ran her foot along the sand, digging a shallow line. "Mom and I got a condo in San Diego. Pretty nice. Exercise center, indoor pool, and private beach. She enrolled me at a school. I start next Monday."

"Sounds good."

Brie's toes dug deeper, wider, the sugary sand giving way to damp clumps. I stood still. Waiting. Listening. The channel grew.

"My parents are getting a divorce," she said.

I leaned against the post on the vacant dock. "I kind of guessed that."

"It's been ugly." Brie kicked at the sand. "My dad, he's been cheating on my mom for years."

"Brie, you don't have to . . ."

Brie turned to me, a painful need pulling at her spectral eyes. "He's had a ton of affairs, always with young women, bodies not brains. Mom always ignored it, always pretended that we were the perfect family. But in December, Mom couldn't ignore it any more. Dad asked for a divorce because—get this—his eighteen-year-old girlfriend is pregnant."

"Oh."

"Yeah. Mom didn't take it too well. She has a hard time with messy situations. She fell into a major funk. Me, too."

"I'm sorry." Not that it was my fault, but I didn't want to see anyone hurting.

Brie climbed out of the trench she'd dug. "I'm not. It was a wake-up call. Mom needed to make some changes in her life, and Dad's pregnant eighteen-year-old girlfriend kind of forced it. Mom's getting stronger."

"And you?"

Brie started walking back to her house. I followed.

"I hate them, you know. I hate my dad's plastic-boobed girl-friend, and I hate the baby. That's pretty sick, isn't it, hating a baby that's not even here yet? But honestly, I hate my dad the most."

"Because you love him the most. When you give someone your love, you give them power over you."

"Don't tell me you've been seeing a therapist, too?"

"Grams." I cocked my head. "Or maybe it was Loretta Hooper Chesterfield Hayes on *Passion Bay*."

"You want to hear something really twisted?" She kicked at the sand again. "I've spent the past six months hating you. Even before the Mistletoe Ball there were times when I couldn't stand to be around you. I hated that you had parents who genuinely loved each other. I hated that you had the world's greatest grandma and five older brothers who adored you. I hated that you had the perfect family life."

Now was not the time to mention the black hole, Parkinson's, and three-wheeled bikes with flat tires.

"I hated how people always gravitated toward you when we used to walk down the hall or sit in the lunchroom." Brie's ghosty face had heated, and two swirls of red dotted her cheeks. "I hated how when the whole school was supposed to hate you, you found a bunch of friends at the radio station, started your own radio empire, and became the most popular girl in the school again."

The hate wasn't mine. It was Brie's. I couldn't control Brie's feelings. I couldn't make her world bright and sunny. Only she could do that.

"Do you still hate me?" Curiosity, not need, fueled the question.

"Truthfully?" Her eyes turned frosty, her mouth hard. "Sometimes."

Not everyone loves Chloe.

Yeah, tell me something I didn't already know.

Call A. Lungren. ASAP.

G.

CHAPTER 23

"SIT."

Ms. Lungren pointed to the chair across from her desk. She wasn't smiling, nor was I as I clicked across the floor of her office in my 1920 red-clay sling-back pinup pumps. Many things had changed over the past three months, but not my need for a good pair of vintage shoes when I needed a little pick-me-up.

Today was the last day of March, and tomorrow I would present my JISP oral presentation, which I'd officially named, *Shut Up and Listen: A Junior Independent Study Project by a Queen Without a Castle.*

Last week I'd quietly finished my written JISP, using the copious notes I'd taken during my time with KDRS 88.8 The Edge. I'd documented my promotional efforts, kept track of the rise in calls, and even did another survey last week at lunch table fourteen. The data was impressive. Ninety-nine point eight percent of respondents had heard of the station. Only two claimed total cluelessness. One was a foreign exchange student, the other a senior stoner. Yeah, the fire probably had a wee bit to do with KDRS's widespread notoriety, but that was one bad day. Okay, one catastrophic day, but before the fire, people were listening to the station. They were excited about my talk shows and calling in. And, yes, I was making menudo out of cow intestines.

In addition to facts and figures, my JISP included my thoughts about the people of KDRS. I shared my feelings about Frack conquering his stutter and Clementine using the station as a launching point for her career. I wrote about Duncan finding fun and Haley finding people who noticed her, not her belly. And I wrote about me, about how getting a voice on radio made me shut up and listen.

I'd bundled the entire report, a hefty twenty-nine pages in Times New Roman 12, into a folder complete with graphs and listener fan mail. This morning my written JISP sat squarely on A. Lungren's desk, the cover page slashed with her red spiky writing, like she'd taken her little kitty claws to it. I crossed my ankles and pressed my lips together. I did what I could. It wasn't the time for pleading or arguing or jokes. Worst-case scenario: Ms. Lungren fails me, my parents go ballistic, I never get into Harvard, and the world will see that I'm not as brilliant as the rest of my family.

Deep breath in. Don't worry about things you can't control. Deep breath out.

Ms. Lungren slid her paws over my report. "Your JISP has been quite the adventure, hasn't it?"

I tore my gaze from the bleeding pages. "Yes." I didn't expect to play Garbage Games and make friends with a fire-breathing dragon and have my heart dip and sway like I was on a roller coaster. I didn't expect to care about whether or not the station breathed its last breath.

Ms. Lungren skimmed through my JISP pages. More red. I swallowed my heart, which had traveled up my throat.

"KDRS ended up being something you're passionate about, it seems," she said.

I nodded. Passion was, after all, the number one criteria for a JISP. In my report I shared my passion for the station and the staff. I bared my heart and wrote about what it felt like to be a queen without a castle.

Ms. Lungren slipped her cat-eye glasses from her twitching nose, letting them swing on the chain hanging around her neck. "But it certainly didn't turn out all right in the end, did it?"

I shook my head and bit my tongue. I'd executed an in-depth study, and I'd shown leadership and networking skills with the goal of making a meaningful contribution to my community. It was all there in my report and on my sleeve.

Tears welled in my eyes.

I wished Duncan were here.

"I'm sorry," I said. Those two words unleashed more apologies I couldn't hold back. "I'm sorry about the fire. I'm sorry Brad's stupid crush hurt him. I'm sorry Clementine won't have a radio station to run her senior year. I'm sorry Haley's DVDs burned, especially all those movies from 1939, which really is the best year ever in film history. I'm sorry Duncan won't have a place to go when people like Stu come around. I'm sorry . . ." On and on the words flowed.

"Are you done?" Ms. Lungren asked when my apology tapered off.

No more words. No more tears. I nodded.

"Good." Ms. Lungren closed my JISP report. "No matter how hard we try, some things don't go as planned. It's a real-world lesson, Chloe, hard, but real."

The real world hurt. I knuckled away the tears. "So what now? Is there any way I can salvage a pass on my JISP? Maybe I can do the shoe project this summer."

"Excuse me?"

I pointed to the bludgeoned report. "Aren't you failing me?"

"Fail?" Ms. Lungren's kitty nose twitched. "Not yet, unless you perform dismally on the orals." She leaned toward me. "You are giving your oral presentation tomorrow, aren't you?" Her face and voice were suddenly lionlike.

"But all that red? It doesn't look like you were too happy with my written report."

"Oh, those are my notes." She tapped my folder. "Your JISP got me thinking about the importance of specialized programs like the radio station. I've been talking to school admin. They indicated there are no funds for a new station, and it's clear Mr. Martinez's heart isn't in radio. But admin, along with the school district, believe in the spirit of the station and they'd like to see the program not limited to the Del Rey School students. They're considering a magnet program open to high school students throughout town." She wore a cat-who-ate-the-canary grin. "So I've been talking to Clementine and researching student-run radio stations. Most of the traditional high school radio stations that were so successful in the eighties and nineties have been shut down because of aging equipment and budget cuts. We're seeing more and more high schools turn to streaming content on the Internet. This change could actually save the station."

"Torching the station is one way to bring about change," I said.

"Not the ideal way. But at its heart, a JISP is designed to create positive change or action. This change in transmission and turning the station into a magnet program could very well be what needs to happen to keep KDRS on the air. Change can be a great thing."

Yes, the world was full of change. You lost best friends. You gained new ones. Grandmas gave up tuna cans and gave life to black holes. Boys with broad shoulders and heavy loads could find fun with garbage and girls with poppy-colored hair.

Ms. Lungren reached into her desk drawer and pulled out a folder. "Assuming these changes take place, I need to make sure you're on board."

"Excuse me?"

"If this new program gets district approval, we'll need to have a few knowledgeable staffers in key positions for next year. Clementine has already agreed to be GM, and while it's still to be decided if there will be talk-show format programs, I was hoping you'd take on the role of business manager."

I uncrossed my ankles, then crossed them again. "Honestly, I'd love to stay on with the radio station, but I don't think Clementine would go for it." Radio was her life. To me it was a hobby, albeit a fun one. I knew I didn't want to be a doctor, like my brothers, but I couldn't see myself in radio, either. With all the free time I had the past few weeks, I managed to crank out an A-plus in econ. Maybe someday I'd run a business, like Dos Hermanas.

Ms. Lungren's nose twitched. "Why would you say Clementine wouldn't go for it?"

"She hates me."

"That's silly. Everyone likes you."

I choked out a laugh. Had Ms. Lungren found the catnip?

"Chloe, this isn't a joke."

I continued to laugh until my chest ached, because sometimes you needed to laugh.

Dark, musty air swallowed me as I walked into the Del Rey School auditorium. I squinted through the semidarkness to the chairs in front, where the three-member JISP review board sat before the stage, lit by a single spotlight. The oral presentation scheduled before mine had ended, and a very relieved junior walked offstage into the arms of family and friends gathered in support all things JISP-y.

I hitched the bag that contained the single prop for my JISP. Today I donned the most vintage of all my shoes. On my feet sparkled a pair of French kid beaded one-strap Grecian pumps, circa 1890. Sometimes a girl needed the strength of shoes that survived more than a century to help her get through a fifteen-minute JISP.

When I reached the front of the auditorium, Ms. Lungren looked at me and smiled. She sat in the middle seat, a laptop balanced on her knees. On either side sat teachers who I probably would have recognized if I wasn't so nervous. All I could concentrate on was the booming of my heart. It sounded like a basketball whooshing through a metal hoop and broadcast over a loud speaker at full blast.

"Are you ready, Ms. Camden?" Ms. Lungren asked. Her earnest face screamed, *You can do it, Chloe!*

I nodded.

One of the other teachers looked around and frowned. "Are you sure?"

I shifted from one marvelous Grecian pump to the other, refusing to look at the empty auditorium seats behind the JISP review board. Dad was out of town at a conference, and Mom had gotten called into emergency surgery. Of course, Grams couldn't drive. As for friends, that was laughable. A part of me had hoped Duncan would make it home for my JISP, but compared to what his mom was going through, my JISP was of miniscule importance.

"Yes, I'm ready." With a sharp nod, I walked up the stage steps and positioned myself in the center of the spotlight. I didn't need the easels or projection screen, because I hadn't brought any display boards or a PowerPoint presentation. I set my bag on the podium.

Deep breath in. Deep breath out. Repeat. Four times.

As I opened my mouth, footsteps clattered down the aisle.

When you're onstage in the spotlight, you can't see into the audience. I squinted and shaded my face with my hands.

Grams! The smile froze halfway to my lips. Had she stolen a car?

A shape shifted behind Grams. I squinted, and something gently tugged at the center of my chest. Merce. The smart one. This time, she stopped what she was doing and gave Grams a ride. I wanted to rush off the stage and hug her. The door opened again, and a group shuffled into seats in the shadowy middle section: Clementine, followed by Haley, Taysom, Frick, and Frack.

I steadied my hands on the podium to keep from pumping them in the air. No one, not even the vilest of villainesses, deserved to be alone for her oral JISP presentation. My throat swelled, and I couldn't speak. I silently ticked off the rules for natural-sounding delivery Clem pounded into my head all those weeks ago. Breathe between units of thought. Don't look down at notes, because it'll close airways. Imagine I'm talking to a friend.

I focused on that shadowy middle place in the center of the auditorium. "Sometimes change sneaks up on you, carried in on the breath of spring, sliding through the sun-soaked waves of summer, breezing along the whisper and crackle of fall. Other times change prefers a more direct route. It comes down fast and hard." I reached into my bag and took out my lone prop. *Wham!* "Like a ginormous hammer . . ."

As I walked away from the stage, Ms. Lungren was purring with delight, and Grams met me in the aisle.

"I'm glad you could make it," I said with a giant hug.

"Thank Mercedes," Grams said. "She called me this morning to find out when your JISP was scheduled, and when she discovered I didn't have a ride, she offered in a heartbeat."

Merce stepped out from the shadows.

The radio staffers hadn't left their seats. They were giving me private time with Merce.

This afternoon Merce didn't look agitated like the day she'd been searching for Brie. She looked at peace and happy, like she had at the bonfire the night of the Tardeada. "So why'd you come?" I asked.

Her mouth quirked in a half smile. "You make me laugh."

So simple and true. I spent much of last year trying to put a smile on Merce's face after her mother died.

"And I need to tell you . . ." Merce reached into her backpack and took out a bag of Twizzlers. "I'm sorry."

Two simple words with the power to change worlds. I took the bag and broke open the plastic.

"At first I bought into Brie's anger, because it was everywhere. I couldn't get out of it. And when she fell into that funk and started missing school, you'd already started hanging out with your radio friends, and I found myself a social mutant, like in elementary school, all alone."

A strange, awed expression replaced her pinched features. "But being alone ended up being a good thing. I learned I wasn't the social zero I'd been in sixth grade. Somewhere over the past few years I learned how to be a friend, and I found some people, some great people, who wanted to be friends with me. For the first time, I didn't feel like I was living in anyone's shadow." Her head shook in a series of slow wags. "You and Brie, you both cast pretty long shadows. Sometimes it was a very dark place to be. It's hard to be number three."

"You were never number three." I handed her a Twizzler. "At least I never thought so."

"No, but I did, and that's what counted. And that's what I needed to change." Merce tucked her Twizzler into her pocket. "It was a great JISP, Chloe. Congratulations. Maybe I'll see you around."

I peeked at the radio staffers. Clem frowned. Haley held a giant sucker, a rainbow-swirled one on a half-inch-wide stick. Frick and Frack thumb-wrestled. Taysom was carrying a skunk. Why was Taysom carrying a skunk? I wanted to find out because these were my people, my clan.

"Maybe," I told Merce before she walked away.

One by one the staffers left their seats. Haley handed me the sucker. "You may want to save it until after we eat."

"Clem made reservations for all of us at Dos Hermanas," Taysom said as we jostled out of the auditorium.

Every inch of my body, from my pin curls to my Grecian pumps, jiggled in a happy dance. "Celebrating the world's most wonderful JISP?" I asked with a waggle of my eyebrows.

Clementine rolled her eyes and fell in step beside me, letting the others go ahead. Her nose ring wriggled a few times before she sliced the air with her outstretched palm and said, "*Whooooosh!*"

"And that sound effect signifies . . ."

"Your freakin' royal roller skates." Clem's curls bounced as she shook her head. "The radio station gets torched, but you crank out a freakin' amazing JISP, and you get a do-gooder guidance counselor on our side who thinks she can change the world, which she probably freakin' can."

I bent in a deep bow. "I aim to freakin' please."

Clem yanked none too softly on my arm. "Come on, I'm hungry."

Beyond Clem's dragon snarl, Frick and Frack bickered, while Taysom hummed some tune to Grams, and Haley made a raspberry sound. The sound of my clan. Something light and feathery flicked inside my chest as I followed Clem into the parking lot. "Seriously, Clem, did you plan a get-together at Dos Hermanas to celebrate my JISP?"

"No, Queenie, we're celebrating justice." That light in her eyes, the one she wore when she was tracking or writing her news stories, blazed. "You remember Brad, the love scribe? He visited me last week. He's kind of shy and quiet, but it's clear he felt horrible about the station fire. After I finally got him to open up, Brad told me about the girl he was crushing on, and it seems she has a boyfriend, but not a very nice one. The guy's ultra-possessive, severely hot headed, and has had run-ins with the boys with badges."

"Are you saying Brad's crush's *boyfriend* set the station on fire?"

"I told Investigator Cargill, and he's looking into it, but the boyfriend doesn't sound nice."

Definitely not nice. Not like Duncan. Who was loyal to those he cared about. I knew if he could, he would have been here.

We reached the others, who were already waiting around Clem's old station wagon. "You want a ride to Dos Hermanas?" Clementine asked.

Even though I had my car, I was about to hop in Clem's dragon mobile when I heard a soft squeak that blotted out every other noise, smell, and vision. I turned as a bike with mismatched pedals and a duct-taped seat jangled to a stop behind me.

"Did I miss it?" Duncan asked in a winded rush, his nubby scarf hanging off one shoulder.

I grabbed the handlebars to keep from throwing myself at him. "Miss what?" I asked with a quirk of my eyebrow. I wanted to hear his voice, which I hadn't heard in far too long. That's another thing about starting to fall in love, that person's voice was everything. A soothing lullaby, a cause for celebration.

"Your JISP. Wasn't it today? Clem sent me an e-mail that your JISP oral presentation was scheduled for April first?" That vertical line striped his forehead. "Hey, is this a joke?"

This time I reached out and smoothed the line, then trailed my fingers along his cheek and to the center of his chest, where I grabbed his scarf. "Nope, it was today, and, yes, you missed it." I pulled him closer. "But I can give you a command performance later if you want."

Duncan made a wonderful, low, rumbly sound at the back of his throat. "I, uh, want." He nuzzled his cheek along my hair.

"How's your mom?" Hardly romantic, but important.

"Not fixed, but good enough for me to take off. I got off the bus an hour ago, but my chain slipped. I fixed it, then had a flat tire and a loose gear shifter. When I got that fixed, I—"

I placed a hand on either side of his face. "Duncan."

"What?"

"Shut up."

He did. Long enough to kiss me. It felt even better than I remembered.

"Come on, people," Taysom yelled from the middle seat of Clem's dragon mobile. "Haley's starving, and she's going to start gnawing on the seats if you don't get in gear."

Duncan and I reluctantly parted. As he locked his bike to the bike rack, I remembered something I'd been carrying around for weeks.

I took out the orange-and-white-striped scarf that matched the ones I made for Grams, Zach, Sam, Max, Jeremy, Luke, Ana, Josie, Mom, Dad, Grams's neighbor Noreen, and Ms. Lungren. I slipped it around his neck. It was even nubbier than Duncan's mom's, and the heart at the bottom looked more like a seagull. "It's too late for Valentine's Day, so we'll call it an April Fool's Day present."

Duncan rubbed his cheek along the uneven stitches. As we ran to Clem's dragon mobile, my 1890s Grecian pumps didn't touch the ground.

Acknowledgments

Special thanks to Douglas Potter, Tara Bulleigh, and the students of 98.7 KWXL Radio at Pueblo Magnet High School in Tucson for allowing me into your fascinating corner of the radio world, and to the faculty, staff, and my comrades at the Walter Cronkite School of Journalism and Mass Communication for nurturing my love of words and quest for truth. I raise my inkwell to the smart, talented women of Romance Writers of America who have been my compass on this journey and to *Chloe*'s early readers: Susan Colebank, Diana Davidson, Anastasia Foxe, Susan Lanier, Paula Slone, and R. R. Smythe. Hugs to Maggie Lehrman and the wonderful team at Amulet Books for their wisdom and creativity and for believing in a girl with a big heart and great shoes. Smoochies to agent Jill Corcoran for enthusiasm and support that leave me humbled. Buckets of love to Kelsey, Kate, and Catherine for helping me fall in love with young adult books all over again and for letting me be a fly on your walls. Finally, my heart to Lee, for putting your dream on hold so I could pursue mine.

About the Author

Young adult author Shelley Coriell writes stories about teens on the edge of love, life-changing moments, and a little bit of crazy. A six-time Romance Writers of America Golden Heart finalist, Shelley lives in Arizona with her family and the world's neediest rescue Weimaraner. When she's not writing, she bakes high-calorie, high-fat desserts and gives speeches and workshops about the joys and business of writing. *Welcome, Caller, This Is Chloe* is her debut novel. You can find Shelley online at www.shelleycoriell.com.

This book was designed by Maria T. Middleton. The text is set in 11-point Filosofia, a modern interpretation of the eighteenth-century classical typeface Bodoni. Filosofia was created by Zuzana Licko in 1996. The main display fonts are Helvetica Rounded, Helvetica Neue Condensed Black, and Shag Mystery.

This book was printed and bound by R.R. Donnelley in Crawfordsville, Indiana. Its production was overseen by Erin Vandeveer.